VOICES OF DISCORD

Voices of Discord

Canadian Short Stories from the 1930s

Edited by Donna Phillips

Introduction by Kenneth J. Hughes

NEW HOGTOWN PRESS
TORONTO

© New Hogtown Press 1979

All rights reserved. Every reasonable care has been taken to trace ownership of copyright material. Information that will enable the publisher to rectify any omission will be welcome.

The publisher thanks the following for permission to reprint the indicated material: Luella Bruce Creighton for "Hydro;" Sinclair Ross for "Circus in Town;" Dyson Carter for "East Nine;" *The Canadian Forum* for the stories by Bertram Brooker, Mary Quayle Innis, A.M. Klein, and L.A. MacKay; and Dorothy Livesay for "Case Supervisor" and "The Waiting Room."

Cover graphic is taken from *Masses* (May - June 1933).

Canadian Cataloguing in Publication Data

Main entry under title:
Voices of discord
ISBN 0-919940-12-9 pa.
1. Short stories, Canadian (English) - 1914 - 1967.*
2. Depressions - 1929 - Canada - Fiction.
I. Phillips, Donna, 1939 -
PS8327.V65   C813'.01   C79-094714-5
PR9197.3.V65

New Hogtown Press receives financial assistance from the Ontario Arts Council.

printed and bound in Canada

CONTENTS

Donna Phillips, Preface/9
Kenneth J. Hughes, Introduction/11
Leonard Speir, Dream of the Air Meter/45
B. Gluckman, Juggernaut/49
A. Miller, Night Shift/54
J.K. Thomas, Production/57
Ruby Ronan, One-Day Service/62
Dyson Carter, East Nine/68
Matt Murray Armstrong, The Rail/87
Bertram Brooker, Mrs. Hungerford's Milk/92
Alice Butala, A Day in Town/101
Sinclair Ross, Circus in Town/108
John Ravenhill, The Hero Returns/113
Dorothy Livesay, The Waiting Room/119
L.A. MacKay, Another Man's Poison/126
Luella Bruce Creighton, Hydro/134
Mary Quayle Innis, The Gift/143
Mary Quayle Innis, The Party/151
Maurice Lesser, Bread Line/158
James Hinton, Meat!/163
Kimball McIlroy, Late November/170
Mary Quayle Innis, Staver/173
A.M. Klein, Beggars I Have Known/182
Larry Lawson, Burp's Busy Day/187

VOICES OF DISCORD

George Winslade, Rainbow Chasing/194
Dorothy Livesay, Case Supervisor/199
Emanuel Berkenfeld, Camp is Wonderful for Growing Boys/209
Simon Marcson, Dream Train/217

VOICES OF DISCORD

PREFACE

The 26 stories in this collection have been reprinted from four Canadian periodicals that were an important publishing forum for authors in the 1930s and an equally important source for their readers: *New Frontier, Masses, Canadian Forum,* and the *Queen's Quarterly*. Although the latter journals continue to publish, the first two have long since ceased to appear. The difficulty involved in gaining access to the stories is only one of our reasons for making this collection available.

The most important reason for this anthology is to share with contemporary readers the images and perceptions of popular authors of the 1930s. Many of them are now well known names in Canadian letters: Bertram Brooker, Sinclair Ross, L.A. MacKay, Mary Quayle Innis, Luella Bruce Creighton, Dorothy Livesay, A.M. Klein. But when these stories were written, they and their not-so-famous colleagues were young writers trying to convey not only the atmosphere of the Depression but also the central concerns of the people—poverty, the alienation of industrial workers, the memory of world war, the threat of fascism and renewed war.

These stories offer a fascinating view of Depression-era experiences. They have been selected to illustrate both the range of narrative form and the variety of themes present in the fiction of the 1930s. For all of us, especially for the generations without direct knowledge of the Depression, this anthology presents an important picture, a picture of life that is richer and more complex than the dustbowl-workcamp outline of the Depression that is so often all we see.

Donna Phillips
Dugald, Manitoba

KENNETH J. HUGHES

INTRODUCTION

Despite the tentative efforts of a few good minds in the sphere of practical literary criticism, Canadian socialist scholars still face some difficult tasks. Not only do they have to establish a critical left tradition and come to terms with the larger tradition of English literature, but they must also begin the process of defining the English-Canadian literary tradition itself. In England the literary tradition was defined in the nineteenth and early twentieth centuries by liberal intellectuals who appropriated English literature and directly or indirectly put it into the service of capitalism. By contrast, the liberal intellectual establishment in Canada ensured that service would be rendered to the British and American empires and their respective literatures, a process that still continues. This colonial mentality guaranteed the general neglect of Canadian literature. In fact, literary (and general artistic) continentalism has been encouraged by the liberals throughout this century.

The basic task for the left with respect to literature is clear enough: literature must be appropriated in the name of the Canadian people in order to serve the Canadian people rather than the ruling establishment. But most assuredly the process of appropriating Canadian literature, of defining a left literary and critical tradition, will not be accomplished if we start out with some of the narrowly dogmatic notions that continue to plague the left here. In particular, we shall not get very far if we insist on approaching Canadian literature from within the framework of an ideological "correct-linism."

This idea of the "correct line" looms large in the history of the left in Canada. It may be described as the dogmatic imposition of fixed solutions selected from or interpreted out of "sacred" texts in an attempt to resolve problems in a concrete, living, and changing reality. Instead of engaging in a dialectical relationship with concrete reality, as Marx himself did, typically the correct-linist interposes sacred dogma between the objective world and his own and other subjectivities. This approach prevents him from developing a theory which can serve as a reliable guide to action.

As in politics, so in literature: all too often aesthetic prescription with no basis in concrete reality has taken the place of genuine theory derived from a serious analysis of specific literary texts and their contexts. The result has been a double tragedy for both literary creation and literary criticism.

In the realm of literary creation, prescription has frequently diverted artists from the task of mastering the artistic process itself, a process without which art is not possible. First of all, prescription has undoubtedly caused many budding writers to forget what they knew intuitively: that they could draw artistic sustenance from *anywhere*, because every character and situation in life is saturated with the political, the ideological, and the potentially artistic. Following from this initial restriction in area of interest, politically committed writers have then frequently developed an unhealthy sense of obligation. After having set their characters in action, they seem to ask themselves periodically if they are being ideologically strong enough or correct enough.

The situation in literary criticism has frequently been no better. Armed with some notion of "socialist realism", the keepers of the revolutionary consciousness soon discover that concrete literary works fail to meet their arbitrary standards, and thus the texts are given only a superficial analysis before being dismissed for their alleged inadequacy. The failure to subject literary *works* to serious analysis guarantees that the *practice* of literature will never challenge the prescriptive *theory* of literature. In this way, vulgar Marxism is substituted for a genuine dialectical approach and as one version of the correct line gives way to another, no one ends up any wiser. Meanwhile, the whole field of literature has been left clear for idealist critics of all kinds to ignore, to analyze out of existence, or to neutralize whatever might serve as a potential threat to their crippled intellectual order.

Fortunately, writers tend to be an unruly and independent lot, who often enough do what they want, regardless of political and aesthetic prescriptions. Knowing Canada better than the prescribers, most of our writers from the 1930s also knew that the working class in Canada was not large enough to win any revolutionary confrontation with the capitalist establishment. They therefore also knew that any serious politicization must unite diverse groups and classes such as petit-bourgeois farmers, bourgeois professionals (Bethune is perhaps the best known), petit-bourgeois individuals in service industries, shopkeepers, craftsmen, skilled and unskilled members of the working class, and the truly dispossessed of the *lumpenproletariat*. Neither did most of our writers forget the problems of race and the status of women. They knew that diverse persons, groups, and classes had to be made to understand each other in order to bring them into a politically useful—let alone actually revolutionary—alliance born of mutual interest. And that is why in the representative works selected for this collection we find such diverse but interrelated subjects and themes as the workings of middle- and working-class minds, the problems of women, life in the sweatshops, factories, and homes, and life among the beggars.

In fact, all the stories in this collection are part of a radical tradition. Whatever the specific limitations of any single piece, and whatever the prescriptive notions of the correct-linist, Canadian writers well understood what they were trying to do. Each went as far as his or her own intellectual and ideological development and objective conditions would allow. All were concerned with bringing about change and were therefore progressive, albeit in different degrees and in different ways. Indeed, the situation is much more complicated than simply separating progressive from non-progressive writers because all too often a specific writer will be progressive until he or she reaches the outer limits of his world vision or ideology and then will turn reactionary. Thus we have a situation in which a writer can be both radical and reactionary at the same time. The correct-linist resolves this problem clumsily by rejecting all of such a writer's works.

To rectify the mistakes of correct-linism, Canadian literature needs an intelligent reassessment by the left. In this process of re-evaluation, the concept of critical realism will be as important to us as that of socialist realism. Arnold Kettle has written in his essay on Dickens:

By *Socialist Realism*, in the field of literature, I assume we mean literature written from the point of view of the class-conscious working class, whose socialist consciousness illuminates their whole view of the nature of the world and of the potentialities of mankind. By *Critical Realism* I assume we mean literature written in the era of class society from a point of view which, while not fully socialist, is nevertheless sufficiently critical of class society to reveal important truths about that society and to contribute to the freeing of the human consciousness from the limitations which class society has imposed on it.[1]

Each of the stories in this volume fits into one or other of these categories quite comfortably.

Common to both socialist realism and critical realism is the concept of the individual character as type. Because a writer deals with apparently isolated characters, and seeks to deal in psychological depth with those characters, does not mean that the writer necessarily upholds bourgeois individualism. As Kettle remarks in the same paper: "There is, of course, no contradiction between this general presentation of a character as a type and his presentation as a unique and even eccentric individual."[2] In his "Intellectual Physiognomy of Literary Characters," Georg Lukacs says, "general, typical phenomena must at the same time be particular actions, the personal passions of definite individuals."[3] Engels was saying the same thing in his letter to Margaret Harkness, in which he offered criticism of her novel *City Girl*: "Realism, to my mind, implies, besides truth of detail, the truth in reproduction of typical characters under typical circumstances."[4] Because of space limitations of the magazines in which the following stories appeared, the degree of particularization of characters varies, and therefore the degree of obviousness of the general as opposed to the particular varies. But in all cases it is finally the general, the typical, the shared, and the representative nature of the individual character that counts.

Equally important is the relationship between form and content. And here even Engels could over-generalize. In the same letter to Margaret Harkness, he remarks, "I am far from finding fault with your not having written a purely socialist novel ... to glorify the social and political views of the authors. That is not at all what I mean. The more the author's views are concealed, the better for the work of art. The realism I allude to may creep out even in spite of the author's views."[5] Here Engels eliminates the possibilities of a certain kind of working-class literature. For forgotten is the oral tradition of working-class life that seems to require narratorial intrusion. As a matter of fact, in the mainline English tradition, the novels of Austen, Dickens, and others would have to go if the prescription against narratorial intrusion were to become absolute literary law. Agitprop theatre and such forms would be unthinkable.

So far, then, as certain stories in this collection have a genuinely old-style working-class base, they have their roots in an oral tradition. In pubs or on the factory floor, for example, the narrator commonly notes any new faces in his audience and interrupts his tale as he sees fit to clarify a point for these new persons. Essentially this style resembles that of the tribal storyteller. What is wrong with the most misguided and propagandistic of literary works from the 1930s is that their writers use this aspect of the oral tradition so clumsily in the realm of print. While in person the careful intonation, modulation, gestures of the living narrator will carry a heavy load of propaganda without being unduly obtrusive, the same narration placed in print tends to become less "real." And the less real the narrator becomes, the more his interpretive or exhortatory intrusions can appear to be heavy-handed propaganda. Obviously great care is required when the narrator breaks into the story.

Narratorial intrusions can be explained by the origins of some of these stories in the working-class oral tradition and by the nature of audiences that the stories were aimed at. It is also important to remember, however, the space limitations faced by our writers in the badly-financed magazines that required them to get to the point quickly. Bearing these two considerations in mind, we see the stories below divide into one or more of the following kinds: 1) those with no narratorial intrusion; 2) those in which the intrusions blemish the work; 3) those in which the intrusions are effectively drawn from the oral tradition and used for purposes of economy in a very short story, in particular to explain a fact of working-class life which is alien to an audience of bourgeois readers; and 4) a special variety in which the working-class oral tradition and the old bourgeois tradition of narratorial intrusion come together for literary purposes.

The following survey of some of the more interesting stories is intended to offer a sense of the variety of stories from the 1930s, an understanding of how that literature works, and an insight into the strengths and weaknesses of representative stories. It assumes, of course, that some stories from the left are decidedly worth preserving and transmitting as part of a full Canadian literary tradition.

Several of the stories in this collection take us to the heart of mechanized, dehumanized life under industrial capitalism. The first is the brief, excellent one by Leonard Spier with the unlikely title, "A Dream of the Air Meter: A Revolutionary Fable." The "Dream" is obviously a political dream allegory in the tradition stretching back at least to the fourteenth century of William Langland's "Piers Plowman." In addition, it shares qualities with science fiction—the journey into a strange world, and the dystopian or nightmarish inversion of the traditional utopia.

Clearly the two worlds in this story are in fact the two worlds of two different social classes. The narrator, apparently petit-bourgeois, allies himself with the working-class victim to throw off the yoke of the corporations and their capitalist state. Were this all there was to the story, however, it could not be as compelling as it is.

As Stewart Ewan has indicated,[6] capitalism began as a system of economic control but up to the twentieth century did not attempt to invade and dominate directly the many other areas of life beyond the workplace. Gradually, however, increasing industrialism took away human skills and work satisfaction and made the human a mechanical function of the machine. The world of Taylorism had arrived. Man as machine is what we find represented in this story, but Spier goes further than this for he has the corporations, through the air meter, control the life of the individual at all times. He points to the increasing development of the new means of manipulation and control by corporations, as well as the increasing dominance of steadily expanding and very regulatory state bureaucracies. The answer to the problem of domination becomes clear from the allusion to the Communist Manifesto when the narrator says to the creature, "You have nothing to lose but that weight on your neck."

B. Gluckman's "Juggernaut" is also a most interesting story. Two years before Lewis Mumford's speculations on the socio-economic implications of the clock[7] and 35 years before E. P. Thompson's splendid paper on time, work-discipline, and industrial capitalism,[8] Gluckman gives us a quintessential, multi-dimensional account of the role of clock time in the transformation of men into machines. One passage in particular makes most obvious the implications of time and discipline, both industrial and social:

"Here's your badge and tool checks," says Harry, "and mind the clock."

Ah! the clock. The clock must be punched. Every eight hours. Every morning ... every night. Sorrow, joy, mothers, fathers, children, sisters, volcanoes, cataclysms ... the metallic clang of the clock-punch drowns them all.

The line moves on ... four feet to the minute ... and body and entrails are already concealing the bare chassis. In go the engines, on go the fenders and wheels ... one by one, with automatic precision.

We see the clock-time of industrial man overriding day and night, concepts belonging to the unruly and shifting natural order of time observed traditionally by the farmers. In the realm of production, therefore, quantitive time dominates qualitative time. It is possible to feel joy at seeing the sun rise when it casts its pale light on a cold winter morn, or despair at yet another snowstorm as the darkness disappears, but it is not possible to *feel* anything about an abstract, precise 8:30 on the clock. Yet clock time invades all areas and disciplines feelings ("sorrow, joy"), human relations of all kinds ("mothers, fathers, children, sisters") and human responses to the unmeasured and unpredictable aspects of nature ("volcanoes, catalysms"). Above all, of course, quantitative clock time dominates production ("The line moves on ... four feet to the minute"), and therefore it dominates men. "In go the engines, on go the fenders and wheels ... one by one, with automatic precision." But there is no sense here of human involvement. It is as if the components put themselves together. That, of course, is exactly the point: there are no men here while the line runs, only machine-like extensions of machines who work "with automatic precision."

We read that "the clock must be punched" and we cannot help but observe that "punching" is associated with physical violence in one of its meanings. Quite apart from the violence clock time does to the feelings of these men, there is a literal physical violence born of the unnatural —and time-measured—factory setting. The mediator between the ruling class and the working class, the foreman, is a man of violence. In this battlefront in the war of classes, a command from him to "get on with the job" brings an insult back from a German: "There is no hesitation. His [the foreman's] lips shut tightly and his eyes narrow, he hurls a bunched hand into the face of the other." When the German "whips out a knife" we see that "Again the fist flashes to the face and the blow thuds home with crunching impact." This physical violence—and the obvious dismissal and subsequent unemployment—is the external discipline that is applied until unruly former agriculturalists and craftsmen internalize thoroughly the discipline of the clock and accept the passive (but productive) role the monopoly capitalist system has prepared for them.

Families must eat, and therefore men must work, and in order to work they must accept the discipline of the clock. Accepting the discipline of the clock means accepting a new mental framework that transcends all previous ties with external nature and modifies human nature so as to change relationships between relatives and friends. All this is in the interest of generating wages for the worker, but, above all, surplus value for the capitalist. A major theme of the story, therefore, is alienation and its origins.

Why call the work "Juggernaut?" The *Shorter Oxford English Dictionary* defines the title word as being derived from the Sanskrit "Jagannatha," which is a compound of jagat (world) and natha (lord, protector), and therefore means "lord of the world." The word has come to mean "Anything to which persons blindly devote themselves, or are ruthlessly sacrificed." Somewhat prophetically, industrialism has become "lord of the world" (in both monopoly capitalist and state capitalist societies) and it has all along—thus far—been a system to which generations have been ruthlessly sacrificed.

A. Miller's "Night Shift" has the brevity of "A Dream of the Air Meter." "LOGS! LOGS! LOGS! Lookit 'em come. Blast 'em," the story begins, and we are introduced to a theme from the factory floor that was common to the thirties (and is still very much with us): the speed-up of the production line. And if the matter of money is treated humorously in this story, there is still an underlying grim seriousness whenever it is mentioned. In the factory dining hall we hear:

> "Say, Molly," Slim whispered to one of the waitresses, "what chance to take you to the dance Saturday night?"
> "Yuh gotta make some more dough, big boy, before yuh can tag along with me," Molly retorted with a laugh.

Slim's standard mode of speech contrasts with the dialect of Molly. Her speech is that of the molls in the gangster films of the thirties (hence her name). Indeed, with her laugh she consciously adopts the role of gangster's moll.

Despite the humour, there is a clear sense of the way in which the cash nexus is advancing to become the sole link connecting different individuals in an increasingly alienated world. Now money was needed to pay for the organized "entertainment" characteristic of the new world of alienation. There is in Molly's answer a direct reference to the costs of going to a dance and an implication of the cost of movies through her impersonation. But this story is important also for the way in which Molly so easily adopts the role of gangster's moll. We see here the alienation function of Hollywood movies as persons are weaned from local cultures and standards and made to accept the "universal" norms set by an imperialist culture, an imperialist culture on the rise under the guise of democracy and people's art.

Money, of course, appears ironically at the end of this story:

> The nightshift went into breakfast with cigars in their faces. "Ho Slim," shouted one of the day gang, "what's on—everybody smoking cigars?"
> "We made an extra profit of one to two thousand dollars on the shift, and they give us a lousy ten cent cigar. We cut a million feet."

The cigar is an early version of the "worker incentive" and the dining hall is generally new to the period and represents the ideology of corporate welfarism, a "fringe benefit" designed to keep workers loyal and happy. There is plenty of room for the irony at the end.

INTRODUCTION

With "Production" by J. K. Thomas, we are again on the factory floor, this time in a tomato canning factory employing both men and women. And here again what is being produced is not simply a commodity, but a society of a kind. For the main theme we see that the technological rationality of the factory produces a system so narrow—it must exclude so much—that it has no room for human frailties, in this case a very human pregnancy. What this system requires is perfect human machines, that the women be treated like machines: "Every woman wore a card pinned on her back. Having checked the basin [of tomatoes], the inspector punched a hole in the card, and Sally sent the basin off on the roller." Here we are not far from the creature in Spier's "A Dream of the Air Meter." Moreover, once again, the obvious instrument of this narrow technological rationality is the clock. For when Helen is late and sick because she is suffering normal human physical difficulties—i.e., when she is not a machine—she is fired by Blore, the manager and foreman of the plant. " 'But please, sir, I need the job.' She caught at his arm. He answers, 'Get out, and stay out.' " His is the power behind the clock and he treats her as an example to the rest. If they do not discipline themselves to conform to the will of the system, they too will be without income. And in this environment of fear even the inspector wanted to keep his job and therefore kept his mouth shut.

"East Nine" by Dyson Carter takes us straight to the shop floor in a dramatically convincing opening:

Everywhere pulleys rattled incessantly. The vibration of the floor, the screaming of the knives and the flicker as the belt shot up and over, up and over, merged into one continuous rhythm of feeling, sound, and sight. The whole rickety plant roared as though an express train thundered through its dismal bowels. Old Sam's mill was busy.

The words "belt shot up and over, up and over" have an onomatopoeic quality that captures the rhythms of the process it describes. As if in answer to a question asked, the last sentence, "Old Sam's mill was busy," is perfect understatement following the preceding description.

One of the controlling images of the story is that of the industrial factories and support systems as a battleground in a continuing war: "Doctor Fraser was a compensation man, trained in the dressing stations of the [First World] war, an expert in patching the unpublicized by-products of industry." (Included here is the notion of men as *products*—by-products—of the system.) Fraser, in fact,

> patched and scraped and re-patched until legs and arms could be moved. Just enough, you understand, so it wouldn't be a total disability. The queer remains, like the vets who make poppies and wicker chairs, would be put into offices, learning to write with their left hands or sitting stiffly erect in steel belts, until they could be let out during a slack period. It was cheaper to have them on relief.

Again, the military imagery emerges: "Morale, in the ranks of the class warriors of the Compensation Ward is as important as morale elsewhere." And

> Dan, the oldest orderly on the staff, an ex-Royal Navy man, remarked to Ma Thompson that it [the Ward] reminded him of the unholy night at Jutland when he had bandaged sweating men on the deck of a half-sunk cruiser, scrawling letters home for the dying crew while they prayed against hope that the can wouldn't sink.

Carter's purpose in distributing these effective images throughout his story seems to have been to suggest the ubiquitous presence of the military mentality in capitalist society.

Wardle, the Communist in the East Nine Ward, says ironically: "Tomorrow we will send a delegation to take it up with the Commissar for Heavy Industry. All in favour of execution for demanding this worker to repair a motor while running?" Despite this scene and the "Aye" chorus of the men, this is not a story that simple-mindedly presents a caricature capitalist villain, Sam. Sam himself is made to be a victim of necessity. Necessity, in the form of the contractual imperative, causes Sam to tell Carl to fix the brace while the machine is running. He would, indeed, do it himself if he had to, as he tells Carl. Thus Carter points intelligently to the capitalist system itself rather than simply to a single supporter of that system as the problem. In one sense Sam is a victim as much as his men, and he is tied to his men in a union of opposites.

At the back of events in the hospital is an attack—again a correctly aimed one—on the capitalist system, and one that tackles the system on its own grounds. For in addition to the inhumanity, the system is shown to be inefficient, irrational, careless. Were it otherwise Carl would not have died.

The conclusion to the story is a prose poem of great beauty, worthy of standing with the best literature of the past. (For full effect it needs to be read aloud.) We are as far here from crude narratorial intrusion as it is possible to get.

In "The Rail" the factory haunts the worker in his leisure hours. Matt Murray Armstrong creates a working-class narrator, Paul, who visits Niagara Falls with his wife and son. As a result of Paul's advanced state of anomie his wife and child remain shadowy figures on the edge of his confused consciousness. Indeed, the outer world of both nature and society comes to match the inner state of a life made meaningless by the monotony of repetitious industrial labour:

Everything merges and goes around. The Sunday afternoon crowds, jostling, laughing, pouring past me. That stream of cars which rolls steadily by, from every Province, every State, gliding along, gliding endlessly along like the water over the Falls, always going around, going around in a dreary circle, getting nowhere, ending nowhere. Like the damnable job which is eating away my days, my years. My life. (Punch in. Start the machine. Watch it run, watch it run. Shut it off. Punch out... Eat, sleep, work, punch in, punch out. Life!) Without end. Without change. Around and around, each year closing in on me more and more. Stifling me.

Paul's mind is drifting toward suicide, and we see the connection between the world of work and the desired world of "victory," of suicidal escape, of the man in space. He throws a pebble over the side and then his handkerchief, which he watches as it slowly drifts downwards:

> It was like the dreams I sometimes have after being at the Falls, when I seem to float along the crest of the cataract and out into that unknown world of purity which must exist there. That unattainable world. It is a beautiful, satisfying experience... Clean... Pure... So vastly different from that far distant, dreary circle of eating, working, sleeping, punch in, punch out. My head is whirling. I know that my feet are on the bottom rail. But I cannot stop. I have no desire to stop.

By now, as in a movie shot, potential physical act of self-destruction gives way to dream as the narrator collapses, unconscious.

The story closes with the tolling ring of "Tomorrow is Monday again." The death in life of industrial production makes death itself adopt the guise of freedom in this inverted world. Paul represents the human spirit revolting at the attempt to mechanize him. While his obsession with suicide is somewhat less than revolutionary, it nonetheless is a common enough human response to the process of dehumanization, and his thoughts and actions make the reader consider their causes. Here is where the process of politicization of a reader begins.

Many short story writers from this decade also turned to the farm, and the agonies of rural life during the Depression, for thematic material. "Mrs. Hungerford's Milk" by Bertram Brooker is a particularly successful story, one that seems to be the essence of simplicity itself. One of the obvious qualities about this work that helps it give body to a convincing illusion of reality is the appropriateness of details. As Joe approached the house "He took off his hat with a sort of swoop and pitched it, like a quoit, aiming for the stoop outside the kitchen door, but it fell just short and rolled in a puddle. 'To hell with it,' he said." The little scene is perfect, as is the description of his drink from the rain barrel: "He went to the rain-water barrel and dipped himself a basin of water. With one swoop of the basin he skimmed the dead insects aside and plunged it down deep, bringing it up quickly to keep the dead flies out of it." Those who have tried will know that this is exactly how it is done. Again, at the beginning of Joe's anger because of the failure to deliver the milk on time, "Hettie held out the plate so that the steam would float under his nose. 'Come on in and get started, Joe,' she said. 'This'll all be cold.' " The act is a convincing piece of feminine diplomacy economically done by Brooker.

Such scenes are important for the creation of the living reality which is the story, but they are not the source of the work's power. Nor does it lie simply in three individual characters who are particularized sufficiently so that they and the conflict in which they are involved become thoroughly credible. Nor again is the stress on an individual family the key we are seeking to the strength of the work. For what we need to observe about "Mrs. Hungerford's Milk" is that the individual characters are also types, and on top of this the family that they constitute is also a type of the family in a particular social class at a critical historical juncture.

First we note that Joe keeps cows, which are tended by his wife and daughter, and that he has a small but not very lucrative cartage business. He is, in fact, a figure in transition between a rural and an urban way of life, for one "business" makes him an agrarian, petit-bourgeois, independent commodity producer (milk) and the other an urban petit-bourgeois entrepreneur. The key to Joe's character as individual and as type, however, is that he is the embodiment in literature of Leo Johnson's thesis about the decline of the old petite bourgeoisie.[9]

We see signs of decline at the beginning of the story:

It looked good around the yard. Some folks would be all for painting the house; but he liked the grey, old, blistered sheathing. He liked the marks of weather over everything, the stains of wear and time, the bleached boards, the sinking steps. It was all right.

Joe can aestheticize his decaying house as much as he likes, but the fact remains that the property is running down. Moreover, he has decided on a course of action that will ensure his failure to survive in the competition for existence in his world:

Ramshackle, his brother called it. But that was just him. He was a baker in the East end. He was a fusser, his brother was. He'd even got the women up on their ear about things. Said he ought to get a truck and keep up to date. But, what the hell, his brother was spending every nickle he made—keeping up to date!

Here we see that we are in the world of trucks, and it becomes self-evident that, economically, a horse and dray cannot compete for long with a truck. Joe, however, has decided against a truck, and for that reason he will go down in the petit-bourgeois struggle for survival. The mention of the brother "spending every nickle" to keep up to date reinforces the idea of the perilous competitive nature of existence for the petit bourgeois in this society.

Not only is Joe going down in the world in terms of social class, but he is also going down in terms of his sense of his own worth. Outraged, he shouts commands at his wife and daughter, but his violent assertion of authority loses strength and he becomes speechless:

This is *my* say! You keep still. I'm sick of this kind of life. *This* is no life for a man. I won't stand for it—do you hear? I'm going to change it. I'm going to have a wife and daughter that has some respect for the old man—or—or—I'll walk out on you. I'll—I'll—

But by now he realizes his impotence.

The inability to earn decent money does not help Joe to retain his authority over the family, as we see in a short passage: "Hettie stood with her back to the stove, looking at him. 'You'd better quit giving estimates, Joe,' she said, *in a tone you use to a child*. 'Tell 'em it's by the hour. That's the only way you'll ever make anything.'" (Italics added). Quickly Joe changes the subject and asks, "How's the supper?" It would be a mistake, however, to view the Depression as the underlying cause of Joe's loss of authority over his family. To understand Joe's loss of status we should turn to such 1920s Manitoba novels (Brooker lived in Manitoba in his formative years) as Martha Ostenso's *Wild Geese* and Robert Stead's *Grain*, as well as to Leo Johnson's thesis. In the novels we see a younger generation representing the forces of an urban and social democratic egalitarianism rejecting the patriarchal authoritarianism that is the characteristic feature of a petit-bourgeois agrarian society in transition.

The decline of the petite bourgeoisie and the difficulties of earning a living in the Depression make Joe Snell in "Mrs. Hungerford's Milk" the type of declining patriarchy in its latter stages. But the work also looks forward and Joe becomes the essential type for the future as it would be developed by the various forces of monopoly capitalism, particularly advertising, to penetrate, divide, and control the family. The wife becomes a *manager* on the home front while the husband becomes a bread earner out in the world. Clearly Joe is not doing a very good job of earning money to support the family, and clearly his wife speaks to him as a manager, for the general "tone you use to a child" is basically the tone of the manager (superior mind, rationality) to worker (inferior mind, strong body). Little wonder Joe says to himself, "They act like I was just a lodger around the place," for that, in an important sense, is just what he is.

Also set on the drought- and Depression-plagued prairies, Alice Butala's "A Day in Town" is a potentially good story marred by minor but insistent and unsuccessful narratorial intrusions. For example, at the store with his wife the farmer says to the store-keeper:

"Relief man don't seem to be showing up. Guess you hafta let us get some things on tick."

The storekeeper smiled his oily regrets and the pair found themselves standing on the step.

"I could have let them have a bag of flour," mused the merchant, "but they didn't even haggle." He felt a prick—*surely it wasn't his well-trained conscience*. But when another customer came in, he was whistling cheerfully. (Italics added)

We are *told* how to respond to the scene rather than allowed to respond (as the earlier account of the farmer's wife's sufferings in town would make all but the totally insensitive do) with sympathy for the farmer and wife and contempt for the storekeeper. Except for the unnecessary narratorial intrusion, the scene convinces the reader of its reality and it does so in most economical terms.

"A Day in Town" is filled with irony as it progresses through a series of oppositions including the urban versus rural, agrarian petit bourgeois versus merchant petit bourgeois, poverty versus plenty, and male versus female. Given the farm setting it is ironical that the woman places "a loaf and the one remaining *tin* of salmon on the rickety table" (italics added) for her children as she prepares to go to town with her husband. Arriving in town she enters the store:

Gratefully she huddled near the hot stove in the store and held out her hands to its warmth. She looked about. Vigorous children eating cornflakes, impossibly fat babies drinking canned milk, a lady calmly reading while an electric washer did the work. Aunt Jemima coaxingly urging you to make pancakes by mixing water with a packaged preparation.

Through the advertising we see the illusions of abundance that the capitalist system has about itself and this contrasts with the brutal realities of the last tin of salmon back on the farm. Again, the leisured lady (presumably youth and beauty) in the advertisement represents a generalized illusion in contrast with which stands the grubby reality of the farmer's wife. Not to be missed here is the way in which the farmer's wife, the *type* of the prairie farmer's wife in the period, must see the joint products of her and her husband's labours reflected back at her in alienated, unobtainable form, an alienated form that the colourful vitality of the advertising "art" work attempts to gloss over. It is here that we see the significance of the "*tin* of salmon" and the "*canned* milk." Through large-scale canning, products have been transformed by capitalist entrepreneurs and returned back at a substantially higher price to those who laboured to produce them in the first place.

The advertisement, in fact, is destiny staring the petit-bourgeois farmer's wife in the face. For both she and her husband are destined to join the work force in the cities and their small farm will become part of a larger, high-technology agrarian capitalist unit. One of the agents of this rural-urban transformation is the storekeeper who will not extend credit (the story does not suggest the point, but he was doomed, too, with the eventual rise of supermarkets). The pressures forcing removal from the land to the cities are everywhere and are captured in the story by the inability of the woman to find a place in which to rest and stay warm. She is turned out of the store because it is lunchtime, out of the waiting room of the railway station when the "station agent came to the wicket and glared at her," and out of the post office when she reads a poster warning against loitering. Both private and state institutions join hands to tell the small farmers that they are not wanted. And that the point is to remove them from the land we learn with the notice in the post office: "A Sale of Land for taxes told its own story. She idly studied the postal rates. Three cents on a two-ounce letter. My, that was half a cent more than she was allowed for a meal." These small farmers lead a clearly marginal existence and it is obviously only a matter of time before they go into the cities and down in social class.

As social types the storekeeper and his wife represent an historical phase of capitalism in its transition from an emphasis on primary accumulation and production in the mercantile and industrial phase to the consumption phase of monopoly capitalism in the recent past. The storekeeper's wife represents the acquisitive, possessive Calvinist phase while the storekeeper stands for the consumption phase as we see in the reference to parties when we meet the storekeeper's "designing hussy" friend. Here we meet with a simulated beauty and youth actually in the context of advertising. For the big fat babies stare down on the "designing hussy" who "seemed as though [she was] one of the cardboard figures...come to life." The woman "was forty-five, but all her friends assured her that viewed from the rear and at a distance you couldn't tell she was a day over seventeen." There is not a little irony in this observation, but it does not detract from the increasing emphasis in this society on youth and beauty. The "shabby black coat of the farmer's wife" who has the "dull ache in her back" stands in contrast with the obviously urban "Permanent wave, modish house dress, trim silken ankles, high-heeled pumps...."

Patriarchal family relations stand out in this story also, for

While his wife had been dodging fearfully from one inhospitable shelter to another, he had been taking his ease in the restaurant. There men were able to congregate and settle the serious questions of the day. There was talk, laughter, games, and congenial company.

Earlier the archetypal (but affluent) version of patriarchy had confronted her in the post office when "the Royal Family gazed down at her from a poster advertising cornstarch." Here we have the suggestion of the connection between patriarchy and monarchy, monarchy and capitalism (and because this is Canada, monarchy and imperialism).

A few simple words in this story speak of the dehumanized inhumanity of this society. We read that the woman "Gratefully... *huddled* near the hot stove" and later "she *scuttled* back across the street" (italics added) and we get the feeling that this is not a human being under observation but an animal or an insect. In such ways is a cruel society indicted. Again, the narrator speaks for the woman and says, "All *praise* to the railway company that provides, among numerous other *blessings*, a toilet in each town." The italicized words commonly appear together in the context of praises to God, but in this despiritualized world there is not a little irony in the replacement of God by the railway company, not to mention the object for which praise is given: a toilet.

Sinclair Ross' "Circus in Town" also has at its heart the decline of the small independent agricultural commodity producer and the decline of patriarchy. Common to other prairie works from the 1920s onwards also is the attraction of the city and its ways for a younger generation.

In the eleven-year old Jenny we find a vivid, young imagination responding freely to the arrival of the circus in town but being repressed by the cold and narrow economic realities of the old family life in the form of her father. Rebuffed by her father as she excitedly runs to tell him of the arrival of the circus, Jenny dashes away to talk to her mother, whose calm understanding of the situation speaks volumes about what she herself has at an earlier date repressed in order to accommodate herself to farm life. "What's wrong?" the puzzled father asks when he senses the hostile environment as he enters the house. "Wrong?" the mother retorts, with great passion. "You—and the farm—and the debts."

What we see here in fact is the disintegration of the old pioneering farm unit. For if the mother and father are at odds, it soon becomes obvious that son and daughter, Tom and Jenny, share the value system of neither the one nor the other. They simply leave the house when the parents argue. The mother, of course, sees how this society seeks to reproduce itself when she says of Jenny to her husband: "Look at her clothes and her bare feet! Your own daughter! Why don't you take hold—do something? Nothing ahead of her but chickens and cows." Here the patriarch's authority is being stripped away. In fact, she has already said the opposite to Jenny: "Never mind, Jenny...your day's going to come. You won't spend all your life among chickens and cows or I'm not the woman I think I am." Here the mother projects her own repressed ambitions on the daughter and simultaneously, if implicitly, recognizes that a new freedom from the old toil is possible in the new world that is emerging.

So convincing an illusion of reality is this little gem of a short story that it tends to lull our critical faculties into a state such that we can accept this illusion of reality as reality itself. But while the story works supremely well as art, it finally falls short on the side of truth because of its petit-bourgeois world vision. Certainly we cannot fault Ross when he reveals the repression of women and when he clearly sympathizes with the young. He is, however, quite unfair in making the father here the villain. The father is what he is, and he has the debts that he has, because of the larger economic necessities of the time over which he could apparently have no control. The freedom from the patriarchal-style control of the father which Ross describes is real enough, but the failure to see that the father is himself manipulated as victim by larger economic forces only dismantles the old family in the name of freedom ultimately to put the same family in the hands of the advertisers and other hirelings of monopoly capitalism. Thus, freedom from the historically necessary and simple slavery of prairie patriarchal society gives way in real life to a more subtle and complex form of slavery in monopoly capitalist society. This, of course, is to bring out the historical implications of the limits of Ross' vision. So far as he went he was on the side of freedom. In the long run, he didn't go far enough.

In L.A.MacKay's "Another Man's Poison" the country confronts the city. Four men from rural Ontario, on their way to the Canadian National Exhibition, stop in Toronto to look up the brother of one of the men, who is found in abject poverty but who refuses to return to the country with them. Evidently the country may be "One Man's Meat," but it is "Another Man's Poison": the brother insists, "What? Me? After living in the city, go and squat in a dead-alive hole like that? You must think I'm crazy."

The title of the story, however, is ambiguous in relation to the object that it seeks to describe, and it is here that we move to the true significance of this short story. For as Bill and Charlie and Ernie separate the fighting brothers, they laugh at the scene. They then go to the Ex. and they find it to be "a darn good show too" but not "a patch on that [the fight of the brothers] for fun." Indeed, a week later Bill still laughs at the scene as he tells his story. In fact, this laughter takes us to the heart of the story as we note the ironic interplay between the narrator and the frame of the story on the one hand and the story that is told on the other. The narrator reveals an utter callousness, an inhuman indifference to the garbage-picking animal existence of these human beings because it is not his poison but "Another Man's Poison" and therefore he does not need to think about it. The narrator and his friends are like Conlon in Kimball McIlroy's "Late November," the storekeeper and sundry figures in Alice Butala's "A Day in Town," and the narrator in John Ravenhill's "The Hero Returns."

Other stories in this collection draw us into the urban experience in Depression Canada. "Hydro" by Luella Bruce Creighton introduces us to a working-class family and community without any bourgeois characters. It begins with a melancholy and ironic reversal of the bourgeois calculating principle that aims at material gain. Here a mere five dollars is necessary to have the Hydro turned back on, and Mrs. Hainer wants it on because she fears having her new baby by the light of an oil lamp. We have here a kind of calculus of Depression poverty as Mrs. Hainer tries the different combinations of cash, persons, and events in her mind. The crux of the matter is that if the baby comes when it is due her husband will not be able to do the three days' work he has been promised. He will therefore not be able to earn the money to pay the Hydro. What to do? In the event, a characteristic working-class community spirit, a spirit of mutual help in shared adversity, comes to her in the form of neighbours. The hero of this story, in fact, is the community spirit itself.

Mrs. Hainer is well drawn as a simple ordinary woman who unsuspectingly accepts the exploitive capitalist world at its own evaluation:

Then when Joe got the trouble in his toobs, the cough, chronic bronchitis, the doctor said, he lost his job at the radio factory. He used to do spray painting, and lacquer. He was off six weeks, and they let him out. Joe didn't get another job. Times got hard, then.

This is a finely controlled piece of irony in which we, the readers, are made to do a lot of work. For *we* must make the connection between the spray painting and lung troubles, and we must also draw the socio-economic implications of "chronic bronchitis" and the devastatingly simple but explosive words, "the doctor said," which follow. The simple Mrs. Hainer may be fooled, but we must not be. The author intends that we be reminded by this irony of the way in which doctors served the interests of the ruling class by deliberately failing to diagnose industrial diseases as industrial diseases so as to avoid paying compensation. All in all, "Hydro" is a very sensitive portrayal of the inner and outer dimensions of certain aspects of working-class life in the period.

Urban, bourgeois culture was often grist for the writer's mill in the 1930s. In "The Gift" Mary Quayle Innis has a single character rise in social class and shift in social consciousness to reveal the difference between working-class minds and their bourgeois counterparts. Very simply, Judith is the familiar bourgeois variety of the consumer common to our own day. Alienated, she has lost contact with life as struggle and she has therefore lost contact with life. Having deliberately developed into a bourgeois individual, she has become an isolated being with nothing left to do but search for gratification of her whimsical needs. In her story "The Party" Innis takes us inside a tragedy for such types. In her calculating and callous fashion Ethel wants to throw a party

> to pay their social debt to Mildred and Earl for the trip to Lake Simcoe, yes that, and to the Rhyners for the dinner ... but principally, honestly, to show their friends that while so many people were out of work and selling their cars and moving into cheaper houses and wearing old dresses, Todd had his job the same as ever and they could afford just as much as they ever had.

The party over, the irony of the situation reveals itself when Todd hands her his lay-off notice. The message of this story to its bourgeois readers is clear: you may believe that you are safe but you are not. No one is safe within the framework of capitalism.

"Bread Line" by Maurice Lesser introduces us to a bourgeois who learns nothing from experience. Cheever Ingram has seen better days of good apartments, fine clothes, money, and all the rest. Now he stands in line with

INTRODUCTION

sixty other men outside a religious mission awaiting his turn for stew.

> Somebody prodded him with a compelling forefinger. Cheever turned, snarling, he was weak from scanted sleep, and hunger twisted his nerves to quick peaks.
> "What's the matter?" he flared.
> "Hey, ya don't need to bite my head off." It was a puffy little man, behind him.

Reluctantly involved in this conversation, Cheever learns from the man that

> "Every guy that gets in here tonight gets a' overcoat along wit' the mulligan" [stew]. The puffy little face suddenly drew up in pleats of enthusiasm. "Jeese, ain't that somethin'?"
> Cheever grunted—"Maybe," he said. "Got a cigarette?"
> The habitual fear of the down-and-outer made a swift furtive mask in the other's eyes. "Ain't got a thing, pal, s' help me," he whined. "This was even the last chew I had."
> Cheever thought, I can't blame the old mooch. I'd probably hold out myself if I had any smokes and he asked me.

This scene needs to be watched carefully, for thus far the so-called "old mooch" has given Cheever information about the overcoat and asked for nothing in return, while Cheever has tried to "mooch" a cigarette off the so-called mooch. What Cheever does, in fact, is to project onto others his own value system. If a mooch is one who seeks to satisfy his material needs without labour and at the expense of others, then clearly Cheever is the mooch here.

Cheever's mooching is part of a broader ethic of acquisitiveness as we see when he spots his old camel-hair coat and recalls the secret pocket he had his tailor put into it, a pocket in which he always kept a one-hundred-dollar bill. Having condemned the people running the mission ("These confirmed, more-blessed-to-give-than-receivers ... they were all the same"), even if he mooches their food, he cannot wait to get his hands on the hundred-dollar bill he believes to be in the pocket. This he intends to spend on himself: "He was thinking, as he ran, in pictures of food, baths, clean linen." Ironically, when he gets the coat and feels in the secret pocket he pulls out the paper, "Good for One Meal, and One Night's Lodging at the Lighthouse Rescue Station." Whereas he had sought to escape briefly to the illusions of his affluent past with the hundred dollars, the chit represents the immediate present that he will not accept. There is not a little irony also in the possibility that the better-to-give-than-receivers received a hundred dollars while the mooching better-to-receive-than-giver must continue to mooch.

Kimball McIlroy's "Late November" takes as its theme the closed universe of the unthinkingly callous and of a certain kind of bourgeois personality. Conlon is obviously retired and possesses an adequate income. Every day for two years he has gone to the park and bought peanuts on the way, as he does on this late November day. The group of unemployed men on the corner are sense impressions to him that remain unanalyzed. The names of the dead on the cenotaph have no meaning for him. Thus is he cut off from both the living and the dead, from culture and history. However, he does enjoy feeding the squirrels who know him and expect him every day. The hungry old man who watches him and asks for some peanuts Conlon quickly categorizes as "a bum," and with him he reluctantly shares the briefest of secondary relationships. Truly human relationships central to a sane world are inverted in this story. The work is successful in that it does not stoop to preaching but lets the bourgeois character reveal itself in action.

In "Staver" Mary Quayle Innis presents another fascinating story of bourgeois and working-class minds, which does not quite come off because of a basically unresolved tension between a quasi-Freudian sexual strain and a Marxist class line. The vision Innis set out to develop is not fully realized. We meet a weak bourgeois husband, a strong bourgeois wife, and a physically strong and attractive proletarian. The latter's refusal to eat the lady's apple (the new Adam in a new Eden theme) suggests the sexual theme but this is not synchronized with the class theme in which the working-class type demands work from the bourgeois type (woman) but refuses to offer any sign of subservience.

A. M. Klein's "Beggars I Have Known" carries us further into the world of the unemployed. It is a discursive essay filled with ironies. The key to the technique is as old as the hills. Klein will delight and persuade, and he will do so in that order. The first two sentences set the tone: "I get along very well with beggars. Perhaps it is because they feel I shall soon be one of them." We smile inwardly because this begins the process of inverting the normal order of things. Instead of the narrator's saying of beggars "there but for the grace of God go I," here the beggars say of the speaker, "there by decree of necessity goes a man who will shortly be one of us." Very insidiously, Klein undermines false petit-bourgeois notions of security and superiority and suggests that appearances cannot hide reality from the beggar, who emerges a figure of wisdom: "Whenever I pass a panhandler on the street he buttonholes me. Even when I say, No, I can't spare a dime, he never feels resentful. He knows I am telling the truth, even if I am wearing a new suit." As he gets into his stride Klein takes us into the underworld of beggars that, not surprisingly, comes to reflect the larger capitalist society. A "couple of guys ... who are nothing more than racketeers ... will give begging a bad name." We smile at this and expect more, so we read on:

Tommy Kinsella, who is a real returned soldier, lost his [military] badge and all he can show are two sawed-off legs.... He's a funny case too this Tommy. He doesn't seem to mind his stumps very much, but he's always complaining about getting T. B. because his nose is so near to the ground.

While we are laughing delightedly at the pair who will give begging a bad name, we have the savage knife of persuasion shoved into our ribs as we read about Tommy.

The same process characterizes the invitation to become a beggar:

As a matter of fact, they have often asked me to become one of them. They don't mind a little extra competition if it comes from a decent fellow, and they lead me to believe that I am such a fellow. They tell me, too, that it is a very happy profession, that you are out in the open all day, that you have no overhead expense, and that you can never be laid off because you are working for yourself. They've planned a union for beggars, but have found it impossible. It's a capitalistic society, they say. But even without a union, one can make a nice living. You can't strike in your trade, I said. People would be happy if you quit work. Would they, though? they said. A rich man can't live without a beggar. He needs him to protect his conscience.

The notion of the little kingdom of beggardom as having the problems of the larger society delights in the literary sense that it puts to us the over-familiar in very unfamiliar form and makes us see it in a new way. While we are smiling at this we have the social function of beggary in capitalist society put to us and we learn beyond any doubt that beggars are not simply individuals who, for whatever reason, have personally chosen their mode of life. They are a structural part of the capitalist society that created them.

The ironic, thirties upshot of all this comes at the conclusion where the narrator realizes that he is not qualified to become a beggar:

I have no ailments, I am not blind, I am not crippled, I am perfectly healthy. Only I am poor; and that's like being blind and crippled. Worse, because you feel helpless without any excuse. But I can't become a beggar; I can't stop pitying myself.

This in contrast with the beggar's earlier assertion: "Our superiority over those who give us money is this: they still pity us, but we have stopped pitying ourselves." The self-pity leads to a debilitating inaction and the speaker reveals himself as a victim of structural defects in the capitalist order. "Beggars I Have Known" transcends the time and place of its creation.

Irony turns to satire in Larry Lawson's "Burp's Busy Day," a deliberately distorted and consciously created caricature of a contemporary capitalist and politician. Lawson presumably names his character Burp to imply both the windy result of his habitual over-eating as well as to suggest the wind-baggish nature of this oily politician. The story would seem to have been written with a distinctly Depression-style, unemployed working-class audience in mind. The sardonic wit of "He ordered a light repast, consomme, sole, a little cold chicken, salad, cheese, and coffee" tends to get lost on an audience which does not particularly fear where its next bite is coming from. Hard times would quickly revive an understanding of this feature of the work. As it is, the tendency for the story is to head, deliberately, in the direction of a silly Ruritarian comedy, for we meet Burp's man, Persimons, discover his chauffeur, Jitters, and see Burp go to the Bloaters Club, while all the time we hear the unceasing refrain of "Sir, Sir, Sir," the outward sign of social differences and required deference in this society.

All the ironies are there for as he drove by, the well-dressed Burp "did not notice a group of *shabbily dressed men* outside the capitol gates being watched by another group of *smartly dressed police*" (italics added). The night before Burp had "been at an official dinner, a small party of twelve with only eight courses...." This morning he meets a delegation from the unemployment camps: "Twelve men who looked as though they had been sleeping for weeks in their clothes...." The model for the twelve is that of Christ's disciples, and befitting a class-divided society we have two sets of them here, the twelve capitalists of the night before and the twelve destitute, unemployed workers.

From the ante-chambers of high politics, Dorothy Livesay's "Case Supervisor" takes us into another crucial sector of the state in Depression Canada—the welfare system. We enter the consciousness of Miss Chilton, a case supervisor, a kind of platoon commander in the battle of the welfare budget. At the top are the remote but all-powerful businessmen who control the system and threaten to administer it themselves if demands for funds are not reduced. Beneath them is the sharp Miss McQueen who rules over the bureaucracy and plays off one case supervisor against another in an effort to please the businessmen and be "professional." Beneath her are the two case supervisors, the reserved Miss Chilton and the more extroverted and better-liked Miss Dogherty. Beneath these two are a number of social workers, including Miss Cherry, who do most of the actual visiting and investigating. Miss Chilton is thus caught as a mediator between the demands of the needy poor (through her subordinates) on one side and the demands (through her superior) of the greedy rich who do not want to support welfare on the other. As the story demonstrates, there is no escaping the generalized crisis, not even at the movies. Miss Chilton is torn between the demands of the system (represented by Miss McQueen) to treat the poor and suffering as objects, and a human desire (represented by her subordinate, Miss Cherry) to treat them as fellow humans in distress. The inner anxiety thus generated seems to have Miss Chilton heading for a breakdown. The story does not attempt any solutions to the problems it raises, for that is not its purpose, but rather seeks to analyze and thus demonstrate the subjective and objective dimensions of a specific social situation to indicate that even what might appear to be cold and inhumanly objective bureaucrats are potentially available for politicization if the pressure on them becomes too great. We must note that Livesay herself was a social worker. She knows whereof she speaks!

The collection closes, as it began, in the realm of dreams. "Dream Train" by Simon Marcson (son of Marx?) presents us with a college-trained bourgeois who has found his destiny with the working class as an organizer and agitator in the class struggle. Head on a log he crosses the country in an empty coal car at night. Between sleeping and waking he leaps backwards and forwards in time to the world of bourgeois illusion in which he had been raised ("fairy castle, of knights, beautiful damsels, and dragons") to books ("paths to civilization's treasure-houses"), to a recognition of the reality of dehumanization in his society, to his lost love ("Hers was a beauty that pervaded.... Poets described it....."—a common poetic theme of romanticism) to class struggle, to agitation, to jail and so on.

The train cutting through the night and the fields of "Canadian grain" becomes more than a train; it becomes a symbol of the country, Canada, grubbily working its way towards socialist enlightenment. Marcson fragments his sentences and piles scene upon scene to create a verbal montage effect. From fragments towards wholeness, from dream to reality is his theme—but not yet.

NOTES

1. Arnold Kettle, "Dickens and the Popular Tradition," in David Craig, ed., *Marxists on Literature: An Anthology* (Harmondsworth: Penguin, 1975), 214.
2. *Ibid.*, 233.
3. Georg Lukacs, "The Intellectual Physiognomy of Literary Characters," in Lee Baxandall, ed., *Radical Perspectives in the Arts* (Harmondsworth: Penguin, 1972), 94-95.
4. Friedrich Engels, "Letter to Margaret Harkness," reprinted in Craig, *Marxists on Literature*, 269.
5. *Ibid.*, 270.
6. Stuart Ewan, *Captains of Consciousness* (New York: McGraw-Hill, 1976).
7. Lewis Mumford, *Technics and Civilization* (New York: Harcourt, Brace, 1934).
8. E. P. Thompson, "Time, Work Discipline, and Industrial Capitalism," *Past and Present*, 38 (December 1967), 56-97.
9. Leo Johnson, "The Development of Class in Canada in the Twentieth Century," in Gary Teeple, ed., *Capitalism and the National Question in Canada* (Toronto: University of Toronto Press, 1972), 141-183.

VOICES OF DISCORD

LEONARD SPIER

DREAM OF THE AIR METER
A REVOLUTIONARY FABLE

It was a beautiful day, cool and invigorating; one of those half-sad days of late September. The air was heavy with dust. As usual, it seemed to sweep along like a swift current. By this fact I thought I knew where I was. This proved incorrect however, for approaching me staggered a spectacle I have yet to witness in my own home land.

At first glance it was a man like myself. Yet it was hardly that which made me pause and stare in astonishment. Its back, or rather the back of the man, was bent as though bearing a burden. Which it was. Attached in some fashion, to the nape of the man's neck, was a device not dissimilar to our common gas meter, but small and compact, though evidently of great weight. I had no time to examine it closely, for my attention was immediately summoned to the countenance of the individual, down which, in spite of the cool weather, trickled streams of perspiration. His bulging eyes were screaming with anguish, and, as several blood-vessels had already burst, minute rivulets of blood were visible. His face was reddish-purple. It was turning black, when by this fact and by his desperate contortions, it finally became apparent that the man was strangling.

Only after a long moment of mingled terror and perplexity, could I determine what his agonized gestures signified. Who would believe it! The upper side of the mechanism that he bore upon his back, carried a small slot for coins. He was imploring me to place a nickel into this tiny scissure, and of course I did so. His expression immediately registered relief. Strangulation ceased. His eyes and the colour of his skin became more normal. It was not long before he could talk, and make me deep-felt declarations of gratitude.

But a greater shock awaited me. When I inquired what his ailment was, he answered in a tone of surprise that there was nothing internally wrong with him. It was his air meter. As I expressed complete ignorance of this contraption, he explained that in this land, not only soil, gas, electricity, food and water were monopolized by corporations and taxed by the state, but likewise the air!

This was achieved by simply attaching and sealing an air meter to each citizen. At a given length of time a coin must be fed the meter. Should the citizen fail to do this, a pair of wires, otherwise loosely fitted about his neck, are suddenly drawn tense by the mechanism, and slowly but relentlessly prevent him from absorbing air. Once a week a collector from the General Air Company comes around to empty the meter of its contents, a small percentage of which goes to the government's tin box. It is also his job to detach the machines from the necks of those subscribers who have expired with their subscriptions.

The man then told me that somehow, through an unknown calamity, he was discharged from his job. He supposed it might be fate. And as he had spent his last cent, he had nothing left wherewith he might gratify the hungry air meter. Consequently, the plight in which I had found him.

By the time he concluded his explanations, the meter was already clamoring for another contribution, and the man began to gasp. I then asked: "Why don't you cut the wires and destroy the machine? You have nothing to lose but that weight on your neck."

He looked at me half tearfully: "No, I can't. It might

give me a shock. Beside, it's against the law to tamper with the damned thing."

"But you don't mean to say that if the law required you to choke to death, you are still going to respect it?"

He deliberated a moment, while his gasping became heavier, and then remarked with decision: "Very well. You dislodge it, and I won't resist."

"But I'm afraid that that can't be done. You'll have to help."

Then, without waiting for a reply, I continued: "Here, while you prevent the wires from choking you, I'll take that stone lying next to the curb, and smash the machine."

His reply was to place the fingers of both his hands around the wires which were throttling him. It was hard for him to grasp the wires, and they were already drawn tensely. But he succeeded. Then I clutched the stone, and while holding the machine in one hand and the stone in the other, began to strike. The machine was by no means dogmatically inorganic; on the contrary, it seemed to be possessed of a diabolic animation. With the result that through its cunning, I often missed the mark, striking my own hand instead, and bruising myself on the jagged and broken fragments.

One peculiar aspect of the struggle was that the more effectively I smashed the obstinate thing, and the more unrecognizable it became, the more tenaciously did it draw its deathly tentacles about the neck of my friend. These wires had already torn through the flesh of his fingers and were threatening to saw their way through the bone. Blood streamed down his hands and wrists and dripped to the pavement. But he was breathing more freely than before.

Finally I said: "All right, friend, one more round and this fight will be over."

He responded by massing his remaining strength in one great tug upon the wires, while I, at the same time, smashed with all my might. Then, with a loud grating sound, followed by a report, the wires were torn free while the machine crashed to the street and rolled into the gutter.

At this point, I awoke. The sun had erected great blazing shafts of light across the ceiling of my room.

Masses (May-June 1933)

B. GLUCKMAN

JUGGERNAUT

You certainly wouldn't think if you saw it on the first links of the line, that it was the fetus of an automobile. To Stephen Tuomi the Finn and Henry McNab the Scotchman, who work opposite each other, it resembles nothing more than a bare frame of steel that requires numerous punchholes and rivets. These punchholes and rivets will keep two families that comprise in all twelve human beings. So they swing their heavy rivetters slung from the rail above and carry on their work with absolute unconcern for the nerve-wracking tattoo as steel hammers against steel.

The factory is in the dull roar of full production. Wheels, bodies, and parts litter the floorspace in orderly piles. Blue neon gas tubes on the girders above the paint-spraying booths substitute for daylight. Underneath goggled workers fire thin coatings of lacquer from their spray-guns onto bodies.... Up, down.... Up, down.... Then across, for eight hours a day. The air is faintly sweet with banana oil from the paint fumes.

Like a giant right angle bend the line winds through the plant ... its nondescript crew shackled by want no less securely than the slaves of galley days.

Outside the barred iron gates stand perhaps two, three hundred men. Broad high-cheekboned Slavic faces, thin swarthy Italians, and the skilful blue innocence of the Nordic. Their faces are heavy and dissatisfied in a vague way. Like tired horses in a thunderstorm.

The gateman is old. The oldest employee of the Company. One day he will die. Then the foreman will go around to the boys and collect contributions for a wreath from the Company, to put on old Charley's bones.

But Charley has lived a long time, and doesn't feel like dying at the moment. He has also seen almost a generation of men standing like patient cattle outside the iron gates, and the sight now makes him irritable.

A car swings off the road and sounds a shrill, imperious note at the knotted group before the gate. They swing readily apart, actuated by the selenium ray of visible power, but press into the gap that has opened in the gate.

"G'wan get back there!" shouts old Charley, "we don't need anybody jest now." He flaps his old arms and they retreat. Muttering darkly to God, but careful that no audible roar escapes, in case old Charley hears and remembers the face. That would mean no job.

A shiny new car hurtles through the doors of the factory, spins crazily at a sudden twirl of the wheel, and screams to an abrupt stop. The inspector climbs out, opens the bonnet and peers inside. He is a long thin man, and wears a conical hat and yellow dust coat that looks like a minister's summer uniform.

A thin column of steamy white smoke crawls lazily into the sky, from the slender stack that stands on the blotchy red squatness of the Powerhouse. Inside the office the switchboard operator is speaking to the Superintendent's department.

"There's a man here who wants to see you about a job," she says.

"Tell him to file an application," he says. "I'm busy just now." She tells him.

"I mus' see the Superintendent," he says, with a thick accent and stolid determination.

"He's busy now."

"Where is his office? I wait."

She shrugs her shoulders, and points to one among the glass-panelled dormitory of offices. He passes a clatter of typewriters and joins a small group on a bench outside the office. After a while the Superintendent, a tall white-haired man with glasses and a jaded air, opens the door of his office.

"Any metal finishers here?" he enquires. The new arrival stands up and follows him in. For about five minutes they talk. Then the Superintendent pushes a buzzer and a small man with a toothbrush moustache comes in.

"Take this man on Harry ... metal finisher." Harry nods the only way. Then begins the ritual.

"Name?"

"MacDonald."

The toothbrush wiggles skeptically. No kilt or heather ever caressed the body with that accent. Still, as Swenson observed to a friend outside the gate "Maybe I tell them I'm Scotchman ... otherwise not get job as Swede."

"Here's your badge and tool checks," says Harry, "and mind the clock."

Ah! the clock. The clock must be punched. Every eight hours. Every morning ... every night. Sorrow, joy, mothers, fathers, children, sisters, volcanoes, cataclysms ... the metallic clang of the clock-punch drowns them all.

The line moves on ... four feet to the minute ... and body and entrails are already concealing the bare chassis. In go the engines, on go the fenders and wheels ... one by one, with automatic precision. The noise is almost an even beat. Only the rivetters scream into the higher registers.

A heavily-built German is helping to fit in steering columns. The men working with him over the chassis seem greatly amused at what he is telling them, and the group stands out for an instant against the clamour and moving background.

The foreman has been watching them and walks up behind the German. He is well set-up himself, with a battered face.

"Quit that foolin' and get on with the job," he orders, with tense muscles. The German looks up sideways and sneers. "Shut your bloody mouth you verdomte—." He uses a foul word. The men can't understand it but they snicker. One delayed minute and the foreman might just as well hand in his badge.

There is no hesitation. His lips shut tightly and his eyes narrow, he hurls a bunched hand into the face of the other. The German falls heavily against a moving chassis, but is up in an instant with bloody mouth and raging eyes. He whips out a knife and makes a mad leap at the foreman. Again the fist flashes to the face and the blow thuds home with crunching impact. The German falls with his head towards the cement floor, but the foreman reaches over quickly and grabs him.

It is all over in perhaps two minutes and the line goes on. The chassis arrive at the turn-table at the right angle bend. The overhead pulleys grip the bodies in their padded teeth, and the trolleys bring them into position above their respective chassis. Then they are slipped on like lids, and the men bolt them into place.

The whistle hoots and the shift changes. It is also the signal for the lunch hour for the salary roll employees and the half-hour of the foremen and shifts.

"Goddamit I told my son ... no cadets for you ... I've done all the fighting you'll ever do ... and if the teacher wants to know who done said it, tell him to speak to me, see?"

If you didn't see you most certainly heard, for old Ed Moore, the boiler-room engineer, is an old salt with a roar like an angry lion. The small group in the lunch-room smile. They are discussing war and conscription. Without benefit of education in the academic sense. Yet with a much greater appreciation of the rhythm of realities. Yesterday they had been discussing sexual perversion. No mention of the term or of Havelock Ellis had been made because they knew not ... yet they quoted cases of the Jones and the Smiths with unconscious facility. Perhaps theory is only a web spun by the spider of historical experience.

A silence falls on them, and they attend to the business of eating. It is a tableau of strong jaws, powerful limbs and a species of content. Workers.

"S'pose we'll work on Good Friday," remarks one of the foremen, "still I don't mind."

"That's all right for you," answers a palefaced billing clerk, half bitterly, "but I don't get paid overtime."

"You've got nothing to complain about," pointed out the shipping foreman, "you're getting full time. As soon as the season is over we'll be laid off while you'll only be on short time. And it's hell when you've got a family."

"There's something wrong somewhere," muttered one of the men, crystallizing all their unspoken thoughts.

Their faces lower until they look once more like the men outside the gate. The enigma of unequal employment and unemployment has taken away the taste of the brown bread sandwiches.

The line moves its cargo slowly forward. The cars are now at the finishing stage. Windshields, cushions, and mascots. It gradually approaches the wooden runway. Yet no trace of haste is apparent among the men. It is a swift symphony.

The front wheels tip over the side and commence to turn. The car tilts downwards. Then at the exact moment a man swings himself behind the steering wheel and guides the car in the right direction.

The eight hours are gone. There is no overtime to tempt anyone to strain. The gates dribble a tired stream of men. A car that they have built stands at the curb.

"Nice bus," says one. "Yeah! I'd like one myself," says the other.

Canadian Forum (October 1932)

A. MILLER

NIGHT SHIFT

"Logs! Logs! Logs! Lookit 'em come. Blast 'em!" Shorty the sawyer was talking to his friend Slim, the oiler. A quarter to twelve on the night shift, and though Shorty was a stocky little man, his gang of ten revolving saws was taking it out of him. He stood before a row of levers on a little platform slightly raised above a broad inclined table. Down the incline, on moving belts, floated slabs and dressed planks of various dimensions.

Shorty's speciality was the cutting of the lumber into certain required lengths. Backwards and forwards, up and down, Shorty moved his levers, and up and down came his saws through the table—two, three, four—sometimes he would have six saws in sight at the one time. And the sweat rolled off his eyebrows; for there was no let-up once the machines were in motion; and if he missed an odd piece he would soon hear about it.

"Only five minutes to go," said Slim.

"Thank cripes," Shorty gasped, "I'm nearly all in."

The whistle blew and the night-shift crews moved over to the cookhouse for supper.

"She's comin' pretty regular tonight, Slim. What's the drive?"

"Oh, I dunno," Slim answered, "but I believe the carriage men have a flea in their ears. Somebody circulated the rumour in the boarding house that the day shift can cut half as much again as the night shift."

The head sawyers, electricians, saw-filers and mechanics sat at one table; the oilers, boom-men, and labourers sat at another. Two comely waitresses were moving briskly between the two with trays of food and pots of coffee.

"Say, Molly," Slim whispered to one of the waitresses, "what chance to take you to the dance Saturday night?"

"Yuh gotta make some more dough, big boy, before yuh can tag along with me," Molly retorted with a laugh.

There was little time for pleasantries in the dining hall.

The business of eating was soon over, and the men hurried back to the mill. At five minutes to one every man was at his post. One or two at the smaller saws were in position holding their respective pieces of lumber, like athletes throwing the discus, ready to start the cut the second the whistle blew.

The siren screamed. The electricians threw in the switches, and immediately everything was in motion. The whirring of the electric motors, the ear-splitting buzzing of the saws, and the clank, clank of the steam-jacks (long cylindrical affairs that tossed logs of six feet diameter as though they were baseball bats), with the thump, thump of the logs coming up from the river on endless chains, made a thunderous funeral dirge for the passing of the monarchs of the forest.

Slim had what was called a snap in the mill—though there was not much money in it. He could fill his forty or fifty lubricators in an hour, and with good oil they would run half a shift. After midnight it was his custom to doze away an hour, oblivious to the row and racket of the machines, on a broad beam among the whirling pulleys about a foot and a half from the roof. "Ho Curley," he called to one of the greasers as he was climbing the ladder, "if ya see the Sup snoopin' around give us a shout."

"Aw right," Curley replied somewhat grouchily.

About an hour later Slim rose on an elbow just in time to

see Curley drawing the Sup's attention to his roost on the beam. Tradition had it at that time that a camp or mill boss had to be a tough guy; so the Sup came up the ladder blasting and swearing in the traditional way. Slim barked and blasted back at him—told him to mind his own business; that his outfit was haywire, and that he could have his (Slim's) time made out in the morning.

Slim then came down from his perch, wandered down to the mill basement, and made a pretense of examining a leaking steam gland.

An hour later the foreman came around with a box of cigars. "What's the gag?" queried Slim, as he bit the end of the perfecto cabbagio.

"Last night ya cut a million feet," said the foreman.

The nightshift went in to breakfast with cigars in their faces. "Ho Slim!" shouted one of the day gang, "What's on—everybody smoking cigars?"

"We made an extra profit of one to two thousand dollars on the shift, and they give us a lousy ten cent cigar. We cut a million feet."

Masses (March-April 1934)

J.K. THOMAS

PRODUCTION

"She's late again," Maggie said, as she tore the skin off a tomato.

"Yeah, she'll get hell when she gets here. The old bastard'll raise hell again," Sally said. She looked furtively behind her. "The poor kid needs looking after."

There was a silence, while they peeled the steamed tomatoes with skilled fingers, cut to the core, and looked for any black spots. The inspector ran his hands through the bowl before punching your ticket, and if there were any black spots there was a row. No use saying anything, he was always right. The firm had a reputation for pure food he would tell you.

Women stood at either side of a long table. A belt rotated along the middle of it bearing large basins of steamed tomatoes. The women operated on the tomatoes rapidly, and for each basin filled to the top, and piled up ("see it's piled up good and plenty," the foreman said) they received four cents. A good worker could make a dollar fifty a day; but she had to move fast and grab the basins quickly.

"He said he'd kick out the next person late," Maggie said.

"Oh, give her time," Sally said. "She can't be more than five minutes late." It seemed later because everybody got to the factory door early. They ran to be there on the dot when the doors opened, as if this was their last chance to enter Paradise. Some of the damned usually waited for an hour or so, on the off-chance of being taken on.

"With her man out of work, she's gotta get here. It's tough luck. Morning sickness gets 'em like that, you know."

"Yeah, I guess so." Maggie paused a moment and regarded her tomato bitterly. Then realizing she had stopped working, she resumed furiously. She was the younger of the two girls and at seventeen had that bright, brief bloom of the factory worker that had completely disappeared from Sally at twenty-six. Maggie's vivacity was in sharp contrast to the grim earnestness of Sally. One had full red lips, the other a thin red line. They both wore old sweaters in the early morning, although they took them off when the sun came up and the steam was on. Yesterday was a scorcher and today promised to be as bad.

"That's one basin," Sally said and sighed. Her lips tightened. "Hi!" she shouted impatiently to the inspector. "Tick me off!"

Every woman wore a card pinned on her back. Having checked the basin, the inspector punched a hole in the card, and Sally sent the basin off on the roller.

Canning tomatoes is a seasonal occupation. The factory is in operation all day and night so that the tomatoes do not rot in the store room. The girls live by piece work for eight hours a day. The Canadian government has a maximum hour law for women; there are two shifts for them; one beginning at six a.m.; the other at three p.m. There is no such law for the men who get twenty cents an hour. They work a fifteen hour day, six a.m. to eleven p.m. (two hours off for food) so that they can make a living wage. Their employers believe in a living wage, you see.

I had drifted into Burlington, on the shores of Lake Ontario, and had been glad enough to get work, even at fiteen hours a day. But by Saturday night, I thought I would never be able to look a tomato in the face again. When you are unloading crates of tomatoes the juice of the squashed ones seeps through your trousers, down your legs, and into your boots. When you get home at night, your trousers are stiff with tomato and your legs are sticky with drying juice. But at eleven o'clock you get too tired to bother about this, especially when you know that you have to get up at five-thirty. Later I was shifted to the inside, and given an apron which kept my thighs dry and feet wet. I had to feed a machine with the peeled tomatoes. I worked next to the women, just opposite Sally, Maggie, and Helen. We three knew about Helen's condition. The two girls had helped her by slipping tomatoes they had peeled into her basin when she felt low. Only good workers were kept on, and any fall off in the production brought Blore yelling around the plant. There were a group of local factories in the company, and Blore had the reputation of having the highest production rate among them.

Helen sneaked in. To me she looked about the same. A tiny unremarkable woman, with a smile that was determinedly bright. She had good features but was not beautiful. You had the impression that in a different setting she would be attractive. She wore an old sweater, a tomato splashed skirt and sneakers. She looked about twenty-four. Her cheeks were white, her dark brown hair was drawn back clumsily, and the deep shadows under her eyes completed the ellipse her eyebrows began.

"Did he see you?" Sally asked quickly, moving aside to make room for Helen.

Helen gathered a basin, some tomatoes, and a knife, looked quickly about her and said "No. When I punched the clock he wasn't in his office." She smiled faintly.

"What a break." Maggie said. "How do you feel?"

"Lousy." Her face fell. "I was sick as a dog. Bill wanted me to stay at home but I knew that would finish me up here." She ripped the skin viciously off a tomato. "I gotta stay as long as I can."

Sally said, "Yeah, I guess you gotta stay."

The factory settled down to its monotonous routine of the day. The machine that sealed the cans persisted in its maddeningly exact rhythm, and its hellish noise. The belt rotated endlessly. The air smelt of boiled tomatoes. The women shifted from foot to foot seeking some relief for their tired feet. Their fingers moved deftly and rapidly. Their faces had a dogged look, except when one knocked on the table with her knife to call the inspector to check her basin; then they would look impatient. It seemed the usual sort of morning, only a little hotter than yesterday.

Suddenly I heard Blore's angry voice at the door.

"Why the hell don't you go to the can before you get here? Always running backwards and forward wasting time. Get on with your work and make it snappy." The woman hurried forward with flushed cheeks and went on with her work mumbling.

Blore, the manager and foreman of the plant, was a short thick-set man, with a powerful build. I suppose I was not very objective, but his eyes seemed as much like pigs' eyes as they could possibly be. He had black hair, a red face, and a voice that could be heard above the roar of the machinery. But it was the eyes that held your attention. He had a habit of walking behind the women, his hands on his hips, stopping behind each one to examine their work and progress. The women would watch the inevitable approach, work silently and furiously when he was behind them, and sigh with relief when he had passed.

He had reached Helen now, and stood behind her. She had just finished her second basin, and fidgeted nervously while the inspector punched her ticket. Blore examined her basin of peeled tomatoes carefully, in silence, then looked at her card.

"Is that all you've done—two basins?" he roared. "The others are on their fourth. What the hell have you been doing?"

Helen hung her head and said nothing. The other women stared at her for a moment with understanding eyes, then went on with their work glancing up furtively to take in the scene. Maggie and Sally tried to appear unconcerned.

"Have you got a tongue? I said what have you been doing?"

She bit her upper lip. "Working, sir." She grabbed a passing basin.

He stopped her and pulled her round to face him. "What time did you get here?" he yelled.

"Twenty after six, but..."

"Late again, eh? I thought I told you you were through if that happened again?"

"Yes sir, but please sir..." She started to cry.

"She's not feeling very well," Sally said.

"Who asked you to interfere? Get on with your work."

"She's a sick woman," Maggie said earnestly.

He turned on Maggie. "For Christ's sake, shut up!" he roared, "or get out!" Then turning to Helen he said, "You're through. Get out."

"But please, sir, I need the job." She caught at his arm. He brushed her arm away with his other hand. She caught at it again desperately, clung to it and would not let it go. Her face was sweaty, and the tears were running down it. She sobbed, "Please don't fire me. Please let me stay!"

Blore drew his arm away. He looked raging mad. Then he yelled at the top of his voice, pointing towards the door, "Get out, and stay out."

Helen looked at him a moment uncertainly, then was sick on the floor.

Sally and Maggie helped her to the door in silence.

Blore turned to the inspector. "Get this muck cleaned up." he said sharply. "Gotta keep the place clean. Get another woman." Then he said something to the inspector in an undertone, behind his hand, and they both laughed. The inspector wanted to keep his job.

— *New Frontier* (July-August 1937)

RUBY RONAN

ONE-DAY SERVICE

Morning begins. The girl's voice is fresh, incisive. "Five Star Cleaners! Just a minute, please. Go ahead: there is your party. Yes, madam, you can have your dress picked up today and have it back the next day. Surely, madam, we guarantee all our work. What is the name please? Mrs. Smith, 145 Smithfield Ave., North Kildonan. Thank you."

The call is put on the spindle. At eight o'clock Mason, the north-end driver, comes into the shipping room to get his pick up. He sorts out the orders, grumbling. "Whew! Look at that. Smithfield Ave.! Why couldn't that damn operator take a call in the city for a change?" As none of the other drivers answer him, he rushes angrily into the office, shoving the call slip under the girl's nose. "Why not pick a call a bit further away?" he drawls.

"Oh, you drivers are always kicking. You know as well as I do that if I refused a call, there would be hell to pay around here. Sling out of here, and stop bothering me." Jeers greet him as he returns to the shipping room. At the same moment the general manager enters from another door.

"Hey! What the hell is this? A meeting? If you want a meeting you can go to the Liberty Temple, not here. Now get out and get your pick ups."

The men bend their heads, pretending to be busy. Only an old timer answers him. "Who asked you to sleep in? We've been waiting here for over half an hour." He is told to make it snappy. The men run out to the waiting trucks.

Mason makes his deliveries doggedly. It is nearly ten o'clock when he reaches Smithfield Ave. As she hands him the dress, Mrs. Smith asks: "And how much will that be?"

"Plain one piece? One dollar, ma'am."

"Oh, but I can get it done at some other cleaners for seventy-five cents and they do just as nice work."

"I'll bet they don't belong to the Dry Cleaners Association." He grins at her. The same old story. "We get fined you know, if we go below the standard price. Tell you what I will do though, seeing as you are an old customer: I'll take the dress for 75 cents, but I'll have to make the bill out for one dollar."

"All right then. You can have the dress. Be sure and make a good job. I must have it back not later than eight-thirty tomorrow night as I have a bridge party on."

"You'll have it back for sure, ma'am! We always give a one day service. Thank you. Good morning."

It is nearly noon when the driver comes in with his load of pick ups. A bill must be made out for each order, and then he comes into the marking room, dumping his load on the table. The room is hot and damp, smelling of gas. Four girls are working in the choked atmosphere, stacking the tables and bins with dirty, smelly clothes. Their hands must move swiftly, touching clean or diseased garments with same speed and accuracy.

They do not speak to each other. Speed and overtime in the summer must make up for the slack winter season, when they work in half-time shifts. Now all they say to each other is "Make it snappy!" The boss has a habit of dropping in, ready to shout, curse and threaten if he scents a mistake. All the girls' energy goes into their work this morning, as the dust penetrates their perspiration-soaked clothes, and the air becomes heavier. The floor is already littered with dust and papers as Charlie, an undersized boy of fifteen or so, cleans out the pockets and brushes the cuffs of suits, stacking them for the cleaning process.

"Wish I was a girl," he is thinking. "They get ten a week for all this sweat. Wish I was a girl. Five dollars don't go far."

Now the cleaner has entered. He is shouting. His body is big and well-built, but his voice is bigger. "Hey! How about those dresses girls? I want a big load as soon as I put these suits through." He has left the door open, so a hot wave of bad air accompanies the deafening noise of the machines.

Flora, tired and hot, is ready to scream. "Shut that damn door! Don't you think it's hot enough in here?" The cleaner pays no attention to her, but wraps his bear-like arms about the large bundle of clothes and carries it into the cleaning room.

The cleaner works swiftly, dumping the bundle into a large washer filled with solvent and benzine-soap solution. He sets the monstrous washer going at full speed. After a while he stops the machine, and dips his hands at full arm's length into the strong solution, to take out the clothes. He then transfers them to an extractor. From there the clothes pass to a revolving dryer, an enormous machine which generates hot air. And now the cleaner can rest a moment, his face ghastly from the gas fumes, his hands blistered and caked from festering sores.

Beside him, in the same room, is the steam cleaner. All day long he stands in high rubber boots, to avoid the pools of grease and water on the floor. Clothes too dirty to be spotted come to him, to be dipped in soapy water and scrubbed with a coarse brush. He works fast, perspiration and water streaming from his scant clothes. His hands are red, shrivelled from constant dipping in hot and cold water, or from solutions of ammonia and acetic.

"All right!" He straightens up, putting the washed clothes into a fast-revolving extractor. Now at last he can leave the unhealthy atmosphere and take the clothes upstairs to the "hot drying room."

As he reaches the dress department, he comes into a real frenzy of industry. He hears the buzzing noises of fans, the banging of the lady spotters, the clanging of the hot irons on the holders as the pressers work swiftly. Ironing boards are lined up on both sides of the room with barely enough space between for a girl to stand and do her work. These pressers wield the heavy hot irons all day without stopping for a rest, for there are hundreds of dresses waiting to be put in readiness for delivery on the same day.

The steam presser stands a moment, watching the commotion made by young girls running from the "hot drying room" to the spotters and pressers, seeing that the "specials" are ready for the stackers, who again must hand them on to the shippers. There is a new girl among them, irritated and clumsy. He stared at her fair, flushed face. "I wonder how long she will think seven dollars a week is worth it?" he thinks to himself.

The girl sees him, becomes self-conscious, stumbles over a chair. The dresses over her arm fall to the dusty floor. A roar of voices. "S-sh! Quick! Here, I'll brush them off. It's all right, kid."

The cleaner moving out of the door, passes the word back: "Here comes the boss."

A sudden lull of voices in the room. The work continues with increased energy. The loud harsh voice of the boss is heard from the foot of the stairs, as he shouts at the marking girls to hurry with their work. His heavy steps are heard on the top stairs and then a renewed shout. "What the hell is this going on here? I could hear you all jabbering downstairs. What do you think I'm paying you for? You all get to work or the whole damn bunch of you get the hell out."

The newcomer stands silent, until another girl pushes her on. The boss continues to shout, working himself up into a temper of profanity. He does not see or feel the black looks cast at him by the workers. He strides across the length of the room. The spotters, pressers, dressmakers, tackers and shippers all seemingly intent on their work, glance sideways at him as he passes. In front of him is the finished line of dresses, waiting to be bagged and sent downstairs for delivery.

"Hey! What the hell is this? One forty-five Smithfield

Ave., marked 12 o'clock special. What is the meaning of this?" He motions to one of the shippers. "It is four o'clock now. What do you think you are going to do? Keep this dress here till six o'clock, when it is wanted for twelve?"

"But Mr. Courtney, it had to be recleaned, and we couldn't possibly run it through for twelve o'clock."

"I don't give a damn. Reclean or not. It is marked for twelve and it has to go at twelve."

"But if we send it out and it is not satisfactory to the customer, you come up here raising hell."

"Who says anything about sending the dress out dirty? Get it ready on time and see that it is a good job. That is what I am paying you money for. Now bag that dress and be quick about it."

The girl shrugs her shoulders helplessly, tears of rage in her eyes. She jerks the bag off the rack, over the dress, and after attaching the bill, slides it down the chute into the shipping room. The boss watches her, shouting: "I'm going down stairs to make sure that dress is delivered immediately. If anything like that happens again I'll fire all you goddam shippers." He means it, for labor is cheap. There are girls begging for any kind of job. He thinks he is safe.

A subdued babble of voices follows, but every girl turns diligently to her work. They seem to be merely tired, hot and worthless machines. But they are thinking, silently. They are unorganized. But day after day these incidents grow, loom larger. There is a silent tension among them, solidarity. Very few among them are getting the Minimum Wage. Yet in the minds of one or two there is the knowledge that "The boss will not enforce the law. We must enforce it." Knowledge grows.

Now it is six o'clock. It is not heralded with a sigh of relief for a good day's work done. Instead, it seems as if most of them are just beginning to work. The drivers come in with another load of pick-ups to be marked for the night's cleaning. They stand about the shipping room waiting to get their loads together. Every one is rushing hither and thither, as if in a fever. There is shouting, cursing and commotion. Finally the general manager loses his temper and orders the drivers to clear out. He checks out their parcels. At last all the trucks are loaded; the drivers start out on the evening's delivery.

The north-end driver finds the boss waiting to see that he takes out Mrs. Smith's parcel. "Twelve o'clock?" he grins. "That was marked twelve so as to be ready for the afternoon delivery." The boss flushes angrily. "Didn't I tell you to mark the articles for the time when you want them?"

"Excuse me, but you did nothing of the sort. You told us to mark them at least one day ahead of time."

"Never mind arguing. Get the hell out of here and deliver the dress," the boss shouts.

The driver starts out. At eight o'clock he reaches the home of Mrs. Smith. "Five Star Cleaners!" The lady takes the bag out of his hand and gives him seventy-five cents. While he looks on she rips the bag off the dress and examines the garment minutely.

"Yes, it is a very nice job. I have a couple more dresses for you to take back to be cleaned."

Masses (September 1933)

DYSON CARTER

EAST NINE

Everywhere pulleys rattled incessantly. The vibration of the floor, the screaming of the knives and the flicker of the belt lacing shot up and over, up and over, merged into one continuous rhythm of feeling, sound and sight. The whole rickety plant roared as though an express train thundered through its dismal bowels. Old Sam's mill was busy. Six thousand frames! In the dingy office Sam and the book-keeper wisecracked over the steno's frowzy head. "God bless the busy little bees!" Sam wheezed, and the salesmen, infected with the return of prosperity, roared approval. Six thousand bee-hive frames for a new apiary. Spot cash. Delivery in two weeks.

They could make it. Sam pushed out into the shop and let the noise flow over him like an invigorating ocean wave. The boys were doing well. Grumbling a bit, but that was a good sign. He moved over to Carl Thorsen's plane. "How's it, kid?" His eyes followed the man's gesture to the high corner where the big thirty-horse thundered in majestic isolation.

"You gotta get that brace fixed," Carl shouted, reaching for a fresh board. "The back's rotten from the water leaking in."

"Right away," the boss agreed. His mind grasped without reflection the disaster that would follow on a major shutdown. "You do it. Get Steve to quit checking. He can handle the plane for a couple hours."

The man looked Sam in the eyes. "You want I should fix the brace while she's on?"

The boss grinned. "Maybe if you're scared, Carl, I can do it myself, eh?" Then, soberly, "We can't throw her off now. The sanders would be out too, they're caught up to you already. Right away, O.K.?"

Carl straightened his back and wiped his hands with a wad of shavings. "I'll get the new ladder," he said, and moved away. In a moment Steve, the clumsy apprentice who never would be able to move beyond that rating in Sam's mill, was standing on the little platform feeding the long white strips of pine along the polished bed. The shriek of agonized wood once more echoed through the plant. Sam nodded contentedly. His boys were good. Lots of trouble this last year, but with the work coming in again that was over. Better than relief, wasn't it? He went back to the office and settled down for a cigar.

Carl, high on the ladder, thumbed his nose down at the men, chuckled, and talked to the big motor as he struggled with the brace bolts. "We couldn't have you comin' down on our heads, baby, could we? Oh, no! You sure got to stand by Sam, honey. You're just like the Mint right now. Keep on like this and maybe we get back three or four wage cuts. Like to see the fat old bastard up here!" He swore at a skinned finger, shifted his weight. Hard job replacing a four-by-four, needs two men. The hole was off centre a bit, but he could force it in with the crowbar. Then he'd go downstairs for half an hour. Sam couldn't say a thing. He understood about fixing braces with the power on, even if the inspectors didn't bother him much. Carl stopped work, listening with admiration to the high whine of thirty horsepower playing with fifty tons of wood-working machinery. She could make it step! A honey for all her grease and grime.

The top rung of the ladder was wired loosely to a water pipe running under the ceiling. It began to move along the pipe. Slowly, you understand. And how could Carl feel it, with the ceiling shaking like nothing in nature? He couldn't.

Not until his feet slipped. "Oh Christ!" he said softly, just as if he knew what would happen when he grabbed for the rafter. Trying to take his weight off the ladder so he could jerk it up straight again. The two-by-four split at a knot and then the whole thing moved to completion like something in the comic page. The belt from the thirty horse was big. When the ladder touched it, it spun Carl over like a piece of paper coming out of a folding machine. Right over with his back against the belt.

Mike, the handsaw man, was the first to see it. The shadow of Carl's big body hurtling into the corner, the slow tangling fall with legs flapping in an idling belt and the crazy way the ladder tumbled down. Mike screamed. But everyone had seen by then, had started running for the switches. Old Sam was out of his chair in the office the instant the complex harmony of the shop became a discordant protest of slowing machinery. He cut the belt himself although there was no need for that. A little time and the mechanic could have got it out of the way. Sam was pale. Sorry for Carl. Sorry for the shutdown. Sorry for the looks of the men. An old-fashioned boss, friendly with the men, old Sam was!

The police ambulance was a long time coming and they couldn't tell whether Carl felt anything or not. He just looked at them, all standing around whispering as men do after an accident. When they lifted him on the stretcher—a hard job, nothing seemed to grip—he swore softly. Filthy curses that relieved the men. "You're O.K. pal!" Steve said, his huge coarse hands trembling like a girl's. "We'll be up to see you!" yelled the boys as they lifted him into the wagon. Then they went back to work, four of them making a scaffold to finish Carl's job. Mike jammed a stick in the lever of the main switch. "Any of you punks come near the juice," he snarled, "and I'll rip you." The brace was repaired in comfort and silence. Old Sam stayed in the office.

The cops gave Carl a piece of inner-tube to chew. No matter how hard he bit he couldn't make his teeth meet, but sometimes he crunched a cheek and the blood spilled over his chin. One of the cops was nervous. Just a young guy, not long on the wagon. He pounded on the window when the heavy ambulance lurched into a snowy rut, but the driver only grinned. He'd driven in France and knew the ruts didn't make much difference. Carl just chewed faster. There were a lot of piano wires in his brain, all pulled tight and he had to keep them from slipping. He knew it would kill him if they all sounded at once. Gnawing helped to keep them stretched. But they were slipping off, one by one, by the time they reached the hospital. Each one went to a different place in his body and stayed there quivering, so that when they hoisted him off on to a wheel bed he screamed. It cleared his head.

"Compensation case," the smoothly starched admitting nurse murmured. She listened to the police describe the accident, filled out a tag and tied it to the bed. A couple of interns came up as she went to phone. One of them lifted the blanket. "Right femur fractured," he said, feeling Carl's leg. The other one nodded and said: "Left one, too." Then they started to paw all over like kids looking for clover leaves. Carl had difficulty in connecting them with his sensations, but when he did the hallway echoed with the language of the mill.

Two younger nurses came towards the bed as the medicos lapsed into embarrassed silence. They chatted for a minute or so and went off to get an order for a hypodermic. Curious men and women hesitated as they passed the little group, glancing at Carl's distorted features and hurrying away, intent on their own suffering. The ceiling of the long hallway began to move past the injured man's gaze, unreal and without meaning as some trick movie shot with crazy perspectives. The nurses were wheeling him into the examination room.

Carl liked the tall blond one. As his sensations began to lose their sharpness he studied her, but whenever he tried to turn his head the bones rasped and something like a dirty grey blanket floated over his eyes. The brandy choked him. Gasping as the spasms shot down his limbs he spluttered the stuff in the nurse's face and over her immaculate white collar. With methodical and expressionless care she wiped his bloody chin and then her own velvet face.

When one of the interns returned with a lank white-haired surgeon, they put a shot in Carl's arm and found that it, too, was smashed. "Lineman?" queried the doctor, bending low over the sweating face. Doctor Fraser was a compensation man, trained in the dressing stations of the war, an expert in patching the unpublicized by-products of industry. He nodded with quick understanding as the nurse sketched the police report, gave a few directions and went quietly on his way.

The tall nurse stayed, absently rubbing Carl's forehead and staring out the window at the pale midwinter sunshine. Ages of time flowed on before the wrecked man became aware of brilliant lights, strange figures, sickening smells. The sharp cold rim of an enamelled pan came up under his chin a split second before he vomited. They were pulling and cutting the clothes from his leaden body. Suddenly a stifling cloud surrounded him. Someone started a thirty horse motor inside his skull. The whine rose to an unendurable pitch. Still higher. Up and up it screamed. Carl flew away on wings of anesthesia.

East Nine faces south and east, looking out over the river and the business district beyond. Its corridors are always filled with shambling men in faded pyjamas and dressing gowns, with crutches and canes, joking, grumbling, rolling innumerable cigarettes. Some of the girls like this ward, others dread it. The Super always prepares the probationers very carefully before they do duty up here. They're sent on the night trick at first, starting in the evening when the wives and children are visiting. That's when it's easiest. In the morning it's a tough flat, the boys are restless and their eyes are hard and bright, giving the nurses everything they'll take. White, wrinkled old Ma Thompson slips around from room to room, cooling the atmosphere, kidding and petting where it's needed, razzing the hard ones.

The boys knew all about Carl before he was rolled off

the elevator. The sick ones hoped he wouldn't be put in with them; the convalescents longed for the diversion of a bad case. The six single rooms were filled, so Number 97, with fourteen beds, won the toss. Blinds were pulled and the stench of ether floated around the screens while three nurses and a couple of orderlies struggled with the fracture boards, spread rubber sheets and lowered Carl's embalmed body to the bed. A pound of plaster and steel for every pound of flesh and blood. It was quite a sight. The old orderly shoved small hard pillows here and there with an experienced hand, marvelling all the while at Doctor Fraser's skill. "Just falling apart," he told the boys outside in the sunroom, "hardly a bone not bust. They ain't half set yet, but they didn't want to keep him under any longer." The men nodded knowingly.

Ma Thompson stayed on late, keeping most of the visitors out in the hall and balcony, taking extra readings for Carl's chart. At nine o'clock she called a special and between the two of them they brought Carl Thorsen, ex-planer, out of the daze. When he grinned, "Hyuh kid!" at the nurse, the old lady sighed and called it a day, going downstairs to sleep near a phone. You couldn't tell in a case like this, and Fraser would raise hell if all was not well in the morning. One by one the men of Ninety-Seven crawled into bed, or had their backs rubbed and tried a new position, lying awake in the dim light listening to the special and her patient.

Carl felt great. The huge mass of plaster was comfortably warm and his brain raced. No more piano wires. Just a sharp prick every two hours as the hypo rammed home. The special—by name June, very nice and very good on jobs like this—had a standing order and she intended to use it up before dawn. A little more each time, and he was a big man. She talked softly, on and off through the night, sympathizing, telling stories, not at all anxious to have the patient fall asleep. You never could tell with shock. Later, early in the morning, she kissed him, thinking of her boy friend and wondering how many nights there'd be at six-fifty per.

When the weary night shift girls came in to wake and bathe the men Carl was still talking. His lips were dry now, the temperature curve sharply up. With one arm free he tried to hold June to the bed, and behind the screen she kissed him again. She went down to breakfast wondering why no woman had been to see a man with an arm and a smile like that. By tomorrow the fever would make him hideous.

When old Sam came up, just before noon, the men sensed him way down the hall. You could tell a boss, somehow, or maybe you just expected him. Nervous and smiling and quickly sober, just like the other visitors, but different. The droning chatter fell off and a sharp hostility permeated the ward. They knew all about the loose brace and the rush order to be filled. Mike and Steve had been up the night before, right after work, with Carl's father and the kids. Anyway, it was nearly always the same. Many a rush job had filled a bed or two in East Nine.

Sam felt old and wary. "Now you take me, f'r instance," Bushy Malone said to one of the boys, just loud enough to be heard as he shuffled past the desk where the boss talked to the Ward Super, "I can take it. Repairin' motors is me dish. Why I tell ye I once changed a wheel on a locomotive while she was hittin' sixty!" The boys laughed harshly. "O' course," the Irishman went on, "I lost me arms and legs and got cork ones instead, but what's that? We've got to speed up out o' this depression, ye lazy dogs."

The mill owner paled with rage. Hadn't he kept Carl three days a week all winter with hardly an order in the shop? Wouldn't the Board pay the hospital expenses? He cleared his throat. "Anything at all you think he needs, nurse, get it. Never mind will the Board pay for extras or not, I will." He marched away, fury and hate burning his stocky round body and speeding him up like 220 volts on a 110 motor. Going down the elevator he composed the ad in his mind, "Wanted: Experienced planer, permanent work if satisfactory; good pay." Sam always paid good, when he had orders. No closed shop for him. Share with the men. Goddam that crippled Irish swine!

From ten o'clock on East Nine was visited by interns.

They waited until Doctor Fraser had been up to inspect his handiwork. Fraser was queer that way. Picked one student each year and wouldn't tolerate any others around him in the theatres or wards. He took his work seriously. Every amputation cost the Board plenty, so Fraser patched and scraped and repatched until legs and arms could be moved. Just enough, you understand, so it wouldn't be total disability. The queer remains, like the vets who make poppies and wicker chairs, would be put into offices, learning to write with their left hands or sitting stiffly erect in steel belts, until they could be let out during a slack period. It was cheaper to have them on relief. Every plant in the province had at least one Fraser specimen. They sent men to him from a thousand miles away. It was hard work. Most of the interns weren't hard enough.

Carl's father came in the afternoon, pale and shaking, tears on his face at the sight of his husky son. The men joked loudly, drawing the old man away. They knew what it was like. Carl's brain was just waking up and his forehead was green with agony, bright fever spots on his cheeks like harlot's rouge. He couldn't understand it. Swollen with pain and fever, his chest struggled against the smothering cast, forcing his heart faster and faster. Each beat sent hell ablaze in his bones.

He couldn't understand it. He listened to the men, sucked water from a china cup with a long spout, held by a nurse; he vomited, drank ginger ale and vomited again. Over and over. Finally they gave him two pints of luke-warm soda, holding his nose and forcing it down, to bring everything up. Instead, it settled him, cooled him off. The boys watched intently, heads half-turned away, of course, but following it all like hawks as you do in a hospital. They were waiting for the break, for the time when the will begins to lose control. When Carl started to groan, just a gasp or two at first, the men looked at each other and nodded, and those who were able went out on the sun balcony to talk it over.

Jack Delong, who had an arm that wouldn't heal, who cried softly all night long before each operation, trembled as he spoke. "My kid's going to be a doc if I have to beat him every day. He'll give guys like us a big shot and finish quick. What th'hell! Dat poor crock be in here two years before they get him rolling. Dieu! Why don't they let him go?"

"Stow it, yellowbelly! You been thinking about your blasted arm so long you got mice in place of your brains." Red, a lanky lead-poisoned Englishman, secretly agreed with Delong's euthanasia theories but couldn't bring himself to open admission. The others argued noisily until thin, worn-out Wardle came in, moving sideways between the chairs as he maneuvered his crutches. He's just come from an hour in the "machine shop," having his useless legs worked in the complicated exercising apparatus familiarly known as the Hot Mamma. He grinned, sitting down, rubbing his knees and looking around at everyone as he always did before speaking.

"I see, boys," he said, "we have another member. If we only had cards we could sign him up properly. Initiation fee, twenty-four hours in hell, and weekly dues of four enemas, two blood tests." He bent over tobacco and paper, rolling the smoke awkwardly. "Tomorrow we will send a delegation to take it up with the Commissar for Heavy Industry. All in favor of execution for demanding this worker to repair a motor while running?"

"Aye!" chorused the men. The roar echoed in the corridor, shocking them all with its intensity. They looked around foolishly. When Ma Thompson came in to lecture them she selected the ringleader from habit. "John Wardle," she said in sudden anger, "if you could stop your agitating for a day or so I'm sure the poor fellow in Ninety-Seven would appreciate it."

The tall man stumbled to his feet. "Ma," he said, "accept my deepest apologies. Some of us, I must admit, are more concerned with the poor man's successors in this retreat than we are with its present inhabitants."

"Yeah," chimed Shorty Renko, waving a fingerless hand, "and wotsa use of being quiet for him? Maybe he be glad of some noise in a while!" He chuckled, enjoying the bitter flavour of his joke. Shorty was Wardle's faithful stooge in countless East Nine arguments, for the communist had put pressure on the Compensation Board, getting the man his treatment, his family bread and shelter. All the men respected him for this and other things, listened eagerly to his lectures on economics. But only a few supported him openly. The Board might yield to pressure, giving what it had to, but not a few soft rewards came for those who used their pull with the big political parties. The majority in East Nine were broken men, for whom union life and struggle were history. They looked ahead to tiny cheques, food for their wives and kids. "Good listeners," Wardle would tell his friends, "but devils to activise. And when they get out, the Board gags them into political sheep." But he kept on trying, telling himself in moments of despair that Lenin himself once lived like this in exile.

Carl didn't pay much attention to things that evening. The interns gave him less dope, tightened the screws stretching his legs and every hour or so tried him with the stethoscope. When the visitors had gone they brought the plaster shears and hacked away a half circle from the top of the cast. It eased the pressure and made way for the sounding instrument. Once an hour the nurses gave him an assortment of drugs. The men fed him with water when he wanted it, which was often, and gave him the bottle. They were very quiet that evening, studying the looks and whispers of the doctors with the experience of old hands. When Delong crawled early into bed, reading his Bible, they let him alone. The frail little coward was looked upon by some as the ward oracle. When he turned to scripture all East Nine heard of it and slept uneasily. Even the lonely souls in the singles were restless, wanting their doors kept open. All night long the call lights flashed above the desks and the nurses earned their pay.

At ten o'clock the special was called again. She hated cases like this with doctors fussing around at all hours. Not a chance to relax and snatch a quarter-hour sleep. She tramped back and forth between Ninety-Seven and the Dispensary, carried an endless succession of bottles to the lavatory and thought with envy of her room-mate's patient, a sleepy old cancer sufferer.

But a little past midnight Carl began to talk, the whole room woke up to hear him and things became more interesting. Every once in a while a passing nurse would stop at the door to listen. Sometimes a fevered voice is remarkably clear and carries far down the hall to the embarrassment of the young probationers who have not become accustomed to the frightful psychoanalysis of delirium. But Carl spoke softly. He murmered to the thirty-horse motor. He whispered to his wife and to the priest who had buried her. No one turned towards him. You can't look at a full-grown man, raving out his life and love in East Nine. Maybe you don't understand. If you can't, put it down to the dim light and the screens around the bed. But that won't explain it. You can't close your eyes, you can't look at each other, so you just stare hard up at the ceiling. And pray to God he'll shut up.

By 3:00 A.M. the men in Ninety-Seven could have recognized Thora, had they met her resurrected body on the street. Even if they were blind men they could have felt her hair and nose and lips, her whole body, and known her as the dead wife of Carl Thorsen. Several times the nurse's hands would rise in startled gestures to her own breasts and neck, caught off guard by some painfully revealing phrase of the rambling mind. One by one the wide-awake men, those who could move under their own power, stumbled out of bed and sought the quiet of the hall or lavatory. Never again would they see a fair Norwegian woman without the memory of that ghastly night rising to blur their vision. Never again could they endure the sight of a woman suckling her child, as Carl's Thora had nursed the baby Sonya. A painter with words, a sculptor with phrases, this planer.

By the time a sickly winter dawn began to fight with the swirling storm outside, all was quiet. Carl was asleep, his temperature was down, and the x-ray department received an order for a head-to-foot picture of one C. Thorsen. Ma Thompson followed Doctor Fraser's standing instructions:

pictures as soon as the patient can be moved, and don't be too conservative.

It was not until nearly noon that there were enough orderlies and nurses available, for East Nine was busy. But they came at last. Carl, clear headed even after two hypos, was lifted onto a huge wheeled bed and sent downstairs. His going raised the ward to sudden gaiety. Card games sprang up, centering around the beds of the more handicapped patients, and crude jokes, laughter, made the work of the nurses lighter. The men held a Board of Trade luncheon, a satirical invention of Wardle's. There were many toasts with cups of weak tea and cocoa, ditties were sung, and when Shorty Renko rendered some workers' marching song in a foreign tongue he was greeted with gusty applause. Temperatures went up, of course, but so did metabolism and the doctors were pleased. Morale in the ranks of the class warriors of the Compensation Ward is as important as morale elsewhere. Thus, it met with official approbation.

Downstairs, meanwhile, far down in the cement hallways of the second basement, Carl waited. The x-ray department was understaffed. The doctor in charge was away at his private office examining the internal organs of some prominent citizen's wife, and the two technicians were taking things easy. Carl was a major job, ten or more plates, no less. So the one who hadn't had lunch early went upstairs; the other fussed changing tubes or making secret signs on record cards. All the while he talked to the specimen on the table, describing the intricate maze of high-voltage wiring and explaining the reason and method for taking the pictures. Carl would nod his head in eager agreement as some point struck him. He was hot. Not fevered, but sweating under the cast with the exertion of holding himself together. The technician obligingly opened a ventilation duct, wheeled the bed under it, and let the patient cool off. The fresh conditioned air was a stimulant to lungs saturated with iodoform and countless pungent odors of the wards. Carl breathed it in, moving his stomach up and down to suck tiny drafts of air down under the cast.

It was two o'clock in the afternoon before all the plates had been taken and they had tucked Carl back into bed again. The ward was still in high spirits and his return did nothing to dampen them, for the night that had passed was temporarily forgotten. The men were having their weekly visit from a member of the Assembled Hosts of Jehovah's Faithful, an obscure sect that made the rounds of the hospital. "Are You Insured in Heaven, Ltd.?" read the current pamphlet. The old fellow propped one up on Carl's chest where he could read it by lowering his eyes nearly out of their sockets. East Nine enjoyed these visits, matching the wits of the Scotchman McCabe against the "reverend." Mac had first become aware of all things religious way back on the Clydeside, after a sound thrashing from the Elders for some dimly remembered misdemeanor. As the years rolled over his sandy head he had accumulated an amazing fund of atheistic information, and all this he had systemized into sermons cleverly adapted to his unwitting victims. He could argue intelligently with a Dean of Theology and equally as well with a street-corner evangelist. Priest, Rabbi and Salvation Army lassie he took in his stride. He knew every doctrine from Buddha to Aimee MacPherson and would work himself up to an oratorical frenzy, leading the faithful into the pitfalls of hell itself, until they closed their eyes and raised their hands in supplication of their particular Deity for deliverance from this disciple of evil. Since his arrival in the hospital—during an argument with his foreman regarding the origin of Lent, Mac had absently slipped his elbow into a high-speed grinder—the ward had maintained a strong front against the succession of doctrinaires that passed through each afternoon.

Today the discussion revolved about the tortures of the doomed, the eternal fires that are reserved for such as McCabe. It was a good topic. Mac was at his best up here where hell on earth abounded. Could the Devil himself equal the handiwork of Industry? The witless knight of the Assembled Hosts did his best, desperately and fatally siding in with Wardle, with whom, as a matter of fact, he was in strong agreement concerning the coming of the millenium, but to no avail. He was trapped and recognized defeat when he saw it. "Repent, before the Gate hath closed forever!" he admonished Carl, and turning over the booklet so that the helpless man could read the back page he buttoned his coat and strode out to more fertile fields. The men amused themselves making paper darts, for which purpose the printed matter of Heaven, Ltd., was particularly suitable; they smoked, chatted with friendlier visitors and debated the supper menu.

"Try a little strained soup, big boy?" The probationer, as pretty and as awkward as a schoolgirl in her neat little blue uniform and ugly black stockings, coaxed Carl to eat for the first time. He didn't want it but the girl was nervous and anxious. Anything to oblige, girls! He wanted water again. Plenty of it, too. Maybe ginger ale or lime juice with ice clinking merrily in the spout cup. But he gurgled the lukewarm broth and grinned his thanks. It tasted very funny, that soup. All evening, while his father and the two children sat beside his bed, Carl tried to puzzle it out. The stuff had seemed to go into his chest. Was his stomach bust? The speculation made him restless and he determined to take it up with the special if she came on again that night. He talked for a while, until that grew difficult, and then turned away and relapsed into silence, pretending weariness. He felt the pressure of a vague but irresistible force surging through him. His father could wait. The children could wait. This was urgent, it needed immediate consideration. Carl Thorsen had to think. Think hard and very, very fast.

Old Sam came up to the ward next morning. Over the phone, he hadn't been able to get any satisfaction. He was worried. The Board had asked him some awkward questions and his men had seemed most pleased to discuss the affair in detail with the Inspector. There was trouble ahead and Sam could smell it.

"No visitors," the desk nurse told him politely. "Mr. Thorsen is very ill. No, the Doctor isn't quite sure just what it is. You can phone this afternoon, sir." And so Sam went wearily away. Didn't he have a family of his own? That he should have to worry about his men as if they were his children!

Today, Doctor Fraser was in one of his pale cold furies. The plates had turned out even worse than he had expected. The whole job would have to be done again, and splices and beef-bone screws put in both legs. Now, complications! He stamped through Ninety-Seven searching for drafts and counting Carl's blankets with his own hands.

"Very strange indeed, Mrs. Thompson," he said with his humorless smile. "There was no sign whatever of congestion yesterday. However, it's done now. Have a special on until I instruct otherwise. I'll be up as soon as I've finished operating and you can call Doctor Morton if anything should develop."

Ma Thompson had already grilled the nurses. No, the windows had not been opened, the blankets had been kept on as directed, only his one exposed arm had been bathed, and so on. It remained for Bushy Malone to give the hint. "He was sweatin' like a cop in July when he went down to be photographed, Ma," he volunteered. "I remember that hole meself. Drafty as a chicken coop and dampish. And he was down there till long after dinner. See if I ain't right, Ma." But the Super of East Nine was not one to waste time investigating the spilling of milk. She was a mopper-up by profession and she proceeded to mop.

Of course there wasn't a great deal that could be done. Carl had fallen asleep early the night before and awakened full of strange and bewildering sensations. Someone, it seemed, had put two rubber hot-water bags inside his chest. Slowly but surely they were filling up. Along about noon time the interns were listening in on those lungs with great interest. They had removed a great deal of the cast, around his chest, for Fraser was no longer omnipotent. Pneumonia! The surgeon steps to one side and another crew takes hold. No sense in bothering about bones until this is over. The medicos invited their student friends up to the ward to get first hand experience. Most instructive case. The pathology department couldn't report for 48 hours, but it was pretty easy to guess. Shock sweeps away the barriers holding back the invisible killers. Before the dinner trays began to arrive they were trundling the oxygen equipment down the hall towards Ninety-Seven.

The day special was homely and very competent. In no time at all there was a rubber tube strapped to Carl's face, the end shoved up a nostril and the little gas bottle bubbling away. He didn't strain quite as much for a while. He figured something was wrong and he took it quietly. All his thinking, about Thora and his old man and the babies, about Sam and the thirty-horse motor, all that had been finished the night before. There was a queer look in Carl's eyes. He watched everything, gazing hungrily into the faces around him.

Around three o'clock Doctor Fraser phoned the father. The old fellow, one grandchild in his arms, the other staggering wildly to keep up with him, half ran to the hospital. They let him look into the ward, then settled him out on the balcony where the men tried to bluff it off and nurses mothered the kids. Carl Thorsen, senior, was like a trapped animal, glaring wildly around and making strange noises deep in his throat. He knew the hopelessness of the struggle here in the East Wing. It had been just like this, three floors below, when they'd called him for Thora. You waited. After a while, a day or two maybe.... He lowered his head and moaned. The men stared out of the windows and smoked furiously.

Wardle was busy that afternoon. He was even late for supper. Taking Malone's tip he had slipped downstairs to the x-ray rooms and chatted amiably to the technicians. He found out all about it easily enough. Even got the name of the man who had opened the window. Were there any nurses in attendance? No, of course not. Where was the Doctor? Were patients in critical condition usually left in charge of the technicians? My, no! They had their own nurse who came down from the Ward to see that the unpleasant business of taking the photos was done as rapidly and carefully as possible. Did the men know Thorsen was in critical condition? That was as far as Wardle could get. He was ordered back to his Ward before a complaint was made to the Hospital Superintendent. Who did he think he was, the Board of Directors? Weren't their bills all paid in East Nine? What do they want, the earth?

Over in the Exercise Room Wardle figured out his plan. He knew an alderman or two, and there might be a commission and a shake-up all around in East Nine. He would write about it to the labour press. The union would organize old Sam's factory. But upstairs? Hell! Things like this upset Wardle. Delong would moon around for a week or more, leading religious discussions. Have you any real proof there is no Eternity? Why must you deny the existence of a God? And thus and thus. He would sit alone for a few days, Wardle would, and do some studying. He got off the machine, put on his bath robe and hobbled upstairs to telephone.

The men slept well enough. The bubbling of the oxygen was soothing to the nerves and the interns were soft-footed at night. But in the hospital you can sleep the clock around and awake with a head full of misery. It was that way in East Nine. The day was one of fierce little squabbles, rows over the food and complaints about dressings and treatments. You couldn't stay in Ninety-Seven. There was that air about the place. Those who were bound to their beds threw magazines on the floor and cursed.

The old man would come in and touch his son's face. "He smiled, Miss!" he would say as the pain of breathing twisted Carl's mouth. Then they would lead him gently away and go back to the soundings and pulse-timing and temperatures. On the balcony most of the men spent the day gathered around Wardle. To his amazement they listened to every word and signed their names to a hastily drawn-up petition. Renko tried to organize a collection committee but the blank sheet for contributions was torn up in furious anger. Shorty, who had seen the War in a Polish village, couldn't make it out. He nearly wept when Wardle himself, in a kind of icy insanity, dug into the basket and ripped the paper strips to minute shreds.

Dan, the oldest orderly on the staff, an ex-Royal Navy man, remarked to Ma Thompson that it reminded him of the unholy night at Jutland when he had bandaged sweating men on the deck of a half-sunk cruiser, scrawling letters home for the dying crew while they prayed against hope that the can wouldn't sink. East Nine didn't get under Dan's skin. He hurried off to get a bed pan, chuckling to himself.

Silence, men! Can't you see it's time. There's the Swedish Lutheran minister. He's going to pray. Why? Ask old McCabe. Only shut up. Just a few words anyway, that's all he'll say, for the old father. No, he won't kneel down. Thorsen might open his eyes and see him if he stands close to the bed ... *my Shepherd, I shall not want*.... What a hideous sound a man's breathing can become! Countless millions of invisible living things swarming through the blood stream of their host ... *the valley of the shadow of death*.... Is it their sound, their insect-humming, that rumbling noise? Suck hard, Lungs! Pump, Heart! ... *I will fear no evil*.... The medicos have it timed. They are watching the clock, listening ... *forever and ever, Amen*.

His lips quiver. The fluttering of a scrap of grey-green paper in the wind. Thora, can you see her, like a Nordic goddess, striding somewhere? Let the brain cells dream! Only a second or two. Yes, to you, Carl. That deep dark shadow, now, you disregard it. Keep the dream. To you, she's coming! You to her. To nothingness.

Turn off the oxygen. It's wanted somewhere else. Straighten your backs, doctors, gentlemen. You young ones wander down nonchalantly and have a drink. You, Ma Thompson, let it lie there just a while. Let all the men file in and look an instant, stiff-jawed and blinking. Time then to raise the windows, phone the morgue, get a fresh mattress.

Fellow man, worker, comrade, farewell. The motor is repaired, the plane sings, the bee-hive profits mount. No longer wretched, no longer of this earth, rest. We of East Nine who struggle and have yet to die, salute you. No volley will be fired. Some other dawn-time the guns will greet your memory. Comrade, farewell.

New Frontier (June 1936)

MATT MURRAY ARMSTRONG

THE RAIL

Restless, I stand beside my wife at the parapet. She is pointing out over the river and explaining everything to the boy—the Suspension Bridge to our left; the American Falls, far across the chasm; Goat Island and the Canadian Falls, almost lost in the mist; and, far below, the *Maid of the Mist* bobbing her way through green and white water to the foot of the cataract. They laugh together. I watch their faces, gleaming wet with spray.

But I must turn away. It is the same today as always, inside me. When I come here, something happens to me, within me. I do not know what happens, or what causes it. It is very puzzling. The Falls themselves? The heart-tightening Gorge? I do not know.

My head whirls. Everything merges and goes around. The Sunday afternoon crowds, jostling, laughing, pouring past me. That stream of cars which rolls steadily by, from every Province, every State, gliding along, gliding endlessly along like the water over the Falls, always going around, going around in a dreary circle, getting nowhere, ending nowhere. Like the damnable job which is eating away my days, my years. My life. (Punch in. Start the machine. Watch it run, watch it run. Shut it off. Punch out. Eat, sleep, work, punch in, punch out. Life!) Without end. Without change. Around and around, each year closing in on me more and more. Stifling me. If there could be something....

"Paul. Paul, do you hear me ? Come along, we're going over the river." It is my wife.

"You want to go over the river?" I mutter, confused.

She looks at me closely. The frown is back to her face. "Yes. I said the river," she says. "Leave the car where it is in the park. We can walk. I want to show Gilbert the American Falls from Luma Island. You can hurry on and buy the bridge tickets."

Luma Island. From where we stand it is just a speck between the American Falls and Goat Island, far across the Gorge, but as I stare it seems to be rushing toward me, growing bigger and bigger, until my eyes seem to absorb every detail of the island. Strangely, my heart leaps. Luma Island!

"Paul!"

Slowly I make my way to buy the tickets. We begin the walk across.

The bridge, is this the one? I am not quite sure. It happened so long ago, when I was a kid, before I had to leave school and go to work in the factory. I do not know just how many years ago it was, or which bridge I saw it from. That part is hazy. It does not matter, anyway.

But no one could ever forget the sight of those black specks of people scrambling ashore like flies when the ice bridge broke and began floating down the river. All but the three. I was standing in the crowd on the bridge when the first two, a man and a woman, whirled under the bridge. They were kneeling on the ice, close together. I think his arm was around her. A man beside me on the bridge said, "Oh, for Christ's sake." I was just a kid. Then they lowered the end of a rope all the distance down into the river and I saw it snap tight against the rail when the third person grabbed it and hung on. After that I watched the rope crawling tight up over the rail as the men heaved on it. It seemed a long time. And I was watching it when it suddenly went slack in their hands. It was crawling up over the rail, inch by inch, then it came up with a rush, curling loose. The men fell in a heap.

They got up looking at each other. Nobody laughed.

Something gripped in my stomach. For a long time I stared at the place on the rail where the rope had rubbed. Then I ran from the bridge.

It doesn't matter which bridge it was.

Delia is nudging me. "We'll keep to the street. It is too muddy through the park."

We are on the slope from the bridge.

"Yes," I agree. "It is too early in the spring. The grass is too tender and young yet." And I said, "Delia dear, do you mind if I let you and Gilbert go on ahead? There is something I need from across the street. I'll catch you at the second bridge."

She does not mind. "But, don't keep us waiting," she says.

The moment they disappear around the bend I strike off through the park toward Prospect Point.

There was an afternoon two years ago. Like the other, this has stayed inside me. I strolled alone near Prospect Point. I stood here. Over there, near the rail alongside the edge of the Falls, two men, a policeman and a civilian, were arguing. The policeman had the other by the arm and was leading him up and away from the water's edge, but when they were only a little way up the slope the civilian jerked free, spun around, sped down the incline, sprang to the top bar of the railing and leaped out over the Falls. Somehow it did not shock me. I don't know why. What struck me first was the imperishable time he seemed to be suspended in mid-air. Actually it could have been no time at all, yet, before he vanished it seemed that the age of a world had passed as I watched. It was a queer feeling. The whole figure of the man exuded triumph. His expression as his body swung around so that I could see his face, the freedom of his limbs, the statuesque posture, all poured out a flow of victory which seemed to rival the regal sweep of the cataract that made it possible. In the theatre I have seen dancers whose act climaxed in a carefully studied pose of triumph. Yes, it was like that. Only, here was no rehearsed pose. That is important. Here, for a background not a dusty backdrop, but the mighty grandeur of Niagara. I could only stand, staring. And suddenly I was staring at the empty, bare rail, and beyond it the rush of water.

Then the policeman's voice trembled at my elbow. "You saw me. I tried to stop him. The lunatic, the poor damned lunatic." His mouth twisted in fear.

I could not trust myself to answer him. I hurried off.

Often I think of that day, trying to understand it. I cannot.

But, Delia will be waiting.

Together we walk along the path through the woods on Goat Island. As we draw nearer to the footpath which leads down the slope to Luma Island my heart begins to pound. My body trembles. The palms of my hands are moist. I cannot understand why this should be. We go down and across the bridge to the tiny island that nestles against the rim of the American Falls.

Except for two young chaps we have the island to ourselves. For a while I stand alongside as Delia points out to the boy the tourists, clad in oilskins, creeping like yellow beetles over the catwalk to the Cave of the Winds, far below. I move away from them, nearer the edge. Out over the falls the sun merges with the spray in a riot of color. I grip the wet railing, tight. It is like gazing into infinity. As I glance back over my shoulder to see where my wife is it comes to my mind that there is something within me that she and those others have not. There must be. It must be that I feel, where they are numb.

A thrill of exhilaration surges through me.

I pick a pebble from the path. Toss it out over the crest of the Falls. It drops like a plummet.

Again I glance back. Surely they cannot see me. I roll my handkerchief into a tight ball. Toss it out. Slowly it drifts away on a rising current of air, wafts downward for a moment, rises again, floating easily as it opens out, but meets the falling water and vanishes. It was like the dreams I sometimes have after being at the Falls, when I seem to float along the crest of the cataract and out into that unknown world of purity which must exist there. That unattainable world. It is a beautiful, satisfying, experience. Clean. Pure. So vastly different from that far distant, dreary circle of eating, working, sleeping, punch in, punch out. My head is whirling. I know that my feet are on the bottom rail. But I cannot stop. I have no desire to stop. The second rail. At last I am within reach of that purified space above the crest of the waterfall, where rainbows are born and live, where all is beauty. My coat is open. My hands reach out. Now the last long step and....

A woman screams. Hands tear at my coat and I am thrown to the gravel pathway.

Slowly I open my eyes. My head throbs. Pain shoots through my body. Everything is misty. Someone helps me to rise. They are leading me across the footbridge and up the slope, my wife on one side, a man on the other. I hear my wife saying, "Thank you. I'll take care of him now." We are standing under the trees. My head clears.

"Paul, do you feel alright? You idiot, Paul," Delia says, but she sounds frightened.

"Yes, I feel fine. I feel just fine."

"Then let's get home, Paul. Let's get home."

Delia takes my arm and we begin the walk back through the woods, across the bridges, toward the international bridge, toward home. We are going home. I feel fine, just fine. If I laugh it will scare Delia again. So I must walk along beside her, quietly.

"You scared Gilbert," Delia says.

"I am sorry, dear. I had a sick spell," I say.

Tomorrow is Monday again.

Canadian Forum (January 1938)

BERTRAM BROOKER

MRS. HUNGERFORD'S MILK

Joe Snell drove his dray into the yard and unhitched the team. The yard was muddy and the hooves of the horses made a sucking sound as they plodded side by side into the stable. Joe followed them in and dipped some oats out of the bin with a rusty basin. After a long day in the sun, the darkness of the stable and the cool smell of wet straw and manure were like a soothing hand passed down over the back of his head. He slapped the shining rump of the roan mare as he went beside her with the oats. On the way home he had tried to cool his parched throat with two glasses of beer. His throat was still dry, but his head was better. He felt like whistling. His head swung lightly on his shoulders as he bent to come out of the stable door.

It was near sundown. The house made a great patch of shadow which fell across the slanting roof of the cow-shed. Long, spindly shadows from the haphazard rails of the fence lay across the straw and mire.

It was nice in the yard with the sun going down and a bit of breeze springing up. The twisted, scrub oaks along by the fence were beginning to sway with it. He took off his hat with a sort of swoop and pitched it, like a quoit, aiming for the stoop outside the kitchen door, but it fell just short and rolled in a puddle. "To hell with it," he said.

It looked good around the yard. Some folks would be all

for painting the house; but he liked the grey, old, blistered sheathing. He liked the marks of weather over everything, the stains of wear and time, the bleached boards, the sinking steps. Ramshackle, his brother called it. But that was just him. He was a baker in the East end. He was a fusser, his brother was. He'd even got the women up on their ear about things. Said he ought to get a truck and keep up to date. But, what the hell, his brother was spending every nickel he made—keeping up to date!

He went to the rainwater barrel and dipped himself a basin of water. With one swoop of the basin he skimmed the dead insects aside and plunged it down deep, bringing it up quickly to keep the dead flies out of it. There was a bench by the kitchen window. While he was bending down washing he could hear Hettie clattering with pans around the stove. When she was quiet he could hear Myrtle humming upstairs.

He dried himself and picked up his hat from the puddle and brushed the mud off it on the bench. He was a heavy, solid man, nearing fifty. He had put on weight these last eight years or so. His middle bulged out of his trousers. His jowls and neck had thickened. The strain of dragging heavy loads on and off his dray for years had driven a crooked wrinkle down between his brows, like a cleft in the trunk of an old tree. His flattened upper lip was drawn tightly across his teeth in a fixed expression, like a clown's smile, forced and permanent.

He went through the woodshed and poked his head into the kitchen, resting his enormous, rough hands on the doorposts. Hettie was at the stove, stirring potatoes in a fry-pan with a long iron fork.

"Hullo, old woman," he said. She was nearly ten years younger than himself, and he liked to tease her. She had kept a young woman's figure in spite of hard work and three babies, two of which they had lost. She managed to look smart with very few clothes because she was always making over her dresses, and was now able to pass them on to Myrtle, who had turned eighteen.

She turned from the stove and sighed when she saw his

strained, worn face. "Pretty tired—eh?" she said.

"Yup," said Joe. "I been on that blasted job of Rutter's all afternoon, since the 2:40 train. Took me three trips."

"I thought you figured two," said Hettie. "I thought you said last week it would be a five-dollar job."

Joe stepped to a broken bit of mirror by the window and began combing his matted hair. "That's what I figured. He asked me for an estimate—and that's what I told him. It's only a couple of blocks to where he's moved to, and he didn't look to have much stuff there in them little offices. But that's just him. He'd got more stuff squeezed into that bit of a shack than most guys would have on a couple of floors. He's a squeezer—that's what he is."

"A squeezer!" said Hettie, laughing. "That's good, Joe."

"They weren't ready—either," Joe grumbled. "That girl he's got—Cassie Williams—a proper fusser she is. Fussing with this and frigging with that—"

"She's not such—"

"Well, anyway," said Joe, raising his voice and beating the air with the comb, "*anyway*—I'll bet it took me a solid hour putting on that last load, with *her* chasing in and out with dribs and drabs of stuff. And when it was all on he came out himself, the little runt, and pulled a five spot out of his pocket. Had it folded up in his vest pocket all ready. You're durn right—*he* knew it was a bargain. 'It's taken longer than I figured,' I says, 'it ain't like stuff you can just throw on. And anyway, it's made three loads, so that'll be seven and a half,' I says."

"Did he come through?"

Joe put the comb down with a whack. "No! *That* guy!" He picked up the comb again and gave it another whack on the shelf. "No *chance*! Said I'd asked him five bucks and five bucks was all I'd get. Looking at me all the time like I was trying to rook him."

"He's a tightwad," Hettie said. "Always was."

Joe squatted his thick body in a chair. "Yup!" he said, with a loose, downward fling of his hand. He had got it off his mind. It didn't matter. He moistened his lips with a loud smack. "Yup!" he said again, with a wry smile. He sat staring at the floor boards, tapping one foot to a tune that was running in his head. He had forgotten what he was waiting for.

Hettie stood with her back to the stove, looking at him. "You'd better quit giving estimates, Joe," she said, in a tone you use to a child. "Tell 'em it's by the hour. That's the only way you'll ever make anything."

A smell of burning recalled her to the stove. Joe stood up and shook himself like a dog coming out of water. "How's the supper?" he said, striding about and flapping his heavy arms.

"Here it is," said Hettie. She was loading up a large plate from two or three pans she had been warming. "We've had ours. It got pretty late—and Myrtle's going to that dance."

Joe stood waiting. His eyes, still gritty from the dust that had been blowing all afternoon, roved about the kitchen. The cleft in his brow suddenly shifted in a crooked, angry line over one eye which had opened wider than the other in a furious stare.

"What's this here?" he said, pointing at a covered milk-pail on the table by the window. "That ain't Mrs. Hungerford's milk—is it?"

Hettie had the plate in her hands, facing him ready to go into the front room where the table was set. "It'll be going over in a minute or two," she said quietly.

"Why ain't it delivered?" Joe demanded. He suddenly felt very angry and strong. The weariness of the long day's work seemed to have left him. Throbbing anger and strength surged through him.

Hettie looked at him in surprise, but kept her voice even. "We was kind of late with the milking," she said, "and Myrtle's been getting ready for the dance."

"But it ain't even dark yet," said Joe.

"It's quite a drive out there," Hettie said. "Must be all of twenty-two miles out to Ormrod's—and after that rain there'll be—"

Joe spread his legs widely apart and stared at her.

"Yeah, but it don't take her all night to get dressed, does it?"

Hettie held out the plate so that the steam would float under his nose. "Come on in and get started, Joe," she said. "This'll all be cold."

He flapped his arms angrily against his sides. "She's getting too high and mighty—is she?—to run over there of a night?"

"No, no," Hettie said quickly. "Don't start that again, Joe. We had to fix up her dress a bit. The poor kid hasn't a thing to wear. She hates going anywhere in the things she's got."

"Sure!" Joe shouted. "That's what I'm a-saying. She's getting too durn high and mighty—chasing around with that Lambert fellow."

"She just wants to look nice—that's all."

"Well, she won't look nice if she don't deliver that milk at the right time—I'm tellin' you. If she can't do a little job like that—"

"You don't need to worry about it," said Hettie. "It'll go over any minute. The paper boy takes it, once in a while, on a Saturday. He goes right to the house to collect on Saturdays."

"That's not good enough!" growled Joe. He started across the floor toward the stairs which went up in the wall just inside the parlour door.

"Here!" cried Hettie, running after him and putting the plate down as she passed the table. "Don't say nothin' to *her*. Don't spoil her evenin' for her."

Joe swung around and glared into her anxious eyes. His head was throbbing. The deep cleft in his brow was twisted in an ugly knot over one eyebrow. "I'm goin' to spoil *somebody's* evenin' if that milk ain't delivered this minute," he bellowed at her.

"They ain't wantin' it," she said, her chin quivering.

"Who gives a hoot whether they're wantin' it or not. That's *their* business. It's *our* business to get it over there right smart after milkin'. He turned away from her and walked over to the bottom of the stairs. "Ho! Myrtle!" he called out.

"Yes, dad," cried a young voice from the room above.

"Don't say nothin' to *her*, Joe," said Hettie, plucking at his shirtsleeves. "You'll get her bawlin' and get her eyes all red and spoil her evenin'. I'll take it over myself, if the boy don't come right away. I'll take it myself, as soon as I've got your supper."

His big, watery eyes were pale with anger as he listened to her. His anger made him feel strong—invincible! His voice, coming out of his great chest, roared in his ears like a torrent. "I ain't goin' to have them Hungerfords kept waitin' for their milk," he shouted. "You talk to *me* about runnin' my business, but where would I be if Dave Hungerford quit gettin' me to do his haulin' for him. He's a durn good customer o' mine, ain't he? And if we're late night after night with the milk, maybe—"

"But we're not late *night after night*."

Joe thrust a square, horny nail under her nose. "A good many nights lately it's been. I told her off only last—last Wednesday, was it?" He turned to the stairs again. "Myrtle!" he shouted. "Come down here. Come on down here!"

"Leave her alone, Joe," said Hettie, getting in front of him and taking hold of his elbows.

He paid no attention to her. He was listening for Myrtle's step on the stairs. He was going to get the two of them together and tell them off. They acted like he was a back number lately. When his brother came around they always sided with him. "Just trying to buck you up a bit, Joe," his brother said. Well, all right, he'd buck up for once and tell them where they got off at.

Myrtle was coming down. He heard her heels, the same as a woman's, on the stairs. She and Hettie were like a couple of sisters, doing everything together, and siding with each other all the time. They'd left him alone a lot lately. "They act like I was just a lodger around the place," he said to himself. He thought of the many nights this summer when he had come home tired and gone to bed early, hardly saying a word to them. They were always working at something or other, and there didn't seem to be anything to talk about, so he'd go to bed. They'd got now so they just went ahead and did things and left him alone.

He wasn't young anymore, and he got tired easier, but he still had a lot of strength. He felt his strength in his head for once, somehow. His head was throbbing with noise. It was full of heavy words that he could throw at them like stones. The words were rattling about in his head and he felt the weight and strength of them and their hard, sharp edges.

Myrtle reached the bottom of the stairs, looked at him, and stood still. She was flushed and panting. She had on the dress they had been fixing up, and Joe hardly knew her. They'd done her hair up different. He had heard them talking about what she ought to do with her hair. She had lost all the little-girl look.

The sight of her shook him. He caught his breath and looked around quickly at Hettie. Her eyes were suddenly alight with love and admiration, and he suddenly saw that they *were* alike, after all. When Hettie's eyes sparkled like that she *did* look like Myrtle. Everybody said she did, but he hadn't been able to see it. Myrtle looked older and she looked younger.

They stood there, waiting for him to speak, but the words like boulders in his head seemed to be rumbling away out of hearing. He felt his strength slipping away.

"You look mighty cute, Myrtle," he said. "Don't she, Hettie?"

"Yes, it's a cute dress," Hettie said. "It's that old grey one of mine—dyed and fixed up."

"Mighty cute," said Joe. He leaned against the wall and kicked his heels back lightly against the wainscotting.

"Better eat your supper, Joe," said Hettie. "It'll be cold."

The mention of the supper brought the throbbing back. "Listen, Myrtle," he said, quickly, before the noise in his head should subside again. "I was just talking to your mother about Hungerford's milk."

"I heard you, dad."

"Well, all right. I don't want any monkey business about it. I don't say much around here any more—but I'm not going to lose a good customer. It's bad enough—these times.

You and your mother got the notion I'm a back number, just because things—"

"Now, Joe," said Hettie, "you're just—"

"Listen to me for once, will you," bellowed Joe. He wanted to get back the strength he had felt a few minutes before. He had felt able to hurt them, then, and he wanted to hurt them. He wanted to fill the house again when he came home, the way he used to, instead of sort of sneaking off to bed to be out of their way. He tried to take hold of himself inside, the way he would take hold of a heavy trunk and up-end it. He wanted that feeling of weight in his hands—to threaten them with its fall. But it wouldn't come. Between the two of them they had softened him—what with the dress, and the hair done different, and the way they looked at each other, and their soft voices.

The noise in his head was gone, but he could make it in his lungs and throat. It would be a shout without strength in it, but he wasn't going to sit down and eat his supper and let them go ahead fixing things to suit themselves.

"Listen to me," he roared. "You think I'm getting to be a stick-in-the-mud, don't you? Eh?"

"You're going to spoil her evening, Joe," pleaded Hettie.

"To hell with her evening. What about *my* evening? What about *me*? Ain't I got nothing coming to me after a hard day's work? What do I get out of it? You ain't got nothing to say to me any more—neither of you—you're all wrapped up in your own doings. You can't even run over with Hungerford's milk. A little job like that! You talk about *me* letting things go to rack and ruin, but—"

"We don't, Joe," said Hettie, her eyes burning into his. "We just—"

Joe raised his arm and flung it downward with enormous force. "This is *my* say! You keep still. I'm sick of this kind of life. *This* is no life for a man. I won't stand for it—do you hear? I'm going to change it. I'm going to have a wife and daughter that has some respect for the old man—or—or—I'll walk out on you. I'll—I'll—"

But he couldn't go on. It was just shouting. It didn't come from any feeling of power inside him. The words poured out of his lungs from nowhere. He wasn't making them up. Nobody was making them up. They just came out of his throat and he let them go. But his throat was dry now. His eyes were smarting. So that they shouldn't see the tears in his eyes he went to the table and scowled down at the plate of food Hettie had put at his usual place. There was a dull ache at the back of his head. He flapped his arms once, violently, to let them know that he was through, and sat down to his supper.

Canadian Forum (January 1934)

ALICE BUTALA

A DAY IN TOWN

The woman emerged from the hole that served as a cellar and placed a loaf and the one remaining tin of salmon on the rickety table. This would do the children until she returned. Another admonition regarding fires, a reminder of the few chores, and she climbed heavily over the wagon wheel to settle herself as best she could on the narrow board that served as a seat. Her husband clucked to the scrawny team and they bumped slowly down the frozen trail on their thirteen-mile trip to town. Yesterday's Chinook had melted all but the last dirty remnants of snow and the landscape was dull and depressing in the bleak morning light. The trail topped a rise and exposed the neighbours' scattered dwellings. With unpainted boards or flapping tarpaper, they crouched among the debris of ashes, cans, slop-water, and worn-out machinery, like old drunkards among empty whiskey-bottles.

Now they descended into the coulee and the woman clung tightly and braced herself to keep from falling over the front of the box, as they clashed over a stone, or dropped heavily into a hole. The last six miles of the road was graded and at this time of the year worse than the trail. It was distinguished by three washouts. The bumps were fearful and nothing but a strongly-built wagon, or a woman who has fought drought conditions for eight years, could have stood it. As it was, she began to feel that dull ache in her back. Everyone who drinks alkali water long enough gets it, but it didn't bother her much unless she rode in the wagon.

The air had a damp chill in it. The woman shuddered and tried to change her position. She was grateful for the shabby black coat even if it was three sizes too large, but she couldn't help wishing the donor had left in the chamois lining. At length the horses, sweating profusely and trembling in every limb, stopped in front of the general store. The woman climbed out stiffly and awkwardly. She was chilled through, and blue with cold.

Gratefully she huddled near the hot stove in the store and held out her hands to its warmth. She looked about. Vigorous children eating cornflakes, impossibly fat babies drinking canned milk, a lady calmly reading while an electric washer did the work. Aunt Jemima coaxingly urging you to make pancakes by mixing water with a packaged preparation. The door opened and for a moment it seemed as though one of the cardboard figures had come to life. Permanent wave, modish house dress, trim silken ankles, high-heeled pumps, the vision flashed a friendly smile at the stolid figure by the stove and turned to the merchant.

"Anybody in town today, Chet?"

"Nope. Deader'n a saloon in prohibition."

"See my little handy-pandies—they're cold."

"Poppa will make them all warm."

Then ensued a friendly interchange of slaps and pats, during which the customer learned that there were no fresh eggs, that the storekeeper had a swell time at the party last night, and that she was a little devil. With a series of squeaks and shrieks and a last mad sally that carried the merchant out from behind the counter and over to the door, the charmer departed, her saucy yellow beret bobbing merrily as she tripped along. She was forty-five, but all her friends assured her that viewed from the rear and at a distance you couldn't tell she was a day over seventeen.

Scarcely had she gone when the door from the warehouse burst open and the merchant's wife bustled in.

Matt surveyed her husband carefully. He wasn't much to look at and the store would have been on the rocks long since without her guiding hand, but no designing hussy was going to make passes at him. The woman by the stove started forward eagerly but Matt only knew her once a year, when she went around to collect chickens for the church supper.

"I'm closing the store while I eat my dinner," explained Chet, not unkindly. "Be open again around 12:30."

The woman passed out into the street. Bent almost double against the rushing wind, by tacking slightly she made her way to her goal. All praise to the railway company that provides, among numerous other blessings, a toilet in each town. The door was open and one half of the structure was occupied by a dirty melting drift of snow that prevented one from closing the door. But who are we to question any haven, if it's free?

The waiting room of the station was hot and clean and the woman sank gratefully on one of the uncomfortable red benches. Soon, however, the station agent came to the wicket and glared at her, his face bilious under the green visor.

She had just got out into the wind a second time, when she felt a heavy impact and a voice exulted, "Geeze, got her right on the bumper."

What the Mardi Gras is to New Orleans or the Santa Anita race track to Hollywood, what an election is to a politician, the period of melting snow is to the boyhood of the village. They know not rink, nor hockey team, skates, skis, nor snowshoes, sleighrides, nor hikes. Everyone on the street is a legitimate target for snowballs, hard as stone.

The woman fled on, reached the store. Locked. The post office was her only hope. Down two houses and across the street. She was just in time to shut the door on a vindictive volley of icy cannonballs. She found herself in a narrow dirty corridor, one side given to little glass doors with dials in their middles, a wicket, and a letter chute. At the far end a little window diffused a gray light through seven years of grime, and enabled the woman to examine the posters on the wall.

A Sale of Land for taxes told its own story. She idly

studied the postal rates. Three cents on a two-ounce letter. My, that was half a cent more than she was allowed for a meal.

Next to it was a poster, with a large photograph of prosperous and happy men standing shoulder high in an oatfield backed by a comfortable farm home, extensive barns, a silo, and an orchard. A smaller inset showed a weather-beaten shack on a dusty knoll. All this farmer had done was turn his farm into a Government holding, allowing vast sums to be spent; irrigation, trees, and intelligent labour had caused the desert to blossom like the rose. Anyone could do the same; the Government was offering free a few caragana seeds.

Her attention was drawn to an elegant announcement that she could, with very little trouble, deposit her savings in a famous bank. A happy family was exclaiming in delight and displaying a bank book with four figures. Next to a notice of a political meeting of the past week, the Royal Family gazed down at her from a poster advertising cornstarch.

Another picture. Strange she hadn't noticed it before. A group of human beings in various shambling poses, spitting, coughing, reading over one another's shoulders—they were in a post office. The caption read "The Loiterers." That anyone would remain in such a place of their own free will was unthinkable; to be libelled for doing so was unbearable.

She opened the door and a snowball crashed at her feet. She slammed it shut and leaned with pounding heart against it.

At this moment Mrs. Smeeks poised a generous spoonful of cottage fluff in the air, pointed it at her spouse and said, "So Twig and his wife are both in town. Their relief slip didn't come this month. He asked three times for it, so the postmistress said. Roads like they are, the relief man won't bother coming today, so they'll come whining to you for credit. They still owe us $15 from last year. We'll never get it out of them. Why should we work and feed them for nothing? We don't get relief. We work hard and there isn't hardly enough turnover from the store for us to take that trip to Yellowstone this summer. If they would only work out their relief on the roads. But no. Even with you carrying ashes all winter that street is a sight."

The view from the window showed the slough called by courtesy a street, with a pile of ashes in the middle, a cindery monument to the voluntary and public-spirited road-worker, C. F. W. Smeeks.

"Besides, these foreigners always have a wad hid somewhere."

The Twigs were of Welsh descent, while Mrs. Smeeks' mixed blood would have given Hitler a nightmare. She had, however, been born in the States.

"At any rate, it isn't up to us to feed them."

Having arrived at this satisfactory conclusion, Mrs. Smeeks fell to and fed herself, and made a very good job of it.

In the post office shrill but diminishing yelps assured the weary waiter that the wolf cubs had found a fresh trail. She scuttled back across the street and into the store. She took off the family overshoes and placed them under the stove, then held her wet feet one at a time up to the welcome warmth.

Tired, wet and hungry, with that dull insistent stab in the region of her kidneys, she felt curiously near to tears. She wondered what kept the relief inspector. She thought of the interview ahead of her, whines and cajolery to be met with bluster and threat. A religious woman, she decided to offer up a prayer to the particular God she worshipped. Today, her mind on the apologies and explanations demanded by the inspector, she prayed. "Thank God I don't seem to be going to have any more kids." She thought of the reconditioned granary that housed her small flock. She thought of the protruding tin smokestack, of the high wind, of her four children in a flaming inferno. She shuddered, and in an excess of remorse wanted to lie down on the dirty floor and grovel, "I didn't mean it, Lord. Please keep them safe. Please forgive me my wicked thoughts."

Her husband came in at last and by common consent

they moved over to the counter. "Relief man don't seem to be showing up. Guess you'll hafta let us get some things on tick."

The storekeeper smiled his oily regrets and the pair found themselves standing on the step.

"I could have let them have a bag of flour," mused the merchant, "but they didn't even haggle." He felt a prick—surely it wasn't his well-trained conscience. But when another customer came in, he was whistling cheerfully.

Mr. Twig's bemused mind remembered the week they had lived on wheat. It wasn't so bad the first day or so but it was too strong for a steady diet. "We might try the Chink's," he said.

While his wife had been dodging fearfully from one inhospitable shelter to another, he had been taking his ease in the restaurant. There men were able to congregate and settle the serious questions of the day. There was talk, laughter, games, and congenial company. The proprietor was a Chinaman. The restaurant changed hands frequently but the owner's name was always the Chink. Women went there but seldom and then on business only.

Mrs. Twig did not feel equal to the ordeal of re-entering the general store. She accompanied her husband.

The current Chink was a young man, polite, affable, obsequious, as became an inferior in this land. He had been given a good education in a Christian school and constantly, but silently, marvelled at a religion that preached need and practised greed. He was working and saving money to attend university.

Mrs. Twig glanced fearfully around at the somewhat dirty and gloomy room. She saw the suggestive brown blobs on the baseboard around the spittoon. She saw one young hoodlum nudge his companion and heard him remark, "See the swell skirt. Ain't she some cutie?" and heard the coarse snigger. But Mr. Twig was not of the mould to do battle for his wife's name, nor had his spouse the temperament that actively resented slurs.

They took Wong Lee aside. This woman was strangely like his own mother—the face wrinkled and dull, the figure prematurely stooped with too-heavy toil. Her hands, rough and red, stretched forth, pleading bread for her little ones. The Chink gave them a half-bag of flour and all the fish he had left; the thaw had made them soft. He added a bag of bull's eyes, those edible marbles beloved of children.

In the wagon again, they turned the horses' heads towards home. The woman thought of the tale she would have to tell her neighbour. Her eyes gleamed.

Canadian Forum (May 1939)

SINCLAIR ROSS

CIRCUS IN TOWN

There was a circus in town, but all of it that reached Jenny was a piece of mud-stained poster, torn by the wind off one of the billboards. A girl in purple tights, erect on a galloping horse, a red-coated brass band, a clown, an elephant torn through the middle. "And did you see the elephant?" she asked her brother Tom, who had found the poster in the street when he was in town marketing the butter and eggs. "Was it really there? And the clown?"

But the ecstatic, eleven-year-old quiver in her voice, and the way she pirouetted on her bare toes as he led the horse out of the buggy shafts, made him feel that perhaps in picking up the poster he had been unworthy of his own seventeen years; so with an offhand shrug of contempt he drawled, "I could see the tents and things, but I didn't bother going over. Good shows don't stop off at the little towns." And then, in a softer tone, as if suddenly touched by her white eagerness, "They all said it wouldn't be much anyway. Maybe a few ponies and an elephant or two—but what's an elephant?"

She wheeled away, resenting his attempt to scoff at the circus. The bit of bright paper had spun a new world before her, excited her, given wild, soaring impetus to her imagination; and now, without in the least understanding herself, she wanted the excitement and the soaring, even though it might stab and rack her, rather than the barren satisfaction of believing that in life there was nothing better, nothing more vivid or dramatic, than her own stableyard.

It was suppertime, her father just in from the field and turning the horses loose at the water trough, so off she sped to him, her bare legs flashing and quick like the pink spokes of a wagon wheel, her throat too tight to cry out, passionate to communicate her excitement, to find response.

But the skittish old roan Billie took fright at the fluttering poster, and her father shouted angrily for her to mind what she was doing and to keep away from the horses. For a minute she stood quite still, cold, impaled by the rebuff; then again she wheeled, and this time, as swiftly as before, ran to the house.

A reek of dark heat, hotter than the summer heat, struck her at the door. "Look" she pierced it shrilly, "What Tom brought me—a circus," and with the poster outstretched she sprang to the stove where her mother was frying pork and eggs and potatoes.

It was not a rebuff this time. Instead, an incredible kind of pity, pity of all things on a day like this. "Never mind, Jenny." A hot hand gentle on her cheek for a minute. "Your day will come yet. You'll not spend all your life among chickens and cows or I'm not the woman I think I am!" And then, bewilderingly, an angry clatter of stove lids that made her shrink away dismayed, in sharp, sudden dread of her father's coming and the storm that was to break.

There was not a word until her father had washed and was sitting down at the table. Then as the platters were clumped in front of him he asked, "What's wrong?" and for answer her mother hurled back, "Wrong? You—and the farm—and the debts—that's what's wrong. There's a circus in town, but we don't go. We don't do anything but work. Other children have things, and see things, and enjoy themselves, but look, look at it, that's how much of the circus my girl gets!"

Jenny dared to be a little indignant at the scornful way her mother pointed to the piece of poster that furtively she had hung over one of the kitchen calendars while waiting for her father. She liked it, it thrilled and quickened her, and now she felt exasperated and guilty that there should be a quarrel about it, her father looking so frightened and foolish, her mother so savage and red.

But even had she been bold enough to attempt an explanation it would have been lost in the din of their voices. Her mother shouted about working her fingers to the bone, and nothing for it but debts and skimping. She didn't mind for herself, but she wanted Jenny to have a chance. "Look at her clothes and bare feet! Your own daughter! Why don't you take hold and do something? Nothing ahead of her but chickens and cows. Have you no shame? Can't you see the big gawky know-nothing she'll be in another ten years?"

Jenny gulped, startled. Ten years from now it was a quite different kind of young lady she intended to be. For a moment there was a sick little ball of consternation down near her midriff, a clammy fear that her mother might be right—and then she was furious. So furious that for the next minute or two the quarrel passed over her. She wasn't gawky, and she wasn't a know-nothing. She was farther on in school than any other girl her age. She could do fractions and percentages, and draw the map of North America with her eyes shut. Her mother to talk, who only last Sunday when she was writing a letter had to ask how to spell "necessary"!

But suddenly the din between her mother and father split still, and it was Tom speaking. Tom unexpected and magisterial, Tom rising to his seventeen years and the incumbency of maintaining adult dignity at their table. "Can't you hold on and let us eat in peace. We've heard all that before. Jenny and I are hungry."

Jenny shivered, it was so fine and brave of Tom—but there was a long terrible minute while she watched her father's face stiffen dumbfounded. She watched—she didn't breathe—she relived the time two or three years ago when for just such bravery Tom had been sent reeling through the door with a welt across his face.

But today, instead of the oath and cry, there was Tom's

voice again, steady, and quiet, and a little scornful. "Come, Jenny, you're not eating anyway. We'll go out and leave them to it."

It was dangerous, she thought swiftly, taking sides was always dangerous, parents weren't to be flouted, but she couldn't help herself. Her pride in Tom was uncontrollable, mastering her discretion. Eyes down, bare feet padding quick and silent, she followed him.

They walked gravely across the yard and sat down on the edge of the water trough, as if their destination had been agreed upon before they started. "It's too bad all right that you couldn't go to the circus," Tom consoled, "but everybody said it wouldn't be much. And maybe some Saturday night before long I'll take you to town with me."

She glanced up puzzled, impatient. Pity again! If only they would keep quiet, just let her have her circus, have it with her if they liked.

That was all, for she wasn't wishing yet. It was too soon. There was a sudden dilation of life within her, a sudden dilation of the world around her—an elephant, a brass band in red coats, half a poster blown off a billboard, and to recapture the moment of its impingement against her was all she wanted, to scale the glamour and wonder of it, slowly, exquisitely, to feel herself unfurl.

"There's Dad now, starting for the barn," Tom nudged her. "Better go and finish your supper. I don't want any more."

Neither did she, but to escape him she went. Uneasily, apprehensive that when she was alone with her mother there might be a reckoning for her having taken sides with Tom. And she was afraid of her mother tonight. Afraid because tonight she felt herself queerly perishable. This sudden dilation of life—it was like a bubble blown vast and fragile. In time it might subside, slowly, safely, or it might even remain blown, gradually strengthening itself, gradually building up the filmy tissues to make its vastness durable, but tonight she was afraid. Afraid that before the hack of her mother's voice it might burst and crumple.

So when she found the kitchen deserted, her mother down cellar putting some of the food away, there was a cool, isolated moment of relief, and then a furtive poise, an alert, blind instinct for survival and escape. She glided across the kitchen, took down the poster from where it still hung over the calendar, and fled with it to the barn.

There was a side door, and near it a ladder to the loft. No one saw her. She lay limp among the hay, listening to her heartbeat subside, and letting the little core of pain in her breast that had come from running, slip away through her senses like the cool grains of wheat that sometimes she sat in the granary trickling through her fingers. It was a big, solemn loft, with gloom and fragrance, and sparrows chattering against its vault of silence like boys flinging pebbles at a well. And there, in its dim, high stillness, she had her circus. Not the kind that would stop off at a little town. Not just a tent and an elephant or two. No—for this was her own circus. The splendid, matchless circus of a little girl who had never seen one.

You'll catch it," said Tom when he found her, "hiding out here instead of helping with the dishes."

And she did, but it couldn't stop her wearing purple tights all night, nor riding Billie round and round the pasture in them. A young, fleet-footed Billie. Caparisoned in gold and blue and scarlet, silver tinkling bells on reins and bridle—neck arched proudly to the music of the band.

Queen's Quarterly (Winter, 1936-1937)

JOHN RAVENHILL

THE HERO RETURNS

Yep! They took Charlie McCann to the crazy house last night. They say it was shell shock that made him act the way he did. Too bad in a way, with his good war record and everything. A lot of folks could have understood it if he'd taken it out on that no good brother of his, but frightenin' the daylights out of us innocent folks around the village was sure a crazy thing to do. Why, when he came in on the stage 'bout an hour before it happened, he acted as nice as you please and went around shaking hands with everybody in the store. We just can't figgur' it out nohow.

Charlie used to work for the farmers roundabouts by the day before he went to the war. He could swing a pitchfork with the best of them, and boys oh boys, he could make the fur fly with an axe in the winter. He was a easy goin' sort, and never had much to say for hisself. He was a good worker all right. A man could put him at a job and didn't have to watch him, so all the farmers liked to get him working for them.

Bill Dyment, down Harrisburg Road a ways, had a little Home girl workin' fer him that they got when she was about twelve years old. Lemme see! I never did know her last name, but everybody called her Ella. A little scrawny mite she wuz, with palish blue eyes and yeller hair. She used t' do washin' and all the dirty work for Bill's wife. When she first come there she weren't high enough to stand over the wash tub, so they rigged up a kind of stool for her to stand on. They had her out learnin' to milk the second day she wuz there. Bill used to say she could strip a cow better'n he could hisself.

Charlie was down there thrashin' one fall and the first thing yuh know, he and her up and married. Charlie bought that old shack across from McClemmins' and fixed it up a little. It used to be funny to see them come into the store, her hangin' onto his hand like a kid. She allus had a comb stuck in the front of her hair and a bit o' rag holding it together at the back. She had three kids purty regular, and they seemed to get along good. She weren't a good cook, but Charlie got most of his meals at places where he worked so it didn't matter much.

Let me see. Charlie wuz one of the first to go from the village. The boys were hanging around the store waitin' fer the mail to come in, and Charlie wuz standin' there listening to them gabbing. All we ever talked about in them days wuz the war. Young Jim Weatherilt walks in all decked out in his new officer's uniform and starts talkin' to the bunch; tryin' to get them to jine up. The boys couldn't make up their minds and Jim got purty excited. He steps up close to Charlie and looks him in the eye and sez: "How about it, Charlie," he sez, "your King and country need you," he sez. "I never thought about it," Charlie sez, kind o' slow, the way he used to talk. But the first thing yuh know they were all shakin' hands with Jim and promisin' to meet him in town in the mornin'.

Charlie never writ home all the time he wuz away, but seein' as how he could hardly sign his own name and Ella couldn't read anyway, it didn't matter much. Bill Dyment never was much fer book learnin' anyhow, though he sent Ella to school fer a couple of weeks one winter when she first came to them. Every month regular, she got a check from the guv'ment fer forty-five dollars so she didn't do bad. She cashed it here in the store, and I let her run credit every month and took it off the check.

Well sir! This brother of Charlie's farmed a few acres o' land down Harrisburg way. Him and Charlie hadn't bin on speakin' terms fer a long ways back. It seems Bill, he beat Charlie out once on a deal over a cow. When Charlie got married, he bought this cow offa Bill, and when he got it home he found out it had caked udders and wouldn't milk. Folks said it wuz a dirty trick to beat your own brother on a deal like that. But nob'dy had much good to say about Bill McCann. There wuz a purty hard tale goin' around about the way he treated a Barnardo Home boy he had with him fer a while. They took the lad back. He ran away from Bill one night and made his way to Harrisburg. They say he wuz all covered with sores and bruises where Bill had beat him. One of the Home officers went down to see Bill about it, but Bill met him at the door with a shotgun, so the feller went away from there in a hurry.

Well, one day I wuz lookin' out the store window and I seed Bill go by in his buggy. The spokes were a rattlin' to beat the band, and the old nag's bones were stickin' out so far yuh could 'o' played a tune on 'em. He druv up to Charlie's shack and ties up to the fence and goes inside. I thought it wuz funny him visitin' Ella when him an' Charlie wuzn't on speakin' terms, but then I figgured maybe Bill had got a change of heart and were kind o' lookin' after Charlie's wife while he wuz away.

Purty soon Bill took to drivin' into the village regular, and then Ella stopped cashin' her check here at the store. Of course I never said nothin' to nobody, fer me bein' the postmaster an' all I knew lots about people's business I weren't supposed to tell. Her bill wuz run away up around forty dollars now this last three months and I kind o' thought I'd better see some cash. The next time she wuz in the store I told her about it. I sez to her, I sez: "Ella," I sez, "where do yuh cash yer check now?" She looks at me with her buck teeth makin' me think of a woodchuck: 'Bill's cashin' it fer me down at Harrisburg,' she sez. And I sez to her real firm like: "Well, Ella," I sez, "yuh better bring some cash in here."

In a couple o' days she brings over ten dollars on account, and after that I didn't see so much of her. She still runs a bill but keeps sendin' the biggest kid over fer the groceries. So, betimes I had to shut down on her fer the bill got up around fifty dollars, and I didn't like the look o' things. Well sir, the kids used to come in fer half a pound of butter and maybe five cents worth of coal oil until they got to be a nuisance. They even come over one day with six cents fer half a loaf of bread. I wuz beginnin' to figgur' where the money wuz goin', but it weren't my place to go speakin' to Bill. No siree! Yuh wouldn't catch me crossin' that feller fer anything.

I wuz gettin' purty worried about the bill she owed, so when the end of the month comes with her check in the mail, I goes over with the letter and tells her I want the bill paid. I asks her if she'd give the check to me, and she nods her head, so I writes her name on the back and she makes her mark. She don't say nothin' at all; just stands there kind o' starin' with her little pale eyes blinkin' and then she begins to cry, so I wuz glad to be goin'. I sent her over some skeeter nettin' the next day with the kids and told them to tell her to tack it on the windows fer the shack was just black with flies, and dirty!—it stunk.

Well, the next day I wuz feelin' kind o' worried, fer I figgured that maybe Bill might git sore when he comes up and finds Ella had give me her check, so I kept watch on things purty close. 'Long about three o'clock I seed Bill drive past to the shack, so I goes into the house and gets the old double barreled gun and hid it down behind the counter. I didn't want no words with Bill, but I figgured on bein' prepared like. Bill stayed a while and when he comes out and drives on past the store I felt a heap relieved. Young Geordie McClemmins wuz sittin' out front with some of the boys, and I heard him say somep'n 'bout crackin' a louse on her belly and the boys laffed. Then it struck me that Ella looked kind o' fat and dumpy when I seen her about the check.

It soon got around the village that Ella was with foal. Jake Stillman told me as how his old woman said they wuz all talkin' about it at the missionary meetin' the women folks held regular. They said it wuz terrible to allow goin's on like that in the village. Some said they ought to tar and feather

her and ride her out o' the village on a rail, but the men folk didn't take that sort o' talk serious, and purty soon it died down. Bill still kept comin' to see Ella, but none of us dast say anything to him. We wuz all a-skeared of him. I noticed he wuz always there the day she got her check.

Things must o' bin gettin' purty bad at the McCann shack. I didn't allow Ella to run no bill, and all they bought wouldn't keep a chipmunk alive. The biggest girl used to come over with the younger ones taggin' along, and buy a bit o' this and that. Their noses wuz allus runnin' and they didn't look as if they ever got their faces washed. Poor scrawny little divils they wuz, kind o' pinched lookin' around the nose, and big starey eyes. I wuz thinkin' that Charlie'd better get back soon or they wouldn't be here to welcome him. We heared Charlie had bin sent to England. Yuh see, he'd bin wounded bad at Vimy. They say he killed fifteen Germans hisself, and got a lot of medals. When Ella got the telegram she brung it over fer me to read to her. I could see Ella wuz comin' along, and couldn't help thinkin' her goin' to have a baby you might say out o' thin air, wouldn't help matters none.

Ella's kid come along that fall just three days before Charlie got back home. Old Doc Williams come out from Harrisburg, and after it wuz over he come over here to the store and started cussin' me fer a fair. Yuh never seen the like of it, and the store full o' women too. Yuh'd almost o' thought I wuz to blame fer Ella havin' the kid. He made a remark about us bein' a lot of psalm singin' hypocrites and such like I couldn't make head or tail of. But he allus wuz a mean old coot, and nobody took him serious, but some of the women were purty sore.

Well sir, just like I told yuh, the afternoon Charlie come home he gets off the stage and comes into the store as nice as you please; shakin' hands with everybody and grinnin' at them. He wuz the same old Charlie, 'ceptin' he had his right hand off above the wrist an' had to shake hands left-handed. None of us said nothin' 'bout the new kid, fer the old Doc wuz over at the shack and we figgured he would break the news to Charlie better'n we could.

We all watched from the window while Charlie walks over to the shack and goes in. He stayed fer a time and then come out and starts fer the store walkin' slow like. He comes in lookin kind o' shamed and stood at the counter and nearly bought me out. When I got all the stuff ready he pulled out a big roll o' bills and paid me right up to date. I felt purty good about gettin' the money so I sez to him jokin' like, I sez: "Well! You'll find it purty quiet 'round here," I sez, "after killin' all them Germans." He didn't even smile at that; just stood there starin' funny at me till he reminded me the way a horse looked I had oncet that broke its leg and I had to shoot it. Then young Geordie McClemmins pipes up; Geordie wuz allus a great one fer kiddin'. He sez, "how's the kid, Charlie," he sez just like that—not meanin' a thing by it, but Charlie chased him half a mile down the Harrisburg road, and Geordie had to jump the fence to get away.

We wuz all standin' watchin' in front of the store when Charlie comes back, and he cusses and swears and shakes his fist at us, then he runs over to the shack and comes out with one of them automatic revolvers they used in the war and starts fer us blazin' away somethin' turrible. I tell you! We got into the store mighty quick and locked the door on him. He had to shoot with his left hand or he'd like to killed us all. He never come near us though, and the sherriff didn't have no trouble at all takin' him to town. Nobody ever thought Charlie would pull a dirty trick like that on his neighbors—'tweren't christian like. Crazy as a loon, he wuz.

Canadian Forum (March 1938)

DOROTHY LIVESAY

THE WAITING ROOM

Now that we're waiting, now that she's sitting still, now she's frightened.... Maybe it's only the way her hands are folded, fingers sitting up stiff like stubble. But she isn't looking at me any more or at the dingy station benches opposite, or the cold stove. She's looking somewhere backward into the farm maybe on a spring morning. Like the day I saw her drying her pale hair in the sunlight, calling back the dog from barking. "Is your father home?" I said. "My husband's out in the back field, ploughing." That's the way she answered. That's all there was to say.

I went back alone and found him, plodding in the slate-colored furrows. He might have been her father. His figure was slight, shrivelled up almost the way a tree gets when the wind has had its say. Wisps of reddish hair stood up around the crown of his head which was bald and burned a mahogany colour by the sun. His eyes were light blue, almost lost in creases. He didn't pay any attention to me till I called him.

"You're Mr. Farley?"

"That's right."

"Jim Caruthers told me to come and see you."

"Well, the soil ain't going to stand still under my feet. What've you got to say?"

"I understand you're one of the farmers that lost a lot of

cattle to the government ... caught with tuberculosis."

"Are you another one one of them government inspectors?"

"No. Nothing like that. I'm a representative of the Farmers' Alliance.

"What's that?"

"A union of farmers who...."

"I ain't int'rested in unions."

"You're interested in getting a fair price for your cattle."

"Maybe so. But I can look after my own interests."

"Some of the farmers up the line figured a petition might help...."

"What they figure ain't got nothing to do with my arithmetic." He turned emphatically to the horse, lifted the reins. "*He* can't wait, no more than I can. We've got to keep on going."

I watched him push the horse ahead, his head bowed like the animal's, aiming for the fence and maneuvering the turn nicely. Before he had it completed I was on my way back, around the barn.

She was at the pump, filling a pail with water till it splashed over her feet.

"Find him?"

"Yes thanks." Maybe she knew I hadn't got what I wanted, whatever it was.

"Have you had ... any dinner?" she asked, hesitating. It was well past noon.

"Well, no." But I'll hit the village soon."

"You might as well have what's left. Come right into the kitchen now, and set down." She had greenish sort of eyes, flecked like stones are under water. Her mouth was full and wide when she smiled. I followed her right in not saying anything. I took a chair by the window.

"You're strange to these parts, maybe?"

"Yes. I'm from up Green Valley way."

"I thought you were a stranger." She smiled, as if that was a happy discovery. She was busy heating something on the stove, and I watched the sun falling in a shaft through the open door, onto the oilcloth worn to a glossy brown. She moved quickly to and fro in the sun, her feet flickering in and out like the spring leaves.

"There, it's ready." And when I sat down it was like I used to feel years back, after bringing the cows home; a peaceful feeling, knowing all the beasts would be shut away soon, to rest; and voices would be quiet. I hadn't felt so welcome for a long time.

"Is it all right?"

"Yes," I said, thinking of the union. "It's going to be fine." Then I began talking to her about it. This part of the country is far from headquarters, so I hadn't been able to talk the situation over with anyone. It was all done by letter-writing. And now here I was telling her all about it as if she was Pete himself; and she listening with quiet eyes, or asking questions like a man would. I must have talked over an hour, first about crops, then cattle, then asking her about different farmers.

"McEachern feels it bad," she told me. "He was down to the store cursin' because they had half his stock branded. He even wrote a letter to McNally, that's our representative.... But I wouldn't trust Heely if I was you, he makes promises easy. And Jim, yes Jim Caruthers fears nobody, he'd help a neighbor if it took his last sack of flour."

"Your husband doesn't seem to like unions," I said at last, mentioning him for the first time. She took a quick breath.

"Well, it's all new like, the idea. Arthur's cautious. But the things you say are different. They're what we think, but we don't somehow put it into words...." She pushed back her chair then, moving from the table, troubled maybe at the way I looked at her.

"You've always lived on a farm?" I questioned.

"I? Yes. I never got educated like the rest. I was the eldest. I started working out when I was fourteen. After a while I got this job, as housekeeper. I wasn't green. But livin' alone here...."

She feels at home with me, I was thinking. She's told me

everything.

After that I stood by the doorway, looking out to the apple orchard where the pink bloom was bursting from the hard brown veins.

"Good-bye." I said. I forgot to thank her for the meal.

It must have been getting on towards fall when there was a convention of farmers at Broutville. We met in an abandoned sawmill, fixed up as a temporary hall with flat wooden benches. Over all the sweet raw scent of wood still penetrated, and from the rocks down below the sound of water ran like a tune in the back of your head.

Pete had come from Toronto, his big, loose body sprawling behind the table, his words few and far between as he shook hands with delegates, his eyes smiling.

"Why, he ain't no different from us farmers," Sam Copperhead was saying to me, over in a corner where registration was going on.

"What were you scared of?" I asked him.

"Thought he might have an English accent. That wouldn't go good, you know, Adam."

"You've taught me how to go wary, Sam. Pete will learn too. Hell, remember how I used to wave my fist at the boys, and shout socialism?"

Sam grinned. "You got over that in Godsill. The men around there haven't forgotten you yet.... Here's Jim Caruthers now." I had only time to shake hands with him before the gavel sounded. We sat down, knees wide apart on the wooden benches. Late that afternoon Jim stood up to report.

"I'll say right at the start I've never been to a meetin' like this before. I've sat right through church meetin's and never opened my trap. I've listened to the minister preach and the Tory and Grit candidates spiel, year in and year out; they couldn't make me talk. For all they knew I didn't do any thinkin' at all. And mebbe that's right. Mebbe I didn't. On the day of Pentecost they say everybody spoke in divers tongues, and when I see all us farming men sitting here together and not fightin', but talkin' about how to keep our land from the mortgage companies and stoppin' evictions and keepin' up the price of milk, then to me it's like learnin' a new language you allus wanted to know. But somehow you couldn't get your tongue around it. Now I kin say I feel real happy. I've learned to talk...."

What he was saying after that I didn't hear. In the dust of the room I felt that welcome feeling. I remembered the pale, smooth way her hair was in the sunshine, and how she had said, "We couldn't put it into flesh and blood words."

Maybe there isn't anything to it, the way a mood like that will come over you. A person you'd almost forgotten comes right up beside you, fresh as morning, so your mind just naturally starts a conversation.... Take us sitting here now. Her dress is touching my hand, her cheek curves close to mine. But I can feel her distance from me, it's like a mountain you can almost touch, but you must walk miles to reach. She was nearer to me in that old sawmill than she is now.

Jim drove me back to Godsill in the old Ford in time for the alfalfa reaping; in time to see McEachern evicted and squatting on Arthur Farley's land. He patched up an old strawberry shed and put his family in it. With Farley growling at him every day and May slipping up unbeknownst to him, with fresh eggs and milk.

Perhaps she has forgotten now, the day he shoved them off. It was October and he had no more use for them working the land. The sky was that brazen kind of blue, sharp as a scythe. The wind was busy whittling the trees bare, you knew what was coming. And in the midst of it the McEacherns were out piling their worn-down belongings onto the wagon, the kids quiet as mice as the old man hitched up the mare.

May had suddenly left us there, beating her thin legs against the wind, running to Arthur at the barn. I could see her, a small agitated speck, like a part of my own mind jumping. He wouldn't listen at all, then he struck her face. It was as if my own brain was stunned.

I started to run, but she was protecting him, meeting me half-way. "I'm not hurt. Leave him alone. And let me go.

Adam, let me go!" She had shaken herself free from the grip of my hands on her arm, she sprang towards the McEacherns.

After that we met in the bush. The rain and wind seemed to be driving us for shelter towards each other. Her hands would be chill as ice till I wound them under my coat. But when we talked, it was about the Alliance. Because of the McEacherns she was burning to help. She began going round and explaining things to the women, "They think I'm crazy; that this is a man's job. But I'll keep right on!" Then there began to be talk about the two of us, and she couldn't get anywhere with her ideas. "They're all closed up like crabs, Adam. There's no charity in them." That was the only day I saw her crying. She didn't cry at all when I said I was going away.

It used to come over me on train journeys, when your mind is like a compass turning slowly from what's behind to what's ahead. Or on street corners, late at night, leaving a meeting. Mostly I was too busy to think, but sometimes even when you're busy you find yourself alone. There's no one out on the street but yourself. Lamps look dim, a faint breeze might ruffle the trees. You remember a thin person, somebody to warm.

For the winter long she would come upon me like that. In April I was coming into the rooming house out of a green mist, and found a letter on the hall table, forwarded from Toronto. I just held it in my hand unopened, happy for no reason. I went upstairs singing.

Maybe I've never told her enough the difference that letter made. Maybe I should have shouted a hundred times, instead of whispering once, how I threw open the window and stretched my muscles. For you believe in a new life. But it isn't for you, for this generation. And then the new life comes, a letter in your hand.

Dear Adam:

He's all closed up like winter. And I feel young. I love my people. I should stay with them. But I can't any more. I'll come to meet you anywhere. Any way.

And now you've done it, youngling. Now you're sitting facing the hard painted seats, the unlighted stove in the station waiting-room. And I haven't met you yet, the way we used to meet.

She never was frightened before, and now she's frightened. I can feel she's cold and doesn't want to be warmed. So maybe there isn't a new life, it was only something I imagined.

Now she knows I'm watching, her hands loosen. One finds mine, is tight.

"The train will be here in five minutes."

"Yes."

"Are you sure you want to come, May?"

She has a strained look, her face white.

"Maybe there's something you want to tell me, May?"

"Yes, Adam. Before we take the train."

"O.K. Plenty of time."

"I shouldn't come, Adam."

"Don't be crazy."

"No. You mustn't make me come."

"Then you don't want me?"

"Yes! But listen Adam. Listen quickly. Bend your ear down. Please. I'm sorry Adam. But before I left him ... he ... I. We hadn't been all winter, but he.... For the first time, it's *his* child I have...."

She began to cry on my shoulder, short, unrestrained sobs. I rubbed her arm, up and down, to stop the way her body was shaking. A mile away the train whistled faintly.

"You go." She tried to push me aside.

"Aren't you my comrade?" I said.

"I *was*." The train was roaring in our ears, screeching to a stop.

"Then come." She was close, a part of my mind.

We ran towards the train.

New Frontier (December 1936)

L.A. MacKAY

ANOTHER MAN'S POISON

Well, Friday night a bunch of us goes down to get Bill to come over to Listowel and bowl. He's sitting on the front steps, sort of frowning at the flower-beds, and smoking and chewing and spitting away like a good fellow. So we hollers at him to come on over to Listowel and give us a hand, and he gets up looking kind of sorrowful, and come down to the gate and says,

"No use, boys. The old woman says I got to water them flowers tonight if it's the last thing I do. Just because I was down to the Ex. last Tuesday, she thinks I'd ought to stay home the rest of the month."

Then somebody says, "I hear you had a big time down there, Bill."

And Bill says, "Well sir, by golly"—you know the way he does—"well sir, by golly, I never had so much fun in all my born days."

And somebody else says, "You was in swell company anyway, Bill, if that counts for anything. How come you took that old bum of a Jim Elgar down with you anyway?"

Then Bill gets going. "Well," he says, "you know how it is. The old woman's always sending him over something, the last of a batch of biscuits, or the like, when they get dried out; and something she said, he gathered I was going down. So when he come over next day for his pail of buttermilk, like we always give him when we churn, he says sort of casual:

"'I hear you're going to the Toronto Exhibition, Bill.'

"'Well,' I says, 'that's once you didn't hear no lie.'

"'Don't happen to have any more room in your car, do you?' he says.

"'Sure I have,' I says. 'There's only Charlie and Ern coming. Want to hold down the back seat?'

"'Don't mind if I do,' he says. 'I ain't never been to the Ex., and I don't figure maybe I'll get many more chances.'

"'You got a brother in Toronto, ain't you?' I says. 'Why don't you go down and stay with him for a couple of days?'

"'Fat chance of that,' he says, 'even supposing he's alive. I ain't heard from him in four years. I ain't none too anxious for the hospitality he'd give me anyway.'

"'I guess he ain't doing so well, eh,' says I, 'from all I've heard.'

"'If he's got the brains of a jackrabbit,' says Jim, 'which I don't imagine he has, he'll be in jail now and getting a square meal for a change. He didn't have no job, nor no money, nor no nothing, the last I heard, and didn't seem likely to get none.'

"Well, we got away about half past five Tuesday morning, and got into Toronto in good time. I says to Charlie—no, I guess it was Ern:

"'We don't want to go out to the Ex. just yet, till people gets there. Let's just have a cup of coffee somewheres and drive around a bit till about ten o'clock. Pity there ain't somebody in Toronto we could sponge on.'

"Ern says, 'Well, Jim's got a brother, ain't he? Let's go and call on him.'

"'Let's get the coffee first,' says Jim, 'and then maybe we'll be able to stand the shock.'

"So we went into one of them Chinese places and had a cup of what they called coffee, the sort of stuff my old woman wouldn't have give to the pigs. Then we come out, and I says to Jim,

"'Well, Jim, where does your brother live? We got lots of time. Might as well be neighbourly.'

" 'Hell,' says Jim, 'if you ain't no more anxious to see him than what I am, there's lots better things you could do with your time. Let's go and see the morgue, or something cheerful.'

" 'Now Jim,' I says, 'that ain't no way to talk about your brother, what you come all this way to see. Where's he live?'

" 'How should I know? Better ask the police. I know the name of the street he was on four years back, but that ain't no proof he's there now.'

" 'Moved into a sweller neighbourhood, I guess," says Charlie.

" 'I don't know what it's like,' says Jim, 'but you can bet your last pair of boots, if he's moved at all it couldn't be to nowheres worse.'

"Well, we got the name of the street out of him, and asked a cop where it was. He looked it up in a little book he had, and looked at us kind of queer, as if he felt like asking us what we was going there for, but I guess he sort of figured it wasn't none of his business anyway, so he told us how to get there, and we went scouting around somewheres down around the railway tracks till we found it.

"Well sir, by golly, you never saw such a dismal-looking hole in all your born days. Dirt, you never saw anything like it, and the smells would turn a sow's stomach. It was just a row of shacks leaning every which way and peeling off in all directions, and that road hadn't been fixed since the year One. I tell you I was sorry for my springs. Jim didn't know the number of the house; said it was something like nineteen or fifty-seven, or something like that. The numbers only went up to about eighty, so I said we ought to stop the car and Jim get out and go along the street and try 'em all out.

" 'I never seen the man yet,' says Jim, 'that I'd go to all that trouble for, let alone that hound of a Bob. If you've had your fun, what say we turn around and start off for the Ex.? I thought that's what we hired you for, was to take us there.'

"Just then, around the end of the street, come an old man in an old ragged pair of overalls, and a greasy coat and a shirt that looked like it had been sewed on him some time last year, and he'd lost the scissors. He was pushing a sort of barrow thing, with all sorts of paper packages in it. Some of them was unrolled, and it looked to me like he'd been out robbing the garbage cans for his breakfast. After him comes another old chap limping along, mumbling and swearing away through what was left of his teeth, and cussing the other fellow like a good one because he wouldn't give him nothing out of the barrow.

" 'Hell's bells,' says Jim. 'Talk of the devil. There he is.'

" 'Where's who?' says Charlie. 'What's biting you now?'

" 'It's Bob,' says Jim, 'the wooden-legged old beggar limping along behind the cart. Now ain't that a hell of a life for a man's brother to take up with? Sort of makes you proud of your family, don't it?'

"Then he yells out, 'Hello Bob, how's pickings?'

"Bob, he didn't answer, sort of looked round dazed, as if he thought he was hearing things. Then he come over to the car and, not knowing any of the rest of us, he looks sort of doubtful, and says,

" 'Was it me you was wanting?'

"Jim, he leans over then and says, 'Hello Bob, are you so stuck up with living in the city that you don't recognize your own brother?'

" 'Not when I see him riding in a motor car I don't, not unless you stole it. What's the game?'

" 'Oh, we was just on our way out to the Exhibition and thought we'd drop in and see how you was getting along. Your business seems to be picking up. Hawhaw.'

" 'Gee, you're smart, ain't you?'

" 'I'm too damn smart to live in a hole like this, and feed out of other people's garbage pails.'

" 'Well, a man's got to live, ain't he? You don't know anything about the sityation here. This here unemployment, it's something fierce. There's thousands of men tramping the streets in this here city looking for work, and can't get it.'

" 'Gosh, that must make you feel bad. Just about breaks your heart, don't it?'

" 'Yeh, you can laugh all right. You don't know what

suffering is.'

" 'No, sure I don't. Never heard of it. What it it? Something you eat?'

" 'Gosh, you're smart.'

" 'Sure; always did have all the brains of the fam_il_y. Ain't you going to invite us in? Where you living now?'

" 'Sure, come on in everybody, and have a good time. See that shed in there? Better run the car into the lane where you can keep an eye on it and the police won't spot it.'

"He jumps up on the running board, and I runs the car in towards an old shed, with a lot of boxes piled up inside of it.

" 'This here's the parlor,' he says, 'the bedroom's over behind them boxes in the corner.'

"We all climbed out and sat down on some of the boxes.

" 'Well,' says Jim, 'I don't claim to be living in the lap of luxury myself, but I'm damned if I'd put up with the like of this.'

" 'I'd like to see what else you could do here,' says Bob. 'There's lots of people I know that'd be glad to change places with me.'

" 'How many people are there in this here city?' says Jim.

" 'I don't know,' says Bob. 'Well on to a million, I guess.'

" 'You mean to tell me that in just one million people there's some that's bigger fools and more good-for-nothing than what you are? Gosh, I know less about the world than I thought I did.'

" 'I don't see what you got to be so damn proud about.'

" 'Well, I got a house that'll keep out most of the rain, and I got three meals a day, such as they are, and I can keep myself in chewing tobacco.'

" 'Yeh, living in a one-horse burg that nobody ever heard of but the post office, and they have to look twice.'

" 'That don't hurt my feelings none. I got a bed to sleep on, and a day's work when I want it, without having to go scrounging around in garbage cans.'

" 'Yeh, fat lot of work you do. I don't live on my neighbours' charity, anyway. I got some self-respect.'

" 'Sure you have. Slathers of it. Pride and independence, that's you all over. Guess the chap with the wheelbarrow must be one of them neighbours you talk about. Looked like you wouldn't live long on his charity. I'll say this for myself, my neighbours think enough of me to help me out when I ask for it, anyways. Which ain't often.'

"Yeh, I bet they'd help you out. Help you out of town if you give them a chance. Never asked them for a railway ticket, did you? I bet there'd be a public subscription would take you to Vancouver.'

" 'Sure there would, and back again. Look here, Bob, you ain't done nothing to deserve it, and I don't see why you should be anything particular to me now anyways, but I won't see no brother of mine living here like a pig, rooting dead cats out of garbage pails, if I can help it. Come on back with me to a decent place. Bill here'll give you a lift, if you got any clothes decent enough to sit down in the car in. Anyway, there's lots of freight trains any day. I ain't got much of a place, but it's a damn sight better than this, and you'd never go to sleep on an empty belly anyway. What say? Is it a go?'

" 'What? Me? After living in the city, go and squat down in a dead-alive hole like that? You must think I'm crazy.'

" 'I think you're crazy if you don't. It's a fair offer. I ain't asking you to pay anything. What good's it doing you, staying here?'

" 'You never can tell. Something might turn up. There ain't no future there, nothing ahead of you. You get a day's work now and again, maybe, and where does it get you?'

" 'It gets me meat and potatoes and chewing-tobacco anyway, and that's a sight more than you got. What do you want with a future at your age, you old fool? You never held a job two weeks in your life.'

" 'No, but the thing is, there ain't no life there, everything's dead.'

" 'Gosh, it ain't half as dead as this place is, by the smell of it. What the hell do you get by living in the city anyway? Go to the movies every night, and eat in all the swell hotels, don't you?'

" 'No, it ain't that, but there's always something doing, and lots of people about, and things.'

" 'Fat lot of good that does you. And a swell lot of people you hang about with here. Of all the noisy, stinking, rotten holes I ever saw....

" 'Oh, you're a hell of a fine guy, you are. Swanking about so damn superior in other people's cars, and living on charity.'

" 'I'd rather live on charity like a human being than root around like a pig into garbage cans. I make enough anyway that I can offer you charity, you old fool, if you weren't too damn pig-headed to take it.'

" 'Oh shut up, will you, and mind your own damn business. I wouldn't take charity from you, not if I was to drop dead on the street.'

" 'And so you will damn well drop dead on the street before I ever offer you anything again. You ain't fit for no decent man even to talk to acrost the street and up-wind, you stinking, mud-grubbing old....'

"That's as far as he gets, and then the two of them light into it both at once, yelling away at each other as hard as they could pelt. Well sir, by golly, I never heard such language in all my born days as them two old blackguards slung at one another; and I've heard a lot. I can't even remember most of it, but if the old woman wasn't back there I could give you an earful that'd make your hair curl. If you want to hear something artistic, just you go down some time and say to Jim, 'Well, Jim, I hear you saw your brother down in the city.' And you better take some asbestos plugs along for your ears.

"Well sir, them two old stagers got so mad that first thing we knew they was going after one another like good fellows, fists and boots flying all over the yard. Charlie and Ern and I couldn't hardly stand up straight for laughing, but we grabbed aholt of them and pulled them apart and shoved Jim into the car; and Ern sat on him and Charlie kept shoving old Bob off the running-board till I got the car going, and then we went off to the Exhibition. I guess we saw pretty near everything there was to be seen, and it was a darn good show too, but there wasn't anything that was a patch on that for fun. Old Jim didn't rightly cool off till we was all the way home; he kept wanting to go back and beat him up. Laugh, I never laughed so much in all my born days."

Canadian Forum (October 1936)

LUELLA BRUCE CREIGHTON

HYDRO

Mrs. Hainer hoped they would be able to have the Hydro turned on for it. They were four months in arrears. Five dollars it would be, to have it turned on. They didn't have five dollars, and if they had there were so many things. But it would be so nice to have it turned on. Lamps made you kind of nervous, if you weren't used to them. Mrs. Mottson, the lady next door, she let them have all their lamps to use, when they turned it off.

Of course, they weren't bad off, except for that. There was the Relief. Joe worked three days out of twenty. You got tickets for coal and groceries, but there wasn't any real money at all.

With the other three Mrs. Hainer went to the hospital. But Joe was working then, and they could do it. It didn't cost so much, if you had it, in the lovely big clean ward. They washed the floor every day, and it was so clean anyway. A lot of other women had their babies there, too. Sometimes when they walked up and down and yelled, before, it kind of got on your nerves. But everybody has to go through it. It's a natural thing, like, you might say. The nurses were so nice, and Mrs. Hainer never had much trouble with hers.

Afterwards it was so kind of quiet and restful, with nothing to do for nearly two weeks, and all your meals in bed, up to the very last night you were in. The baby came in so clean and pretty, and all the other little babies, in a wagon. Joe came in every evening, and sometimes he brought flowers, from the flower bed. If it was summer. With Julie it was summer, with George, too. Bernice was the winter time, like this one.

Joe got all kind of silly and romantic about her, in the hospital. He said she looked so pretty, with her light brown hair in big long braids over the pink bed jacket. He'd half a mind to marry her himself, he said. As if they hadn't been married all these years. Joe used to be always like that. Great for jokes.

Then when Joe got the trouble in his tubes, the cough, chronic bronchitis, the doctor said, he lost his job at the radio factory. He used to do spray painting, and lacquer. He was off six weeks, and they let him out. Joe didn't get another job. Times got hard, then.

When Mrs. Hainer knew she was going to have it she felt awful bad. They didn't have any savings, and she knew how it would be. She hated like anything to let on to Joe. Not that they didn't like children, but him out of his job, and times so hard. Joe was feeling so poorly, too, at the time.

But if it was coming, it was coming, and there you were. Joe walked straight out of the house, when she told him, and got a bottle. He was ashamed, after. Joe wasn't a drinking man. One thing about Joe, he never took it out on his wife.

Mrs. Hainer had it all figured out. The baby would be born on the twenty-first. Joe's turn on the Waterworks came the sixteenth, three days, with real money. Four dollars a day, for working on the Waterworks, because Joe knew the man. That would be twelve dollars. After they paid the five to have the Hydro turned on again there would be seven dollars over. There was something sort of mean about having a little new baby come into the world by lamplight. When the other three were all born in real hospitals, too. It would likely come at night, and the bedroom was so dark.

Mrs. Hainer didn't go to the doctor until about a month before. She felt just fine. There wasn't any need. She walked to the doctors because she didn't have car tickets. They had no real money at all. It was thirty-one blocks to the doctor's. The doctor was a real nice man, but awful busy.

"Your fourth, eh, Mrs. Hainer?"

"Yes."

"Well, I guess you know what to do, pretty well."

The doctor smiled cheerfully. Mrs. Hainer wondered how the other three were getting along at home. It was too far to bring them. She could walk it, but George was only six, he couldn't. You couldn't put more than two in the carriage. Mrs. Mottson, the lady next door, she said she would come in and keep an eye on them.

The doctor examined Mrs. Hainer. He felt the heartbeats, and put the band around her arm to tell the blood pressure. Mrs. Hainer stared straight ahead of her at the plain white glass curtains. She hated to tell the doctor that she was going to have the baby at home, this time. Probably by lamplight, too.

"Everything seems alright, Mrs. Hainer," the doctor said. "I'd cut down on meat for the next few weeks, and get plenty of orange juice. You can expect your young fella about the sixteenth, I should say. Good-bye, Mrs. Hainer."

Mrs. Hainer walked heavily out through the crowded waiting room. Everyone seemed to stare at her. She put her hands in her pockets when she opened the door. It would be nice to have gloves.

If the baby came the sixteenth she couldn't have the Hydro. Joe couldn't go to the Waterworks, either. Somebody had to look after the other children. So they'd never get the twelve dollars. It went by the alphabet, the Waterworks did. If you missed your turn you didn't get it again for months. Even if you knew the man. A man can't go and say "My wife is having a baby." If there's a job he's got to be there, to get it.

It seemed a long way home from the doctor's office. Mrs. Hainer tried to hurry, but it just seemed as if her feet wouldn't get off the ground. It was colder, going home. The wind was against her. Her coat wasn't any too long for this weather. The coats they had now were a lot more sensible than they were when Joe had bought her that one. Green broadcloth stuff, it was, with a kind of a curly light brown collar. The fur in the collar used to be straight, but once it got wet it went all curly like. Mrs. Hainer thought it was prettier, all curly, anyway, but Joe never liked it so well after. He was proud of that coat. Bought it for her all himself, down in the basement of one of the big stores. Joe was a great one for things like that. If it hadn't been for Joe's tubes, if he'd been able to keep on with the paint spraying, things wouldn't a been with them as they were. A new gift of a child, and the Hydro turned off.

When Mrs. Hainer got to the corner of Stadacona Boulevard she could see the lamplight in her own house. The one with no verandah on it. All the rest of the houses on Stadacona Boulevard had verandahs. The Mottsons, the people next door, even had a little tiny furnace, in their house. But there were no doors between the rooms in the Mottson's house. The bedroom in Mrs. Hainer's house had a door. That was an important thing. They had one more room than the Mottsons, too. They had a room upstairs. Five rooms, altogether, counting the kitchen. The Mottsons only had four, and no doors. But they had a telephone. All the people on Stadacona Boulevard gave a nice Christmas present to Mrs. Mottson, for the use of the telephone. If you can't even pay to have the Hydro turned on you couldn't have a telephone.

It was nice of Mrs. Mottson to come in and light the lamp. In times like this it was lovely to have good neighbours. The doctor must have been wrong about that date. She would be real careful, and likely it would hold off. "I won't tell Joe," she said, "it'd only be worrying him. He's got enough on his mind." Ponderously she hoisted herself up the steep step to the front door, where there should have been a verandah, but there wasn't.

Mrs. Mottson was right at the door to meet her.

"Getting quite a wind up, isn't there," said Mrs. Mottson.

"Seems a little colder."

"Have a cup of tea, dearie, you must be that tired."

Mrs. Hainer lowered herself into a chair. She put her

feet out in front of her. Her ankles were swollen, and her finger puffed out on each side of her wedding ring. It looked odd, with her so thin in the arms, she thought. She drank the tea eagerly. It was good strong tea.

"I *am* a little tuckered," Mrs. Hainer said.

"The children have been good as gold," Mrs. Mottson said, "and I just slipped over home and stirred up these muffins. Have one, Mrs. Hainer. The lady where Doris works, they have them for breakfast, and Doris, she showed me how to make them."

The three children sat on the settee, cramming muffins into their mouths.

"They're real lovely, Mrs. Mottson."

"Have another, Mrs. Hainer. There's nothing to them."

"I'm really ashamed," said Mrs. Hainer, and ate three muffins.

"Was he pleased, then?" enquired Mrs. Mottson.

"He said I was all right. I knew I was, of course. I wouldn't a gone, but for Joe. Just another dollar, it is."

"He can wait for it."

"I guess he knows he'll have to."

"A good doctor, Doctor MacPhail."

"He's a nice man. I'd as soon have him as the next one."

Mrs. Hainer sent the children out to the front to look for their father, while she told Mrs. Mottson what the doctor said about the date.

"If it's right, it'll mean, of course, that Joe can't get the Waterworks."

"Never say a word to him, Mrs. Hainer. We'll see that you're looked after. The nurse'll be here from the City, and we'll see to the other kiddies."

Mrs. Mottson consulted a calendar. "The sixteenth—that'll be Wednesday. It's Doris's half day, that is, and we'll be able to manage just fine."

Mrs. Hainer rested her head on her swollen hands.

"You're too good to us," she said, "may the good Lord reward you."

Joe went off at a quarter to seven the morning of the

sixteenth, and Mrs. Hainer got up at six o'clock and gave him a good breakfast. They had got the relief ticket the day before, and he had porridge, and bacon and a fried egg and fried potatoes, and three big cups of good strong tea. Mrs. Hainer made him up a good lunch, too. With cold bacon and bread, and a ginger ale bottle full of tea, with lots of milk and sugar in it.

"Put hair on your chest, that will," Joe said.

Joe was so glad to be working again. Even for three days. Twelve dollars. He kissed Mrs. Hainer before he went off, and Mrs. Hainer felt suddenly excited and happy again. Just as if she'd just been married to Joe, and he had a job. And she'd been really married to Joe for nearly seven years, and was going to have another baby any day now. And that would be the fourth. And the Hydro was turned off.

With Joe gone Mrs. Hainer thought it would be a good chance to clean the house up properly. She was up so early anyway, and the children were still asleep. She mopped and dusted the parlour, and swept out the bedroom thoroughly. "I'm going to have the house clean, anyway," she said. "Now, while the children aren't right under my feet I believe I'll just wash up the kitchen floor."

When Mrs. Hainer got down on the bit of sacking to wash off the kitchen oilcloth she was suddenly aware that she was going to have her new baby that day. Joe might have gone, and the Hydro might not be turned on, but the baby was coming anyway. Mrs. Hainer got up to her feet, and stood very still in the middle of the kitchen, for a minute. She pressed her wet red hands to her face. Her heart pounded. She never could get over that immense, turbulent excitement when she knew that the moment had come for her to have a baby. She was so filled with curiosity about babies not yet born. Would it be a girl or boy? What would it be like? The knowledge that she was right now, in a few hours, at the farthest, going to see this little secret creature, filled her with intense elation. All alone in the kitchen Mrs. Hainer had her moment of exaltation. Then she wiped her hands, opened the door, and walked carefully across the narrow lawn, to tell

Mrs. Mottson.

"Now you get right into your bed," Mrs. Mottson said, "and I'll look after everything. I'll phone the doctor, Mrs. Hainer, and be right over."

Mrs. Hainer finished washing the kitchen floor before she went to bed. She was glad the bedroom was so clean and neat, and so glad it was daytime. It kind of takes away the scary part of having a baby, when it comes in the daytime. It was lovely of Mrs. Mottson to be there.

The nurse was more than an hour late, and Doctor MacPhail was terribly angry. But he put her under almost right away, and gave it to her himself. He did everything himself. He was a good doctor and a nice man.

Mrs. Hainer was resting very, very quietly. It was lovely to have it all over. And a boy. My, but Joe would be pleased. The doctor had gone into the Mottson's to phone. You could hear his voice booming through. The passage between the houses was so narrow. It was good they had such nice neighbours. The doctor sounded angry about something.

"What the hell is the matter with you people down there? This is the third I've had since two o'clock this morning, and every God-damned nurse late...." It sounded like he slammed the receiver down pretty hard.

The doctor came in again.

"How are you feeling now, Mrs. Hainer? Great little chap you've got there!"

"I think she's sleeping," the nurse said.

Mrs. Hainer smiled to herself. She wasn't sleeping, but she was too tired to talk. The nurse was bending over the baby. She seemed to be putting oil on him, or something.

When Mrs. Hainer woke the nurse had gone until the next morning, and the baby lay pink and shining and squirming in the clothesbasket. Mrs. Mottson sat by the bed. Mrs. Hainer could hear Joe out in the dining-room. He sounded as if he were sending the children to bed. It must be after supper time. Mrs. Mottson lit the lamp on the dresser.

"You've had such a nice sleep, dearie," she said, "wouldn't you like a little drop of soup?"

Mrs. Hainer smiled. "I could take some," she said, "it's too bad for you to bother."

After Mrs. Hainer had her soup Joe came and said, "Well, Gladys, I got in one day's work, anyhow."

"Now, Mr. Hainer," Mrs. Mottson said, "you just go the other two days. Between Doris and me, we'll look after Mrs. Hainer and the boys."

Joe turned away kind of quick, when she said that. "Doris doesn't want to be spending her time off looking after my care," he said. His voice sounded husky. It was hard on Joe, him being always so independent.

"We're glad to do it," Mrs. Mottson said. "If people hadn't been good to us when our Lorraine came I don't know how we'd a did it."

Upstairs Doris was putting the children to bed. "They can see their new brother tomorrow," Mrs. Mottson said.

"How much does he weigh?" asked Mrs. Hainer.

"The nurse said six pounds, five ounces," said Mrs. Mottson.

"Let me see him," Joe said.

"Pick him up careful, Joe."

"Let me feel the heft of him." Joe weighed him carefully in his big hands.

"Doesn't weigh an ounce under eight pounds," Joe pronounced.

"Of course, there's his little clothes," Mrs. Hainer said, doubtfully.

"Them little things? Them little things don't weigh nothing worth counting!"

"Eight pounds!" exclaimed Mrs. Mottson, "think of that!"

"The biggest one *we* ever had," said Joe, proudly.

Joe put the baby back in the clothesbasket. The baby screwed up his face and opened, astonishingly, two jewel bright blue eyes.

"Well, I never!" said Mrs. Mottson, "look at him open his little eyes. Mark my words now, that's a bright young one."

Mrs. Hainer began to laugh a little. "My, I'm so glad he

was born in the daytime," she said, "I was kinda worried about the Hydro being not turned on."

Canadian Forum (June 1932)

MARY QUAYLE INNIS

THE GIFT

When she came down to breakfast, Roy was already at the table. The room was blind with sun, so bright that Judith blinked and bent her head as she ate the neatly-cut grapefruit. What a house this was for sun; it was brighter even on cloudy days than any other house she knew. She had wanted it for that. The high situation, the trees pressed back about an open shield of lawn had promised abundant sunlight. Reaction probably from the dark room she had been living in ten years ago. She and Paul had moved every few months and each bath-sitting-room with its convertible bed and discreet cupboard arranged to conceal dishes and display books had seemed dingier and more airless than the last. Paul who had worshipped the sun—how he would have loved this house. What made her think of that?

"Sorry I have to go," Roy said, rising. Judith, to turn the channel of her thoughts as much as to make a point, exclaimed cheerfully: "Roy, I want something. I want a hundred dollars to buy a bunny coat for evening."

"I thought you had an evening wrap." His voice was patient as though she were one of those ceaselessly demanding wives one reads about in novels.

"Oh, but that gold one is archaic, dear. It looks absolutely matronly. I want a white fur one while I have figure enough to look girlish in it."

"You always look lovely," Roy said cautiously. "Besides, clothes come out of your allowance."

"Not fur coats. A hundred dollars for a fur coat, Roy, is simply ridiculous. I wouldn't ask you if I had a cent left but I haven't. Not much more than a cent."

"I'll see, dear. Things are tight now."

"But I wanted it for Friday," she wailed. "I know your seeing. When have I wanted you to buy me an extra like this, Roy?" She ran after him and laid her hand on his arm. She was laughing as though it were all a joke but she really wanted the money and Roy knew it.

"I'll see," he repeated. "I'll see if I can let you have it."

When he frowned she was inclined to tell him not to bother about it, but then she remembered what he was always spending—on the car and his clubs and golf and travelling. It was silly for her to have to wear the gold cloak which had begun to tarnish. When Roy was gone she thought, as she finished her breakfast, that she didn't demand enough from Roy. He hesitated at such moderate requests that he ought to face more exorbitant ones just for practice. But what a dear he was.

She smiled. Funny how one got used to things. She had worried so once over food bills and had made soups and stews without end. And now it was a new white fur evening coat. She had wondered when she was hopelessly, miserably poor, what she would do if she found herself suddenly rich. People said that poor girls made the most reckless spenders but though the incredible thing had happened to her she hadn't been reckless. Roy wasn't rich—but he had millions compared with what she had always had. She had been thrilled but she had gone quietly.

There was no doubt, of course, that her standard of values had risen steadily. That was natural. She was Roy's wife and Roy was proud of her. But it was queer, looking back, that a second fur coat shouuld be as necessary to her now as one decent pair of stockings had been then.

The mail came. Odd she should have been thinking of Paul that morning, for there was a letter from Paul's mother.

Judith sat looking at the cheap paper and the fine, wavering address in pale, probably watered ink. She had nothing on her conscience as far as the parents of her first husband were concerned. She had written to them several times a year since Paul's death and sent gifts at Christmas. She had done all anybody could. For Paul, too. Funny she should have that defensive feeling about them all, when she had done everything. She opened the letter.

The first words caught her breath. The old man, Paul's father, had been sick for a year and no one had expected a hopeful turn in his illness. Still the news startled and chilled her. The pale, fine writing slanted more sharply than usual down the flimsy page.

"Pa passed away this morning. It was real sudden at the end, but he didn't suffer, I am glad to say. The funeral is Tuesday, half past two. I wish you could come. He would like it. I wish you could come but you are maybe busy. It is God's will and we must submit. Your loving, Mother."

Tuesday was today. The poor little soul with her ground-in habits of economy had not thought of telegraphing or phoning. She would be all alone now. Judith glanced back over the uncertain words. "Passed away." How she hated that. Why couldn't people use the honest verb "to die?" It was a blessing for the old man—bed-fast so long. He had never been the same since Paul died. The loss of his only child had broken a spring somewhere. "He would like it." Her father-in-law had been exceedingly fond of her. All the love that should have been a daughter's he had lavished upon his son's wife. Judith started. If she meant to go she must do so at once. The only morning train that could make the connection left in less than an hour. But of course it was impossible. She had shopping to do, a luncheon engagement, tea at her club and tonight a bridge party. To go out of town—it was nearly a three hours' trip to Bridgeburg— would take the entire day. And of all things, a funeral. She would wire and later send a long letter.

When she was dressed for her shopping, Judith looked into the sun-dazzled mirror at the shining reflection of her big charming room. She and Paul had never imagined that a room could be so beautiful and bright. Paul was haunting her this morning. Frowning a little, as though under compulsion, she hurried to change into a plain black suit and made the telephoned apologies that cleared her day. For a funeral. People would think she was crazy. She took a taxi to the station and just made her train.

At the junction where she changed trains, Judith got a very bad lunch and ordered some flowers. They would be sure not to be delivered in time. She was cindery and in ill humour as the local dragged past white-fenced crossings and between featureless green fields. Yet a sharp edge of recollection was beginning to cut through her displeasure. In spite of herself she remembered here a stone silo with its low-pointed roof, there a dismantled windmill or a smooth, deep pond brimmed with blazing sky. It was eight years since she and Paul had come out to visit his parents for the last time. They had stayed four months because they had no money and no other place to go. She had been very happy when they passed the pond and the windmill in reverse order, going to Paul's new job and their renewed dreams of fulfilment. Within a year after that Paul was dead.

How it was all the same—the station platform and the cheese factory, the red and white houses on their wide, tree-roofed lawns. Judith walked slowly along the village street. It was completely silent, pressed, beaten down by the glaring weight of sunlight. There was not a person or vehicle in sight.

Judith walked slowly, remembering those quiet, sunny rooms which had oppressed her horribly then, because she was tired and ill and dependent. Paul had been quite happy, lying for hours on the grass under the plum tree, with the hard green plums dropping sometimes near his head and an oriole stirring above among the leaves. She had been irritated by his contentment but his mother had been happy to see him there. And the next summer he was dead.

Only in the little side street where the cottage stood, where death waited, life was going on. Neighbours went in and out of the little house and a car stood in front of it. Judith approached diffidently, for the women did not know her and stared forbiddingly. She found her way at last to the back bedroom where her mother-in-law rose from an old carpet-covered rocker, holding out her arms.

"I knew you'd come," she repeated, holding Judith's hand. "He always liked you. He thought as much of you as he did of Paul. Set down, dear. You must be tired."

There were other women in the room, sisters, cousins, some of whom Judith vaguely remembered. They looked disapprovingly from her smart to their own scrubby black, all silent, one or two weeping steadily. The widow did not weep. Her small, deeply wrinkled face was calm though the blue eyes looked moist and faded. She had aged greatly in those eight years. Judith felt the clutch of tears as she held the hard, crooked old fingers and looked about the shabby bedroom in which everything was unaltered. Pins were stuck into the eyelet-embroidered pincushion in the same design—they must be rusted tight in place. The ends of the starched dresser cover hung down rigid as marble. Paul's cradle stood against the wall where it stood when he was a baby. The old woman drew her into the kitchen.

"I want to see you alone a minute, dear. I'm so glad you come. I wanted to tell you, dear, don't look at him. I didn't want to but they made me. He failed terrible. He ain't himself. You remember him the way he was."

"I'd rather," Judith murmured. "He was so good to me."

"He thought the world of you. When he was sick he asked for you over an' over. It seemed like you was the only person he wanted to see."

"I wish I had known," Judith said. Would she have come if she had known, she wondered.

"I never let you know. He wandered so an' if you had come he might not of knowed you. An' I know you're busy. You got your own life."

She stopped and looked round the kitchen as though she wondered what her own life would be like now that its centre was gone.

"How will you manage?" Judith asked softly. People were coming into the parlor, she could hear shuffling steps and a faint flutter of voices. "You can't live here all alone," she added.

"Oh yes, I'll be all right. I got my nieces, an' his sister ain't far away. I don't mind to be alone."

"And have you got—I mean—enough to live on?"

"Oh yes, I'll be all right. I don't need much. Don't you worry about me, dear. I want to give you something. I might not see you to myself again."

"I have to go right back. You won't mind."

"I know, dear. You can get the bus. That makes connections. It's something he left you. It's in his will an' he wanted me to give it to you if you come. He planned it for years—to leave you something. You an' Paul had it so hard."

Judith's eyes burned with sudden tears.

"If the baby'd lived," the old woman went on, "Pa'd of left it to him, but now it's for you."

Judith turned her face away. She had not thought for weeks of the baby; that memory she had almost succeeded in putting away. It had never been a real baby to her, for it had lived less than a month and had done nothing but wail faintly, horribly, all night long, while Paul stamped about and she cried weakly with helplessness. To the old woman who had never seen the baby, it was a real child, with Paul's eyes. She went on, putting a small package into Judith's hand.

"Here it is. Just put it in your purse. He planned it for years—something to leave you when he was gone. He always liked you."

They were drawn back into the mourning company. The minister came up, the widow was led to her place of honour and Judith hid herself behind a row of sharp-eyed neighbour women. When it was over an admiring cousin of Paul's, a feed merchant, who remembered her, offered to drive her to catch the bus. She had only time to kiss her mother-in-law.

"Come an' see me," the widow whispered. She was crying a little now. "Come an' see me, dear. Some time."

"I will. Of course I will." They both knew she never would.

She gained the bus and the junction and at last the train for home. Judith felt that she had been away for years. She relaxed in the comfort of the club car and looked at the bored, well-dressed people around her. She was getting home again to her own world. The unaccustomed, painful events of the day receded like a dark tide. Lights sprang out along the track; Judith stirred out of numbness, went to the dressing room and began to make herself presentable.

At the funeral she had felt that her safe new world was gone, that she was lost and alone again, helpless and vulnerable to pain. It was very comforting to feel the dark dream abate. Only remnants of it clung to her as she arranged her hair and put on her hat. Her mother-in-law must be left very poor, she would have barely enough to live on. But people often had more than one thought, and living was cheap in a small town.

What would Roy be thinking of the message she had left him? He would be annoyed if she didn't get back in time for bridge at the Ellises'. She didn't feel like bridge but Roy would want to go. She would have to get a bite of dinner; in spite of everything she was hungry. The new, shining life clasped her again.

Friday night. What had Roy decided about the white fur coat? A hundred dollars. He was getting stingy. Oh well, of course she could charge it, though he didn't like that. Lights flashed by in a bright stream. They would soon be in. She fished in the purse for her compact and found the little package her mother-in-law had given her. Some little memento. He had planned it for years. Poor old man, he was a dear. Judith took off the careful wrappings and found an envelope. The train was grinding into the station. She looked into the mirror and powdered her face accurately. Really she looked younger than she had done eight years ago. Years younger. She put away the compact and opened the envelope. It contained soft, worn bills creased closely together so that her fingers could scarcely separate them. A hundred dollars.

Canadian Forum (June 1934)

MARY QUAYLE INNIS

THE PARTY

By the time Todd came home, Ethel had the house cleaned and set in such shining and unnatural order that he walked quickly through to the kitchen and sat down there as though he felt at home nowhere else. She had been afraid that he would come in a bad humour because he had been opposed to the party from the beginning, but she had not expected him to look so black, so really furious. He scarcely spoke to her and went on smoking and staring at the floor—not a bit like Todd.

He liked parties usually, but he had been against this one because so many people were out of work and because men were being laid off in his own factory. As if that could affect Todd. As if that were any reason when he had work himself. That was really why she had wanted to give it—to pay their social debt to Mildred and Earl for the trip to Lake Simcoe; yes that, and to the Rhyners for their dinner, though the ice cream had had salt in it—but principally, honestly, to show their friends that while so many people were out of work and selling their cars and moving into cheaper houses and wearing old dresses, Todd had his job the same as ever and they could afford just as much as they ever had. That, of course, was the reason she invited Cousin Jessie and the Cutshaws. They wouldn't mix with the rest of the party at all; she shivered to think of the way Mildred would look at them, too obviously suppressing a giggle. But while she was making this enormous, this unique effort, she simply couldn't waste a particle of it. Every crumb, so to speak, of the party cake must be eaten, and eaten by the right people.

For Ethel hadn't been able to forget the things the Cutshaws and Cousin Jessie had said about Todd before they were married—those nasty, unnecessary, utterly false stories about his drinking and having been jilted by another girl. And how the Cutshaws, with the ghastly freedom of family friends, had prophesied that he would never be able to support Ethel. And now after three years they were really wonderfully well off. Not that they had any money saved —who had? But they hadn't any trouble at all in keeping up the payments on the radio and the rug and the chesterfield set, and her own fur coat was paid for now and so was the bedroom furniture. And there wasn't a piece of it that wasn't better than anything in the Cutshaws' house.

Ethel went down on her knees to wipe up for the last time the margins of the waxed floor. It shone like a dark gold mirror—wonderful what a gloss the rented electric polisher had put on it. But even the electric polisher made you tired. Ethel got up slowly, feeling the taut muscles in her back. Oh, but she was tired already, and there were still the bedrooms to do—both of them because there wouldn't be a corner of the house Cousin Jessie wouldn't explore before she left.

Todd had gone out into the yard and she was thankful for that. Now she could slick up the kitchen before Dickie woke from his nap. But just then Dickie cried out with his usual vehemence and she dressed him and sent him out into the yard, praying that his father would amuse him a little. Dickie did not exist for her today except as a nuisance, an obstacle, something to be kept off the chesterfield. She flew to do the bedrooms but the new blue and gold taffeta bedspread wasn't unfolded before Dickie's expected yell rose and rose. Todd did not move. Ethel ran down and opened the gate. Surely Dickie wouldn't get run over in the next half hour. Although those things always happened when you weren't expecting them.

THE PARTY

The new shade for the piano lamp was in a kind of a huge hat box, packed in yards of crumpled tissue. Ethel unscrewed the old parchment shade and held the new one in its place. Gorgeous—almost too gorgeous. It was as big around as an umbrella and the flame chiffon and gold net and foot-long tassels—oh, it was luscious. There was the bronze elephant for the mantelpiece too; elephants were all the rage.

Todd didn't know she had bought all these new things. She had hoped he wouldn't notice till after people had arrived but the first thing he said when he came in was, "Where'd you get that?" pointing at the flaming lamp shade.

"It changes the whole room," she said, her voice trying to sound light and easy and succeeding a little too well.

"You didn't buy that just for tonight?" he demanded and the corners of his mouth drew back tight and ugly.

"I bought it for all the time," she answered defiantly. After all he had a job; they weren't on the street.

Todd said nothing, she only wished he would. For suddenly he laughed, loudly and not at all as though he were amused.

"The kid's in the street," he said at last. "But of course his getting run over wouldn't stop your party."

With an effort she refrained from answering. Tonight he would be telling her what a success the party had been and what a speedy little hostess she was.

She brought Dickie into the kitchen and made him bread and milk. Todd's eyes made her nervous; he was looking around for signs of a meal and it was true that she had been too much bent on preparations for the party to think about supper.

"I s'pose the kid an' me'll have to eat sandwich crusts," he said.

"No, you won't," she snapped. "There aren't any. I'm getting the sandwiches from Fahey's. I told you that."

He laughed again—that dreadful laugh. He was really trying to be horrid.

"Well, that ought to make their eyes stick out!" he said.

"I s'pose that's what you want."

It was and it wasn't. Fahey's being the most exclusive place in town, of course Mildred would recognize the least crumb of one of its frail triumphs. But Cousin Jessie and Mrs. Cutshaw wouldn't know Fahey's cakes from the corner baker's, and for them she would leave a few of the mauve and silver containers on the kitchen table. There was no use in paying Fahey prices without getting credit for it.

But she wasn't only showing off—that was the part you simply couldn't explain to Todd. It was that once, just once, she wanted to have everything absolutely perfect. Every day she was buying round steak and looking for a really good dollar cleaner. Just this once she wanted to have the kind of bedspread and lamp shade you saw in the movies, the kind of refreshments they probably served at the Government House. Just once she wanted to feel like one of the society women in the picture section of the newspaper. And of course while she went to all the expense of enjoying perfection, she might as well reap a kind of side profit from the envy of the Cutshaws and the Rhyners. Or was their edification her real goal, the satisfaction of her private urge for perfection only a side issue? The question was too difficult. Only she felt depressingly certain that the society hostesses in the paper didn't have backs that ached the way hers did.

"Shovin' the kid in bed already?" Todd demanded truculently.

"It's time. Besides he's tired."

She carried Dickie upstairs and left Todd to make a supper of bread and butter and a couple of boiled eggs.

Fahey's came—their mauve and white motor resplendent at the door, lighting up the whole street. At last it was time to dress. Dickie, feeling excitement in the air and made perverse by his mother's urgency, protested for an hour against sleep. Ethel put on her dress and had a moment of clear happiness before the mirror. It too was new, something she had kept from Todd, and it suited her perfectly. Her hair had been marcelled yesterday and she had on her new silver slippers. She wouldn't wear these things again for ages;

THE PARTY

it was a terribly expensive party. But however you looked at the matter, it was worth it. She ran downstairs to lay out the borrowed cups. If only Todd weren't so cranky. But there was no time to think of anything now.

Mildred in pale green velvet and the Rhyners all a sophisticated glitter, Coles and Thompsons, dressed up to kill. It was something to have put people on their mettle like this. And Mrs. Cutshaw in her old black and satin and Cousin Jessie, with her collar bones, as Todd said, like coat hangers, pointing her thin nose at the pictures and the cushions, taking in everything. The men retired with Todd to the corner of the dining room where she had set the bottle of gin. She had bought a liquor permit just for that but apparently it had been worthwhile. She began to get out the card tables and lay out the new decks. Mrs. Cutshaw was looking for her husband already.

"I hope there isn't anything he can drink," she whispered to Ethel anxiously. "Tell him I want him. Tell him to come right here."

Ethel told him but he said, "Yes, all right," and refilled his glass.

Mrs. Cole had lighted a cigarette. That would take Mrs. Cutshaw's mind off her absent husband, and Cousin Jessie was looking at Mildred's bare back as though she had never seen a back before. Mrs. Thompson didn't look herself; she was pale under the rouge and her forehead was contracted. Mildred said Mr. Thompson had lost his job.

"Heavens," Mrs. Rhyner cried, "There were twenty let out in Fritz's place this week. Fritz'll be next, I guess. My sister's husband's out of work and they got four kids. Thank the Lord you only got one, Ethel."

"Todd's got his job though," Ethel answered. "Here, Mrs. Cole, you play with Fritz. And Mildred over here."

Mrs. Thompson looked as though she wanted to cry but she took a place opposite Mr. Cole and began to shuffle. Cousin Jessie had wandered out into the kitchen, of course.

"My, all them glasses," she said sniffing. "What fancy boxes! Fahey. Did you get your cakes there? I hear they're real dear."

Let Cousin Jessie look—the stage was set for her. She would tell Bess and Aunt Clara and everybody how well Todd was doing. The evening unwound itself like a skein of silk.

They were going and Ethel was glad. She was so tired she could scarcely stand to see them off. Dickie woke with the chatter in the next room where the women were putting on their wraps and Todd went in to quiet him. She had been watching Todd anxiously for the last hour. He had been drinking a lot and his face was fiery red.

"Marvelous party!"

"Great you folks are so well set up when so many aren't."

"Your dress is too sweet for anything, Ethel."

"It was grand, darling. You certainly know how to throw a good time."

They laughed and called to each other as they went out to the cars and Ethel knew that the old man next door would complain tomorrow about being waked up. She didn't care. Three o'clock. The last two hours had been torture but it had gone off all right. The gin bottles were empty and the cakes were wrecked.

Ethel dropped down on the chesterfield and rested her arm upon the new cushion, on which Mildred had spilled ice cream. She wondered if it would clean. Oh, she was tired—one solid ache. She unbuttoned her slipper straps to ease her burning feet. Next week the bills would come in. Ethel shivered.

But it had been a good party—everybody said so—and she had shown them. They had been surprised, you could tell that. She stretched out her wracked body and smiled at the memory of Mrs. Rhyner's face when she saw the Fahey cakes.

Todd came in.

"Satisfied?" he asked and his red face wore a hard, cruel smile.

"Of course? Wasn't it grand." Whatever made him look like that? He wasn't her Todd at all.

"Had a good time? Show off all you want to?"

She stared at him and did not answer.

"Then look here!" he cried and he pulled her upright on the chesterfield and held out a typed slip.

"What is it?" she asked drawing back.

"Take it. I didn't want to spoil your party." He laughed loudly, horribly, and added, "It was in my pay envelope today."

Canadian Forum (June 1931)

MAURICE LESSER

BREAD LINE

Sixty men stood shivering in a crescent queue. A wind that bit with the malice of old teeth, flicked down from a blear sky. Little spurts of snowy rain found weak places in their ragged jackets and made spiteful, sucking noises under their pulpy shoes. Cheever Ingram, about fifty places back, squinted calculatingly through the dusk, toward the head of the line. Like a grotesque slug, it burrowed ever so slowly, into a double doorway, where a yellowish electric sign hiccoughed on and off. Experience taught him that he was still more than a whole hour removed from a bowl of stew, and a place (if he was lucky) by the searing, pot-bellied stove. His chin sulked down on his chest. He almost slept.

Somebody prodded him with a compelling forefinger. Cheever turned, snarling; he was weak from scanted sleep, and hunger twisted his nerves to quick peaks.

"What's the matter?" he flared.

"Hey, ya don't need to bite my head off." It was a puffy little man, behind him. There was a kind of whining snuffle in the voice, and a thin ribbon of tobacco juice ran down the right side of his jaw. "I just wanted to tell yuh, we're dam' lucky we made this line-up tonight."

"How do you mean lucky?" Cheever asked.

"Bennies," the little man said, with an owl-like wink and nod. His rubbery lips jerked back and sent a stream of bug-juice lolloping against a nearby lamp-post. "Every guy that gets in here tonight gets a' overcoat along wit' the mulligan." The puffy little face suddenly drew up in pleats of enthusiasm. "Jeese, ain't that somethin'?"

Cheever grunted. "Maybe," he said. "Got a cigarette?"

The habitual fear of the down-and-outer, made a swift furtive mask in the other's eyes. "Ain't got a thing, pal, s' help me," he whined. "This was even the last chew I had."

Cheever thought, I can't blame the old mooch, I'd probably hold out myself if I had any smokes and he asked me. He dug his hands into his torn pants pockets, and miserably rubbed his cold thighs. He took another look at the head of the line. The men in front moved eagerly, yet slowly, like cattle being goaded up a killing chute. The electric sign over the entrance blinked, teasingly closer. It was made in the shape of a lighthouse. Black spaces left by missing bulbs gave it an uncouth, grinning look. Cheever stared at it through watery eyes, until the words—Rescue Station—a man may be down—Welcome—merged in his eyes, like a smeared prism.

He was close up now, and, through the swinging doors there came little puffs of sour-smelling, heated air. Vaguely, he could hear the professionally hearty voice of somebody, who stood just within the door. It sounded like a phonograph record that had stuck at a worn place. Repetitiously, it boomed, "Welcome, Brother." Cheever's face twisted into a grin when he thought of the owner of the voice. These confirmed, more-blessed-to-give-than-receivers, he thought. They were all the same. This one, despite the big voice, would probably be a little man. It was the big men who had the little voices. But, big or little, their patter was always the same. First, there came the pouncing hand shake, accompanied by a manful pat on the back. After that, the smug little pep talk. Invariably, it was something about a man being down, but never out—silver linings—and then, the playful inquiry about when he had been to church last. To hell with them, Cheever was thinking, what he wanted to do was eat and be warm. Say, come to think of it, maybe the old mooch was right about getting an overcoat with the stew tonight.

Overcoats. His fatigued brain played with the idea. In a fume of unreality, he could see all the overcoats he had ever owned. He saw them packed in a thick, insolent line; as they hung in the wardrobe of his black and silver apartment on the Drive. There were grey and blue ones, and black and brown ones, all vying for favour in his eyes. But his favourite of them all was a silken soft, camel-hair ulster. He wore it whenever he drove the roadster. How warm it had been, and how it had fitted him. How proud little Dubinsky, the tailor, had been of his handiwork. Cheever remembered the day of the fitting.

Through a mouthful of pins, little Dubinsky had said, "Meester Ingram, I kent understand, for why do you want it a secret pocket in the lining?"

Cheever never told him, and he grimaced now at his little vanity. Hiding in that snug little cache there had always been a crisp new hundred-dollar bill. It had been used at various times. Once, as a tip to a taxi-driver, who was willing to trust Cheever the night he forgot his wallet. A dancer in a cabaret who had just lost her job was another recipient. He used it once in a crap game, and another time in a speak-easy, when they wouldn't take his cheque. After every time, he had religiously put another bill back in the place of the used one. It had been a sort of never-go-broke insurance.

And now, thinking of all this he was through the door. Now past the clammy handshake. Stale stewy food, sweaty, unwashed bodies, and wet clothes steaming in the sudden heat, made a conglomerate smell that was almost stifling. Cheever's icy knees still numb from the wind, carried him anxiously toward the steaming copper kettle, at the other end of the room. In his haste, he barged against something solid. He stopped and looked, stupidly. It was a packing case, half full of fusty looking overcoats. They leered up out of the box, like old draggle-tailed hussies, at a place of assignation.

Eyes blinking in the turbid light, Cheever suddenly stiffened. That label? That lining? He strained closer. It couldn't be, but it was. It was the brown camel hair overcoat he had worn so long ago. The one with the secret pocket. What if no one had ever found.... Cheever licked his suddenly dry lips. He pointed a wavering finger.

"That one." Fear, made him speak hoarsely. "Could I have that one, please?"

The tall thin man, with plastered streels of hair who was handing out the coats, looked closer at Cheever. He wasn't quite sure that Cheever had not been drinking. In that event, it was his duty to—Cheever knew what he was thinking.

"I'm not drunk, if that's what you're looking at," he said. The other still stared, pryingly, unbelievingly.

"Honest, Mister, I haven't had a drink for..." Cheever's voice faded, in panic at the thought of losing the coat.

Other men had already lined up behind Cheever. The sight of them, waiting for their coats, more than Cheever's words hastened the thin man's decision. His skinny hands dipped in the packing case and brought out the coat.

"I'll give you the benefit of the doubt, Brother," he said.

Cheever's fingers twisted into lumps of eagerness as he grasped the coat. The acrid smell of a chemical delouser, tanged sharply in his nostrils as he held the coat at arms length, gloatingly. Quickly, he shrugged it on. Then, furtively, he let his hand slide down the facing. Yes, there it was. His questing fingers slid into the cunningly hidden little pocket. Over, and over, some machine-like part of him was praying, "Oh, dear God, let it be there, don't let anyone else...." Suddenly, he felt the wadded crispness of paper under his hand; abruptly he stopped praying. He almost shrieked with relief. His head felt bulged with a swift rush of blood as he forced his way to the door.

The night air felt clean and almost wine-like and now, for no reason that he could think of, Cheever felt himself running. Great, sobbing breaths worked up from his empty stomach and racked him. He was thinking as he ran, in pictures of food, baths, clean linen. All these, right under his hand. The thought slowed him.

Pantingly, he stopped under a light. His groping hand,

clutched the little bit of crisp paper. Fumblingly, he drew it toward him. Straightened out it read—'Good for One Meal, and One Night's Lodging at the Lighthouse Rescue Station.'

Canadian Forum (September 1933)

JAMES HINTON

MEAT!

"Is that meat good meat?" I query suggestively, as we stand looking into the bear's cage.

"Good! You're damned right it's good!" says Chet, his long tawny hair bouncing angrily from the vicious affirmative little jerks he gives his head. "Pure sirloin!"

"But seriously," I insist, "do you think it is fit for decent humans like us?"

"But seriously," he mocks, his little eyes shining like brown agates, "what difference does it make?"

"A great deal of difference, my concupiscent phallicist," I answer patiently. "It is in the cage only a few feet away, as you may see for yourself. And Trotsky is still in hiding. Large chunks of dripping juicy meat to chew and to swallow. With salt and with pepper."

"Oh, for chrissakes!" says Chet with angry impatience, as if he thinks I am again tantalizing his belly for such is my custom when we are hungry that I may momentarily forget my own stomach-burblings in his discomfort. He turns and strides away.

"Wait, Chet. Wait," I say soothingly for he will never listen to my ideas until he has imagined their taste or their feel.

He shambles on with his great lanky strides and I have to run to catch him. I take his arm and he turns impatiently around.

"Now be a good fellow, Chet, and listen. You know my practicality is inveterate and fecund. Here is my idea in a nutshell as the men of business say." I take his arm and encourage him back to Trotsky's cage. "Trotsky," I impress upon him, "eats good meat every day. With the help of a fish line or stick we may also eat meat. Every day. As much as we can eat."

Chet looks down at me with all the stupefied surprise and alarm any idea causes him. I feel as if I had lit a match in a cave.

"Meat," he says speculatively, scratching the short blond whiskers on his chin.

"Yes, meat," I encourage him.

For a moment he stares at me fixedly, intensely.

"Well, why not?" he says brilliantly.

"Certainly! Why not? Trotsky can live on short rations for three months at least. Then summer! And jobs for all!--as I read in the papers. It's the thing!"

We stand staring at the big heap of meat in the cage. The puzzled look on Chet's face has yielded to one of splendid enlightenment. "Should we?" he says suddenly with a big friendly grin that fills his face with a lovable warmth.

"Yes! By heaven, yes! Fresh meat every day and down with the flyflot! And enough to hawk at the houses of the men to feed their dogs and cats. Money for bread and tobacco. What!"

Just then Trotsky comes out of his den, as if he has been listening to our plot. We don't respect him at all; for to us he appears merely a very large piece of innocuous desuetude, wrapped in a rather magnificent fur, with his pin-eye head and baby feet dangling out.

"*He* sure eats well," says Chet, shaking his tawny head sullenly. "Do for a year without eating."

"Agreed then?"

"Agreed," he says firmly.

"Well then, back to town. Strike when the time has ripened—the moment of opportunity."

"What the hell for?" says Chet with sudden anger. "Nobody's going to feed us there."

"But how, how tell me, can we do it now that Trotsky's awake? And at present someone may see us. We'll have to come earlier tomorrow."

"To hell with that noise," says Chet, shaking his large head, his face rubescent, as though I were taking from him a potential meal ticket. I can see at once that in suggesting the plan before we are ready to act I have made a tactical error. Given the savory image, he becomes the amateur communist and there is no such thing as a revolutionary situation. And when he has fortified a resolution by saying, "To hell with that noise," then the decision is definitely not open to suggestion.

"To hell with that noise. I'm not going to wait until tomorrow."

"As you please," I say resignedly for after he has said it twice he becomes the immovable object; and I, unfortunately, am not the irresistible force I used to be. "But if we must do it now, let us at least do it intelligently."

"How 'intelligently?'" he asks still a trifle arrogantly.

"Well, Trotsky's no more than cunning, to be sure. But it's no use giving him the chance to bungle our economic salvation for us. We'll have to do the thing effectually and accurately or he'll have one of our wings. Probably the left if he has his choice."

"Yes," says Chet, "the bastard'll bite off our arms if we give him the chance."

"Fine! Now listen: One of us will go to the other side of the cage and divert his attention in the best way he can. While he is there the other will pull out the meat with a hooked pole or something."

"Agreed," he says simply.

We walk off into the dark cold woods and find two long sticks, one with a branch coming back after the manner of a fish hook, which Chet sharpens to a fine point on a flat rock.

It is agreed tacitly that Chet will tease the bear on the other side while I will take the hooked stick and pull the meat out. But we are forced to wait for over half an hour before the field is clear for action. There are not many around but there seems always to be someone in sight.

First there is an old man with a bald, liver-colored head, paddling a great chest and stomach along with a thick cane. He looks at us closely and we expect him to start expostulating upon the idleness of contemporary youth, how we young 'uns are letting the Empire's Chest slip, and how he won the Boer War. But Chet stares at him with such malicious intensity that he is soon discountenanced and paddles himself off.

A buxom nurse-girl passes with two fair-haired little boys in thick blue coats, blue-eyed, sailor-hatted, brass-buttoned, be-spatted. They want to look at Trotsky but she is embarrassed by Chet's prurient stare. She drags them off with her pretty cheeks flushing. "No dough, no clootch," says Chet quietly with a reflexive anger.

Then there comes a fat-buttocked policeman with shoulders like the neck of a beer bottle, the embodiment of supercilious insectile buffoonery. He stops and looks at us bellicosely and presently asks what we are about.

Before Chet has time to make his customary remark—"Waiting for our Heespano Sweez, slug"—I say politely and with extreme gravity: "I am a student of political economy at the University of British Columbia. My friend is correlating a study of icthyology with temporal phallicism. Having no lectures today we are studying the insidious movements of Trotsky."

"Sure," growls Chet, "but he's constipated today."

And I am afraid there will be trouble shortly.

But the officer does not understand, he does not grasp the humour of the situation. He looks at us suspiciously for some moments, mutters words to the effect that we look more like bums than students, and finally walks away with exaggerated dignity, swinging his stick with superb nonchalance. And he disappears, appropriately enough, into the monkey house.

Before I have time to make certain that there is no one in sight, Chet jumps the fence, runs to the far side of the cage, and begins to growl and snarl savagely, clattering his stick against the bars. Trotsky looks at him cautiously. I jump the fence and stand silently that he may not be distracted. After Trotsky has made certain that Chet is a good deal smaller than himself, he walks over to the stick and begins to cuff it.

I slip in my hooked stick, feeling greatly worried lest some passerby catch us at our hunting. The first time I start to draw the meat away, the hook slips off. I make another attempt and drag a lump as large as my head a few feet nearer the bars. Then I hook it properly and drag it out. It appears to be good meat and I am tempted to eat a portion raw. But knowing the condition of my stomach, I lay it on the ground and look over at Chet. Trotsky is standing at the far end of the cage and Chet is growling with such ferocity that I would hardly be surprised to see him pry apart the bars and jump in to kill the monster. I hook out another piece with one stroke and lay it beside the first. I feel that I should look about again; but the task is too interesting. And then, as I am hooking out a great chunk, the size of several hams, I hear a shrill voice behind me. I feel as discomfited as a worm thrown on a hot sidewalk. I drop the stick and nearly try to crawl into the cage.

I turn and there is a dark-coated, gold-spectacled, old lady shaking a black umbrella at me. "Here! Here, you shameless boy. It's cruel, it's cruel, stealing—from an animal. Shame, shame!" Her voice every second jumps from a normal woman's voice to heights of uncharted, unnamed shrillness.

The sweat springs up all over my face and I am thinking, "Why am I sweating?" My cheeks feel as if they had been laid against hot irons. I stand staring stupidly at her, thinking to myself, "Why must I sweat, why must my cheeks burn with guilt?" And at the same time I am trying to signal to Chet that we have been caught. But he is having such great and rare fun that he is oblivious to all else.

I climb over the fence hoping that she may be placable. But evidently she expects me to attack her for she lifts her umbrella in a defensive gesture and retreats a few paces. She is very short-sighted, bent-nosed, wrinkle-faced, sunken-lipped. She is looking at me over her glasses with large outraged blue eyes.

"It's cruel; it's cruel!" she says with her voice flat one second and intensely shrill the next. "What does it mean? Answer me, young man?"

"Madam," I say finally, trying desperately to focus my brains, "Madam, it is either a matter of eating the bear's meat or eating the bear himself."

"What do you mean!" She opens her wrinkled mouth with such incredulity and her wide blue eyes stare with such amazement that I am sure she has expected me to bellow in Hindustani.

"Oh!" she shrieks softly. "Oh! A Canadian! How cruel! A Canadian."

While she is shrieking in her yodling, robin-like voice, the fact that I am a Canadian and so cruel, Chet has finally noticed that something is amiss and he comes leaping over the fence with his tawny hair waving like a lion's mane, the long stick held spear-like in his hand—a splendid barbarian. The old lady looks so frightened at this juncture that I think she may faint; and I take a step nearer that I may catch her if she falls. But it is quite apparent that she thinks we are about to attack and devour her for she steps back quickly, screaming, "No, no! Help! Don't touch me! Help!"

She becomes quickly entangled in her long black skirts and falls to the ground, still screaming for help. Chet stands staring at her with stupid, incredulous amazement. The policeman comes running from the monkey house, clutching his baton, taking the situation in at a glance. Chet changes the grip on his stick and for a moment his face becomes ugly, brutish with anger. For a moment I am afraid that we are going to get into an awful mess. But his expression of anger passes quickly and he opens his mouth with surprise.

"The meat," he says intently. "The meat!" He bounds over the fence and picks up the two smaller pieces which he tosses to me. He then picks up the large piece and leaps back.

The policeman, without bothering to help up the old woman, or to ask any questions, charges for Chet.

"Students, eh? Yuh bastards!" Chet waits until the uniformed person is lifting his stick to strike and then he swings ahead the large chunk of meat. This chunk catches the policeman directly between the eyes and he staggers backwards with an inchoate shout. Chet follows quickly, agilely powerful, and fells him with a second blow. For a second he stands over his victim as if considering the expediency of rubbing his face with the meat. But then he bursts into laughter and shouts, "Come on!" His eyes are shining with all the famed zest of triumphant youth and he is trying to stop laughing.

We head for the trees at a mad sprint with our three pieces of meat. We are having great difficulty with the gallop because we are roaring with laughter and cannot breathe properly. The officer is still shouting but we plunge into the bushes and soon we can hear him no more.

"Soon," gloats Chet between deep inhalations, "we'll light us a fire."

"We ... can dip it into ... the sea for flavoring," I gasp.

"Meat!" he growls jubilantly.

"Yes—juicy, thick and—dripping! Meat!"

New Frontier (July-August 1937)

KIMBALL McILROY

LATE NOVEMBER

It was snowing when Conlon reached the street—a light, bitter, driven snow that filled the air but failed to cover the sidewalks. On the street it ran along in little clouds behind the passing automobiles, aimlessly.

Conlon turned south toward the park. He walked quickly not because of the cold but because he wanted to walk that way. There was a restlessness in the air, a restlessness which Conlon resented more because it was intangible. It was a part of the day, a part of the snow, a part of the dirty streets.

At the corner where he had to wait for the light he saw men standing in little groups, talking with their coat collars upturned against the wind and the snow. When the light changed he started across the street leaving the men behind him, disinterested, talking, resenting the snow.

Walking again on the deserted sidewalk he plunged his gloved hands deeper into his pockets and buried his chin in his collar.

The park seemed bare in the gloom of late afternoon, the lonely benches forlorn. Only the granite cenotaph stood strong and confident in the midst of the swirling flakes. Conlon stood for a moment looking up at it. He read the names engraved on the solid column, names which meant nothing to him, names which meant nothing to anybody now. The living were concerned with November snow and a cold wind off the Lake.

He walked through the park alone, past the covered bandstand, away from the cenotaph. He followed the cement pathway because it was the easiest and the ground in November is rough and uneven. He walked without thinking, conscious only of the snow and the fallen leaves.

He found a bench away from the others, partly sheltered from the wind and the snow, and sat down, stretching his feet out before him. He took a cigarette from his pocket and lit it, holding the match in cupped hands out of the wind.

Conlon was feeding the squirrels, feeding them as he had fed them every afternoon for two years, from a little paper bag of peanuts in his overcoat pocket. The squirrels in the park expected him now. They waited for him to come, screeching and scrambling through the trees over his head.

He paid five cents for a bag of peanuts on his way to the park. He smoked a cigarette on the bench with the peanuts in his pocket and then he walked to the little clearing and waited for the squirrels to come to him.

He knew them all. There were seven or eight of them who always waited for him. They were tame and unafraid to take the peanuts from his outstretched hand. After the Spring there would be more of them, young and frightened, watching him apprehensively from the haven of the trees.

He squatted comfortably, leaning back on his heels with the bag of peanuts in his left hand. He cracked the nuts dexterously with his right, dropped the shattered shells on the ground and held out the twin kernels for the hungry squirrels.

For a long time he fed them, intent upon what he was doing and oblivious now to the thickening snow. The bag was half empty and his hands were getting cold. He stood up to warm them in his pockets.

Someone was watching them, an old man in a faded blue suit and no overcoat who kept rubbing his bare hands together in the cold. A bum, Conlon thought. He stepped back. "I do this every afternoon. The squirrels come to expect it."

The man nodded, his face blue and expressionless in the wind.

Conlon said, "They're here even in the winter."

"Where else could they go?" The voice was as expressionless as his face. "They've got to stay here same as everyone else, I guess."

Conlon's hands were warm again. He took out the peanuts and tossed one to the waiting squirrels.

"Would it be too much to ask for a couple of those peanuts?"

Conlon said, "Sure." He took a handful out of the paper bag. "They're tame, they'll take them right out of your hand."

The man looked at him for a moment. "I wasn't going to give them to the squirrels. I want to eat them."

Conlon said, "Are you hungry?"

"I guess I'm as hungry as those squirrels."

Conlon felt something tighten inside him. "Here," he said, "take the bag. You can have what's left. I'm sorry there aren't more."

"I don't want them all. Just give me another handful. I'll put them in my pocket and eat them later."

Slowly Conlon gave him all the nuts he could crowd into one hand. The man took them and stuffed them into his pocket. Glancing at the squirrels, he turned and walked away toward the cenotaph at the other end of the park.

Conlon didn't feel like feeding the squirrels any more. He sat on the bench, holding the crushed bag of peanuts in his hand and feeling the snow. He put the bag in his pocket and lit a cigarette.

He felt better when he tasted the smoke.

New Frontier (September 1936)

MARY QUAYLE INNIS

STAVER

When she gave him her old winter coat for his wife, he felt the cloth and said quickly, "Why, it'll be as welcome to her as flowers in May." Instead of mumbling "thanks" and shuffling his feet as most of them did, the young man stood there feeling the coat and looking straight at Edith. His eyes were a light brownish green, almost the colour of citron. He laid the coat over the veranda railing and said, "I'll cut your grass for you."

Edith was startled. "You don't need to do that," she said.

"Where's the mower?"

She watched him from the sunroom window. He was a huge young man, tall and very broad with shoulders that looked as though he wore football pads under his blue shirt. The lawnmower clattered along like a toy in front of him. Edith thought how hard a task her husband made of the grass-cutting. Perhaps she could get this man to come every week. When he finished she offered him fifty cents, half-expecting him to refuse it. He took the coin, looked at it and put it in his pocket.

"Now, what more is there?" he asked, looking at her proudly. "I got to raise $2.25 this week to pay the rent. If we can't pay the rent we got to get out." He looked at her, waiting, and added, "My baby's five months old."

"Why," Edith murmured, "Why, I don't know. My husband usually does the outside work."

He seemed not to hear. "I'll do anything," he said. "I got to raise $2.25 by Saturday."

"Well, come Friday," she said impulsively. "You can clean the cellar."

Staver was his name. Edith thought about him all day. She imagined his wife—very young, with blond hair, and his fat, dark-haired baby. He must have had a good job before the depression, he walked as if he had had everything. It must be hard for him to wear frayed cotton trousers and broken shoes and see his wife wear somebody else's coat. She could save enough out of her allowance to pay him for cutting the grass every week and make a reprieve for Francis who hated doing it. It seemed terrible that a young, intelligent, powerful man should find it a struggle to raise $2.25 a week.

It was ridiculous how she looked forward to Staver's coming. Edith Craigen lived very much alone; she thought sometimes that no old maid in two rooms lived more quietly. Francis had serious digestive trouble and could eat only bland foods and strained soup. When he was gone in the morning, she made a junket or a cup custard for his dinner, washed the breakfast dishes and dusted the house. Then the day was hers—it was more than she knew what to do with. They had few friends as quiet as themselves. Movies hurt Francis's eyes but he liked certain radio concerts and he liked to read. During the day, Edith sewed a little, lay on the chesterfield with a magazine, turned the radio on and turned it off again. One day a week Mrs. MacPhedran came to do the cleaning and Edith dreaded that day when she had to get a substantial lunch, and listen to the woman's cheerful talk.

The young man Staver was something new. She looked forward to his coming like a child waiting for Christmas. When she saw him walk round the house and heard him rap loudly at the back door, her cheeks suddenly burned and she hoped he would not notice how nervous she was. But he noticed nothing. His look encompassed the cellar, tidy already, and condemned it as a poor, unworthy scene for his labours but he said nothing. He opened the windows and started vigorously to work. Only, as she started upstairs, he called out:

"I charge forty cents an hour."

"All right," she answered timidly, "yes, all right."

His clothes were terrible but he was much too big to wear anything of Francis's. She prepared him a substantial lunch out of things that would not be included in relief supplies—eggs and a salad and cake. On one side of the tray she placed a red apple. He could eat that on his way home or this evening for his supper. When he brought the tray back he only said:

"What can I do now? I need a whole day's work."

"I only had the cellar to do You can cut the grass next Friday." She glanced at the tray. "You forgot your apple," she exclaimed. "Put it in your pocket."

He looked at the apple and then at her. "No thanks," he said.

What had she to think about before Staver came to her door? For now, all afternoon, she wondered why he wouldn't take the apple. Perhaps he was angry because she had given him only half a day's work. She would try to think of something for him to do when he cut the grass next week.

Early next morning the phone rang. "Staver speaking. Got anything for me to do today?"

"Why no, I haven't. I told you yesterday...."

"Yes, but I need seventy-five cents more for the rent. I got to pay it today."

"I'm sorry. I haven't got anything."

What would he do, she kept wondering all through Saturday and Sunday. Surely he wouldn't be put out with a little baby for lacking seventy-five cents. It was almost a relief when the phone rang on Monday morning.

"Staver speaking. Any work for me today?"

"Did you—did you get your rent?"

"She let it go over to this week. I got to get three dollars now."

"Well, there's the grass Friday...."

"Couldn't I do it sooner? If you got anything else...."

He came to cut the grass on Tuesday but she had to keep him from coming again on that day for he spoke of Mrs. MacPhedran as "the servant."

"Shanty Irish," Mrs. MacPhedran said. "Look out for that kind."

"You let yourself get roped in," Francis said sourly. When he came in he sniffed at the faint thread of cigarette smoke which Staver left behind him. He smoked a cigarette after his lunch and Edith suspected that he often had one while he was waxing the floors.

"He does the lawn nicely," Edith said.

"That's the trouble. I don't get any exercise and I feel the difference. The doctor said I needed some exercise."

"You never liked to cut the grass."

"Of course I did. I don't see how you think we can afford a man around all the time."

Her allowance was strained to pay Staver but he was a necessity. Her thoughts had lifted out of the old vague round of blue or brown for a dress, paper for the dining room this fall or next spring, and had settled into the round of Staver's problems which seemed far more real and engrossing. She thinned her wardrobe to outfit Mrs. Staver and began to knit the baby sweaters and socks.

Every week the burden of raising the $2.25 pressed upon her like a nightmare. He seemed to find very little work beside what she gave him and she was desperate to find jobs for him. He said nothing, he did whatever she asked, but his green eyes stared proudly through hers till she looked away. For he looked on her not as a woman, not even as a human being. Francis said it was dangerous for her to have the man alone with her in the house. She would not have liked him to know how little dangerous it was. To Staver she was only the means of raising his rent and a clumsy enough instrument, his eyes assured her. But just as the struggle to find work for him grew almost insupportable, the tension relaxed. He said:

"My wife's gone with the baby to her mother's. I'm moving to a smaller room."

His rent was now only a dollar a week. Edith breathed again. But he telephoned as urgently as before and she ventured to ask, "Do you need as much money now your wife's away?"

"More," he said coldly. "A man by himself don't get relief."

When she brought him his lunch he said in a hard, quiet voice, "I ain't had nothing to eat since yesterday morning."

He was being theatrical. It couldn't be as bad as that. She was on edge, thinking of a young man starving while Francis picked at his omelet. But he ate no more than usual and she dared not offer him food to take home.

Edith asked about his wife. "She keeps askin' if I got work," Staver said. He was often sullen now and he would work for a whole day without speaking. Then he got another yard to cut regularly and that helped. It helped until the terrible day of the garden party.

A friend had persuaded her to go to a garden party on the church lawn. On her way she went to speak to Staver who was cutting the grass in the backyard. In her new blue dress and hat, walking in her shining white shoes over the crisp, sharp-smelling grass she wished childishly that Staver would notice her. He turned around.

"I'm going out," she said. "I'll leave the back door open so you can put away the mower. Here's the money."

He took the money and looked at it in the way that annoyed her. It was as though he expected to find the sum not right or one of the coins counterfeit. He looked at the money longer than usual and then he said slowly, staring right at her:

"I think I should get more for this grass-cutting. It's a big lawn. It's worth a dollar."

Her heart gave a leap of anger and she felt all her muscles tighten as though she were going to strike him. Her voice was quite steady.

"You said you wanted forty cents an hour and that's

what I'm paying you."

"Grass-cutting is worth more," he answered obstinately. "It's hard work. I should get a dollar for cutting this lawn. The other place I get a dollar."

She heard her voice rising with anger. "I never paid more than fifty cents before you began to cut it. It's absurd. The other lawn must be bigger."

"Some, but this is harder."

Why harder? She felt the sunny yard and Staver with his blue shirt and staring, insolent green eyes turn like a pinwheel before her. She had never been so angry in her life.

"I won't pay a cent more. If you don't like it, don't come."

She walked proudly to the gate, thankful that her long skirt hid the trembling of her knees. But when her anger was over, like an illness, and weak recovery had set in, she worried what he would do now. But he would telephone tomorrow and come next week as if nothing had happened. A quarrel wouldn't halt Staver. But he neither phoned nor came.

A week. Two weeks. She could not sleep for worry. She saw him on a park bench starving, standing in line in a hostel to receive a bowl of soup, or begging—but Staver would never beg. She began to understand how men could turn to crime. But then why had he been so overbearing and unreasonable about the grass?

Not a sign for three weeks. Perhaps he was dead. But Staver was not the man for despair. He must have a job. She felt sure that he had a job and set about, during sleepless nights and the long, lonely days, to rehabilitate Staver and his family. Yellow oilcloth, dotted muslin curtains, she furnished them in a sunny flat, dressed the wife and baby in pretty clothes, filled the cupboard with food. She thought, as she had often thought during the long, still summer, sitting opposite Francis in the cool room near the lamp, how curious it was that while her husband thought her absorbed in darning his underwear or reading a book on Russia, she should really be downtown with the Stavers. She had lived all summer with them and Francis did not know. He was glad that Staver did not come any more.

"You're well rid of him. He was an insolent fellow."

She looked at Francis sitting, thin and narrow in the big chair, with his green slippers and his nearly bald head.

The next morning she was thinking about the Stavers' new prosperity when she heard the click of the letter flap. It was not time for the postman. On the hall floor lay a folded page from a small notebook, bearing a pencilled note: "My Dear Lady, would you kindly trust me with 50 cts untill the weekend for the purpose of getting some food and Lady excuse me for been a nuisance to you, Thanking you Lady, (Staver)."

She looked quickly through the glass pane of the door. He sat on the step waiting for her answer.

She could not go out for a moment because she was crying. She could not get over feeling that he had had the job she had imagined for him and somehow lost it and that he must be feeling disappointment as well as humiliation. For she could not have believed that Staver would so humiliate himself even when he was starving.

But when her mouth was steady and she could speak to him she found him not humiliated in the least. He stood up and looked at her; he was thinner but as haughty as ever.

"If you haven't got any work," he said impersonally, "I thought maybe you'd let me have fifty cents till Saturday."

"I have got work," Edith assured him quickly in a trembling voice. "You can wax the dining room floor and wipe down the kitchen walls and wash the cellar windows." She did not dare mention grass.

Though he showed no shame, she was sure that he was inwardly ashamed and that he would work willingly as he had done at first. But he had never been satisfied or grateful, he had only tolerated her and done her work scornfully because he had to eat. He was more scornful and impatient than ever. He no longer telephoned but simply came to the door and waited for her to show him work. When he stood there she could hardly deny him and he pressed hard on this discovery, coming two or three days a week.

Edith had to admit to herself that Francis was right. It couldn't go on. Staver was too much for her. She felt feeble and exhausted; Staver had consumed her like a long illness. His need was as great as ever but she could no longer supply it; she had lost strength and heart for the undertaking. When he dragged the lawnmower up the cellar steps his eyes were too scornful to bear. He seemed to feel that she had taken advantage of his necessity and to bear with her niggardliness only because he must. She hesitated to answer the door for fear he might be standing there. Yet all the time she was so sorry for him that she could have wept.

Early one morning in September she went downtown on one of her infrequent shopping trips. As she started up her own street she saw a figure coming toward her about a block away. It was Staver. He was coming away from her house, having found no one in. Suddenly the thing seemed unendurable. She was tired and the sun was hot on the long, unshaded street. She couldn't think of anything for him to do now, she couldn't face him at all. In sheer self-defence, like a small frightened animal popping down a hole, she crossed the street and turned west. She walked quickly with her head turned down. She could hear his footfalls ring in the silent street and for a dreadful second she thought he was following her, but the steps went on. He couldn't have recognized her and she would think of something for him tomorrow. But the next morning he did not come.

She looked for him every day. The old circle of wonder and worry closed round her again. Suppose he was starving; if he grew desperate and did something wrong it would be her fault for having failed him. But perhaps he had a job. Then suddenly she knew what had happened. In a way she had known all the time. He had seen her avoid him that day on the street. No wonder he didn't come.

If only she could reach him to say she still wanted to help him, that her brutal rudeness on that day had been the result of fatigue and a hot sun. In a way it was peaceful without him. Francis was pleased and things went along quietly. But the quiet was dismal. She missed Staver's strong step, his confident movements overhead. He would never come again—she felt a sinking of her spirits that was almost despair. But she tried to remember the time when he had come so often, driving her till she almost wished she would never see him again.

And then in late autumn as she walked on a downtown street with Francis in the evening a great figure brushed quickly past her. She caught a glimpse of him so brief that she could hardly be sure that it was Staver, and yet she was sure. He wore a new overcoat and a new hat and he was walking very fast with his head up as he always did. He must really have got a job this time; some wonderful piece of good fortune had come to him. He would never need her again.

She felt her world go black but she made so little sign that Francis was not interrupted in the remark he was making. But he had to repeat it twice before his wife answered him.

New Frontier (April 1936)

A.M. KLEIN

BEGGARS I HAVE KNOWN

I get along very well with beggars. Perhaps it is because they feel that I shall soon be one of them.

Whenever I pass a panhandler on the street he buttonholes me. Even when I say, No, I can't spare a dime, he never feels resentful. He knows I am telling the truth, even if I am wearing a new suit.

But when I have the change I give it to them. I am not one of those who go around making nasty remarks about beggars just because their mouths smell of beer. I know that when a fellow has only a nickel to his name he would rather, and it's much wiser, too, spend it on a glass of beer, than on a cup of dishwater. Coffee just washes your insides and keeps you awake, whereas beer fills you, tickles your guts and makes you drowsy. It's easier to sleep on hard benches that way, and besides, if your mouth smells of beer the flies don't fly into it when you're asleep with it open.

I remember once when I had a dime between myself and hunger, I thought of how to spend it. If I bought something to eat, I figured, I would be hungry again in no time and would have to walk the streets with an aching belly. So I went into a cheap movie and for four hours forgot all about my hunger, except now and again when I saw on the screen how the rich eat.

There is a man on our street, an old Jew, who lives in the

Home for the Aged. Every day, except Saturday, you can see him walking around the block with his eyes glued to the sidewalk looking for cigarette butts. He keeps the butts in regular cigarette boxes which he picks up in the gutter. Whenever I see him nosing around for his butts, I always give him a brand-new cigarette; sometimes I don't notice him until he turns the corner, and then I run after him to give him his smoke. He always takes my cigarette and then blesses me. I should live to an old age: I should be rich: I should have pleasure from my children. I always feel good when I leave him, because he blesses with so much heart, caressing my shoulder at each blessing, as if he was loading them on my back.

I told him he could pick up a lot of butts outside the Arena on wrestling nights, because the fans go out to have a smoke between bouts and always at midnight there are hundreds of butts on the sidewalk. As a matter of fact, once when I was coming home from a show downtown at twelve o'clock, and walked up by way of Fletcher's Field, a beggar walked up with us and stopped at the Arena to pick up these butts. But the old Jew tells me he can't get out of the Home for the Aged after eight o'clock.

There is a beggar who rings our door-bell on Mondays. To tell the truth I never saw him ring it and I often wonder how he does it because the fingers of both his hands are all chopped off. My mother gives him a nickel—we're poor, too—and he grabs it off with his palms and with the stubs that are left of his fingers. When my brother, who is eating dinner, asks my mother who it was at the door, she always tells him, and begins to describe the buttons of flesh where the fingers should be, and my brother says, Can't you see I'm eating?

I know all the beggars of our city personally. Most of them are real beggars, but some of them are fakes. There are a couple of guys, for example, who patrol Peel and St. Catherine Street, who are nothing more than racketeers and who, if they are ever found out, will give begging a bad name.

These fellows get themselves a pair of returned soldier buttons, and every time they nab a customer they flash the badge and say something about a country fit for heroes to live in. But Tommy Kinsella, on Place d'Armes Square, who is a real returned soldier, lost his badge and all he can show are two sawed-off legs. Everybody pities him, however, when he tries to get on a street car.

He's a funny case, too, this Tommy. He doesn't seem to mind his stumps so very much, but he's always complaining about getting T.B. becase his nose is so near the ground. I suppose you get that way, from trouble.

Then take Steve Szopik. He is the fellow who hangs around our factory and runs messages. Occasionally he gets a sandwich and a Coca Cola. Now he's been trying to break into the beggar game for years. But he can't do it. He just can't get a license. No pull. Everything is politics.

On the other hand, a snob like Burke—the violinist in front of Christ Church Cathedral—has all kinds of pull, and gets a license, and one of the best spots in town. Stuck-up! That's not the word for it. He calls himself a mendicant.

It's the blind beggars who are really handicapped. When you're blind and a beggar you can't run after your clientele; it just passes you by. It doesn't even feel embarrassed. You're blind.

And they can throw into your box whatever they feel like throwing. You can't ever know.

I just can't see old man Rosenbloom. He is blind and is led around by his little boy. He wears dark glasses and carries pencils in his hand. It's the idea of the pencils that I can't get. I imagine that if you are blind you are entitled to charity without giving away presents. Apart from the expense, it's foolish. What does he want, his patrons to write him a letter?

So, as I am saying, I get along swell with beggars. They remember that when I had money I was no piker. They tell me all their secrets: why the doorstep of some churches are more profitable than others; what restaurants throw you out, and which ones give you a hand; how to approach elderly ladies and how to tackle young slickers; where the bookmakers are, and what time the barbutte finishes, and the winners come out; how to feel the denomination of coins; what words to open up your plea with, and what phrases to leave out when the giver doesn't seem to pay any attention; when to talk clearly, and when to mumble; when to be bold and when to be humble; what districts have dogs in their porches; how to shake a coin-cup so that it should make the greatest amount of noise with the least danger of the coins falling out; and numberless other tricks of the trade.

As a matter of fact, they have often asked me to become one of them. They don't mind a little extra competition if it comes from a decent fellow, and they lead me to believe that I am such a fellow. They tell me, too, that it is a very happy profession, that you are out in the open all day, that you have no overhead expense, and that you can never be laid off because you are working for yourself. They've planned a union for beggars, but have found it impossible. It's a capitalistic society, they say. But even without a union, one can make a nice living. You can't strike in your trade, I said. People would be happy if you quit work. Would they, though? they said. A rich man can't live without a beggar. He needs him to protect his conscience.

So they were trying to persuade me to join their ranks. My wife wouldn't stand for it, I said. She always talks about beggars in a sad voice, and gets herself weepy about armless sleeves and folded trouser legs and empty sockets and men with dumb, pitiable expressions.

That's nothing, they said. For us to be blind or crippled is only a school degree, like a doctor's or a lawyer's. That's the way we hang out our shingle. Our superiority over those who give us money is this: they still pity us, but we have stopped pitying ourselves.

Anyway, I said, I'll think about it.

I have been thinking about it. But I am afraid to broach the subject to my wife. I know that she will begin to cry. She is too proud. And I, too, am afraid that I can't afford to take this step—I have no ailments, I am not blind, I am not crippled, I am perfectly healthy. Only I am poor; and that's like being blind and crippled. Worse, because you feel helpless without any excuse. But I can't become a beggar; I can't learn to stop pitying myself.

Canadian Forum (June 1936)

LARRY LAWSON

BURP'S BUSY DAY

"Good morning, Sir."

The Honorable Alexander Burp woke up to hear the water pouring into his bathtub and to see his man, Persimons, raising the blind in his bedroom.

"Ah, good morning, Simons," he answered.

Then he stretched back in bed for another short nap. These were "the best minutes of his whole day," he often said.

He was tired that morning. The night before he had been at an official dinner, a small party of twelve with only eight courses, but tiring nevertheless. From there he had hurried to present prizes to athletes at the Y.M.C.A. and to make a short address. After that he had dropped into Sir Thomas Bolt's party and talked to dowagers. He had also sounded out Sir Thomas as to what he thought about the plan to build a dam on the country's principal waterway. It had been two o'clock before he got home, and here it was eight o'clock already. He sighed, lifted his ponderous bulk from bed, and felt on the floor with the toe of his foot for slippers.

After a light breakfast—fruit, cereal, toast, bacon and tea—Persimons helped him into his overcoat, handed him his silk hat, and turned him over to his chauffeur, Jitters, who was waiting on the doorstep of the Burp mansion.

"Good morning, Sir," said Jitters.

Ah, good morning Jit," said Burp.

The drive to the government offices passed without incident. Burp settled himself back in the corner of his limousine, to glance through the morning papers, and so did not notice a group of shabbily dressed men outside the capitol gates being watched by another group of smartly dressed police.

"Good morning, Sir," said the man who took Burp up to his office in the elevator. Burp nodded.

"Good morning, Sir," said the young lady who sat in Burp's outer office.

"Good morning, my dear," said Burp, and as he passed he patted her sleek blond head.

Seated at his desk in his private office at last, Burp emitted another sigh, and rang for his secretary.

"Good morning, Sir," said a youth who entered with a portfolio of papers under his arm.

"What have we got before us today?" asked Burp.

"Delegates from an association formed at unemployment camps are waiting to see you."

"What, inside the buildings?"

"No Sir. I gave orders that they were to be kept off the grounds."

"Quite right. I can't forget what happened to my dear friend and colleague down east that time. Why, do you know that some of those radicals actually dared to lay hands on him?"

"Will you see the delegation?"

"Let them wait until tomorrow. It might cool them off."

"That is what you said yesterday. Besides, the Mayor of the town has phoned to say he wished you would see them and get them along back to where they came from."

"Oh, well. Let them come in."

Burp drew a handkerchief from his pocket and wiped his hands. Then he poured a glass of water and drank it slowly, standing by a window from which he could see a group of men approaching the building with three mounted police at their head. In a few minutes the secretary had shown them into the office.

"Good morning, Gentlemen," said Burp.

Twelve men who looked as though they had been sleeping for weeks in their clothes stood before him silently.

"What can I do for you?"

A spokesman outlined their petition. Because they had been out of work, and had no food, they had gone to work at relief camps. For eight hours a day of manual labor they received no pay but their bed and board. They also got an allowance of twenty cents a day, for "sweet charity's sake." They had complained about the food and were told it was regular army ration. They had complained about their sleeping quarters, and were told they were quite up to the regular army regulations and that they must remember that "they were really at war fighting the forces of depression." They were told too that they could "desert" and starve again. Their demands were that they be given a working wage, not an allowance, and that they be allowed to buy their own food and supply their own lodgings.

There was a hush as the spokesman finished. Then Burp spoke.

"My men, I am sorry for you. The relief camps were my own invention to help ease your lot. You are suffering. So are we all. Think of the thousands of men who would only be too anxious to take your place in these camps. Would it be fair to them to improve conditions for you and hence to delay the opening of new camps? I think not."

"We don't want talk. We want pay," said the spokesman. Burp glared.

"Now you are becoming unreasonable," he said. "We are doing all we can to help. I, however, will personally speak to the minister of defence and see if he can improve your rations. As to pay, where is the money to come from?"

"We are working. We are not paid for it. We only want value for our services."

"I will speak to the minister. I can do no more now. Perhaps later on." Burp rang for his secretary. "Show these men out," he said.

"Swine," said the spokesman. Other terms of abuse reached Burp's ears from the rest of the delegation. Burp gripped the arms of his chair and said nothing. When the delegation had left, he took off his glasses and polished them. His secretary returned.

"Show in the gentlemen of the press," Burp said.

"Good morning, Sir," chorused another dozen of men as they filed into the room. Instead of looking as though they had been sleeping in their clothes, they merely looked as though they needed sleep.

Burp smiled a greeting, and leaned back comfortably in his chair.

"Anything new today, Sir?" asked a youth.

"Nothing startling. I had a delegation of labor campers here today. They wanted pay. I promised to do what I could."

"Will you elaborate that?"

"No, sorry. I can't at present."

"How about the Title Bill?"

"Nothing new, boys, nothing new."

"But listen, the Post says you are in line for honors."

"Tut, tut. Why I have a title. Ain't I the Honorable?" The press giggled.

"How about the new dam?"

"Nothing new. Well, I guess that's all for today."

The press rose as one man.

"Just a minute. This is not for publication, mind you. I was talking to Sir Thomas Bolt last night. He predicts a distinct upswing in business conditions."

"Was this official?"

"Well, you see, Tom and I are pretty good friends. He had a little party last night, and of course he asked me. He told me after supper."

"Could we interview him?"

"Try, but don't mention my name."

"Thank you, Sir. Good morning, Sir."

The press filed out again. The secretary entered.

"Lunch with Sir Thomas at the Millionaire Club at twelve thirty, Sir," he said.

"Oh, dear. What a bore," said Burp.

The man who took Burp down in the elevator said, "Good afternoon Sir."

The man who held the door open for him said, "Good afternoon, Sir." Jitters standing beside the car, touched his cap. At the club the doorman said "Good afternoon, Sir." The head waiter met him in the hall saying "Good afternoon, Sir." Burp was shown to a table where Sir Thomas Bolt was sitting.

"Good afternoon, Sir," said Burp.

"You're late," snapped Sir Thomas.

"Sorry. I have had such a morning."

He ordered a light repast, consomme sole, a little cold chicken, salad, cheese and coffee. The men ate in silence. When they had finished Sir Thomas spoke.

"Burp," he said. "We have got to come down to cases about that dam. Can't you start work at the river as a relief measure?"

"Why, Tom, I was just wondering where I could find a job for the unemployed. I had a delegation this morning."

"Good. We will wait to capitalize until the ground is cleared and ready. I will put you down for a little."

"A little?"

"Don't worry. I have always treated you right, haven't I?"

Burp agreed. On such mutual confidence and easy acquiescence are the great undertakings of our great country undertaken.

Sir Thomas moved into the lounge with his coffee and started to talk to his fellow members. Burp, seldom at ease among equals, excused himself, and hurried back to his office.

Seated at his desk, he took a sheaf of papers from his drawer, dipped a pen in the ink, and continued his work on his autobiography. He wrote, "At the age of fifty I was offered a title. My first impulse was to decline. But I reconsidered. What, after all, was the bauble, but a recognition from the people? A reward for my services? It was a distinction at which many aimed. Should I, by refusing it, deprive them of yet another incentive? Make them less zealous in their work of bettering the country's welfare? I thought not...."

Burp had not been offered a title but he believed in being prepared.

For three hours Burp wrote. Then his secretary entered.

"You are due for dinner at the Bloaters' Club at seven, Sir," he said.

"Blast," said Burp.

"At nine-thirty you are to accompany the ambassador's party to the horse show."

"That's nice."

"At twelve you are to take the train to Toronto to deal with the Rail matter."

"What's that?"

"You remember that Cavelle has threatened to foreclose on the Rail and Iron works. We have here the correspondence from Sir Thomas Bolt about it. He has large Rail holdings. So have you."

"I will read the letters on the train," said Burp.

He went to the dinner, the horse show, and finally reached the train. He was shown to his private car by a porter who said "Good evening, Sir."

The conductor greeted him with "Good evening, Sir." His secretary met him saying "Good evening, Sir." When he entered his bedroom Persimons said "Good evening, Sir."

Burp was tired. With Persimons' aid he quickly undressed, and knelt down beside his bed. Persimons withdrew.

"Oh Lord," Burp prayed, "Help me in this Thy work, that I may walk in the way of the righteous. My strength is sorely tried in this high place Thou has given me. Be Thou my comforter. And don't let Cavelle foreclose. Amen."

Feeling more rested, Burp rose to his feet as Persimons entered.

"Anything you wish, Sir?" he said.

"No," said Burp, climbing into bed. "Put out out the light."

"Good night, Sir," said Persimons.

As soon as the door had closed behind him, Burp got out of bed and turned on the light. He went to a portfolio where the Cavelle letters were kept, and fished around until he had found a book. He returned to his bed, fixed the pillows, and settled down to read *The Goldfish Murder Case*, by the author of *The Sparrow Murder Case, The Ostrich Murder Case* and *The Monkey Murder Case*.

Burp read for half an hour, and then turned to the back of the book to look at the last chapter. In a few minutes he resumed his place again.

He had had a hard day. The train swayed gently, speeding along at sixty miles an hour. The steady click, click, click of rail joinings came more faintly to his ears. His eyes closed. The book slipped from his hands. He turned his head on the pillow. Burp was asleep.

Masses (March-April 1934)

GEORGE WINSLADE

RAINBOW CHASING

Smoky was broke. He had got up early that morning, before the wife and kids were awake. Relief was cut off. The unemployed organization was scattered. Smoky had tried to hold it together, but all the papers were talking about the return of prosperity and many of the gang had left for over-the-line.

This was the beginning of the last "boom" period, and the chief topic of conversation in the union hall was the building boom in Los Angeles and the chance of getting a quota number.

Worst of all, Smoky's wife was beginning to nag him. She had started again last night when Smoky came home late from the meeting, and she was lying awake, waiting.

"You think more of the reds than you do of your wife and kids—you're flogging a dead horse, I tell you—first thing you know you'll be regular bum." Smoky couldn't stand nagging.

He arrived at the door of the employment office as the clerk opened up for the day. He was determined to take the first job that came along, and failing to land a job he was going to take the seaboard freight out that night going east.

The forenoon was spent discussing the class struggle in the slave market. Along about noon a sailor man blew in. He walked over to the group around Smoky, and inquired, "Any of youse guys want a job on a boat as a flunky?"

Smoky spoke up, "Yeah, I do, Cap. What kind of boat yer got?" Ignoring the inference that he might be a captain, the seafarer replied, "Ever been to sea before?"

"Sure. What d'ye think I came over in, a hack?"

After hiring two more, the sailor led them up to the American consul's office, where their names and pedigrees were recorded. Then they were taken over to a blind pig where the seamen bought a round of drinks.

He told them he was second mate of the *Agnes Dollar*. The ship was a lumber schooner and was carrying a million feet of Robert Dollar's lumber from Dollarton to San Pedro. "How far's that from Los Angeles?" asked Smoky, and learned that Pedro was the harbor of Los Angeles.

"What luck!" mused Smoky as he walked home to get his clobber, "right in my mitt. I can jump her when we get to Pedro—get a job at ten bucks a day—what a chance to make a stake."

His wife knew by the look on his face that he had landed a job. They talked about how they would be able to get on their feet again in the new location, and how long it would take to get quotas for the kids. She packed his clothes, and Smoky threw in a trowel and hammer.

He got to the ship just as the kitchen crew were setting down to supper. The new flunkies ate in silence while the cook gave them the icy stare. Smoky finished eating first and bummed the cook for the makings, which gave him the cue to talk business.

The cook was a Dutchman, and looking Smoky up and down, he asked, "Ever vait on table before?"

"Sure, I used to sling hash in a grease joint on Cordova Street, the Busy Bee."

"Yeah? Vell dats no recommendation," answered the cook, "but I guess youse is the cleanest. You vait on de officers' mess."

Turning to the next he asked: "Vot is you, a Vobbly?"

"Yer goddammed right. Want to see my card?" answered the Wob.

"No, I take yer vord for it. Da firemens looks like a tough gang on this tub—you look after the crew's mess."

The cook eyed the remaining flunky for a full minute, and then exclaimed, "Sprechen zei Deutsch?" The blond boy's face beamed as he gurgled, "Yah."

"Vell, I need help in da galley to peel da spuds."

Paddy Doyle was a slave driver if ever there was one. He got his master's ticket twenty years before and for the last fifteen had sailed Chinese waters. He had left his wife and kids in Shanghai, and was looking forward to white women for a change.

He was strange to this side of the Pacific and had forgotten the coastline. He wasn't taking any chances of sinking the old coffin ship so he took the outside channel down to Pedro. Once past Flattery, he sailed out to sea a hundred miles before he steered south.

Smoky lost his sealegs and his breakfast, too, but this didn't worry him much. Wasn't he going to make a stake? There was a three-year building program in Los Angeles—yeah, the Capitalists were too strong—they were planning their economy on the international scale—yeah. Smoky would have to get some dough—he couldn't develop into a bum—yeah, he'd work, but by God he'd never quit the movement—not for nobody.

Ten days later the *Aggie Dollar* tied up to Hammond's Wharf at Pedro. "What's doing over there on the dock?" cried the Wobbly as they moved in, "see the bulls chasing the workers."

At that moment six bells struck and the cook hollered, "Come and get it." As Smoky placed the soup on the mess room table he heard the skipper grunt, "I'd sooner have a bunch of Chinks any day than these goddam union men. Fifty lumber schooners tied up in harbor on account of a longshoremen's strike. Fat chance we got of discharging our cargo."

Smoky was dragged away from this music by a swift yank from the chief, who had finished his soup and wanted his chow.

It was rumored in the fo'c'sle that the crew would get an advance of a ten spot that night, but Smoky hurried through his supper, stowed his gear and went ashore to find out all about the strike.

He found the meeting of the Wobbly longshoremen on Liberty Hill. He pushed up to the front and listened to every word. He forgot all about making a stake and asked the chairman for five minutes to give the strikers greeting from the longshoremen of Canada.

Next day was Saturday and Smoky began to think of the stake he was going to make. He walked up to the Old Man and touched him for his ten bucks. "Wot in hell do you take me for, a walking bank?" stormed the skipper as he turned into the chart room.

A gang of scab longshoremen walked up the gang plank. "Turn to and man the winches," roared the skipper, who had returned to the deck.

The crew stood round and the spokesman roared back, "We don't man no winches for no scabs."

A short council of war with the stevedores followed, then the captain hollered down the engineroom to the chief to get steam for the winches. But the chief came up on deck and reported that the firemen refused to get up steam for scab longshoremen. So it ended at that.

The flunkies were perched on the deckrail with Smoky telling the Wobbly the difference between the program of the Workers' Party and the I.W.W., when the third engineer came aft.

He was a pretty good scout, the third. He called Smoky over to his cabin and asked if the old man had given him the ten spot yet. He wanted Smoky to do him a favor. He slipped him five dollars and a note, addressed to a girl, asking him to grab a street car and deliver it to his sweetie.

Smoky figured he could trust the third, so he told him his great secret and asked for advice. Should he take his dunnage and shove off now? The third figured it would be better to stick it out over the week-end and push off on Monday. Smoky decided to take the advice.

On his way back to the ship, after an evening at Long Beach, Smoky got back to Liberty Hill just in time to see the cops take Upton Sinclair to the hoosegow for reading the Declaration of Independence! "Liberty Hill," muttered Smoky. "Liberty Hell!"

Old Robert Dollar himself came aboard on Sunday morning and had a consultation with the skipper. As soon as Bob Dollar left, the captain ordered steam and pulled out into midstream. He dropped anchor astern of one of Uncle Sam's cruisers and awaited orders.

The message came, "Proceed to 'Frisco. Cargo is sold."

Smoky cursed all shipowners, masters, mates and engineers on the seven seas. What about the stake now? He couldn't get ashore.

The cargo was discharged at Frisco and word was passed around that the ship was sold, too. All hands were signed off and transportation tickets given to port of hire. Which meant that Smoky had to go back to Vancouver.

The skipper was to be the last to leave and turn the boat over to the new owners. He kept Smoky to help him pack his gear. All the mess gave Smoky a tip of five dollars, except the old man.

Smoky was helping the old man pack his clobber, when a chippy walked up the gangplank and inquired for Captain Doyle. The skipper left with the girl and called to Smoky to finish packing his bag and send it to the Ambassador. Smoky answered, "Aye, aye, sir!"

Under the mate's bunk was a big seabag. In this Smoky packed all the silk pajamas, silk underwear, shirts and socks. In the skipper's bag he piled all the junk and left it in the mess room.

He sailed for home on the *H.F. Alexandra* and began to prepare for the next depression.

Masses (July-August 1932)

DOROTHY LIVESAY

CASE SUPERVISOR

Last night she had escaped to a movie. But it was no escape. The news reels flashed by as if unrolling from her own mind: war, breadlines, crisis, drought—and yet again those letters in thundering black type—CRISIS.

After that she laughed hysterically at Popeye. And the comedy, which should have lifted her into ease, into deep-sofaed and luxuriant rooms, remote as an aquarium—the comedy began where she had left off. A girl was climbing Mrs. Rooney's rickety stairs, turning a door handle slowly, afraid to protrude herself into the threadbare room. A girl was hot and angry after standing all day long behind a counter. This was to be department store love, just above the landlord's dispossess, just above the breadline....

As quivering scenes melted and were speeded up, held still and shot across the eyes, she found herself tensely clutching the chair seat. It could not end the same way—it must not. With Mrs. Rooney fighting her daughter for the rent. And "I'm going to have fun when I'm young—see? I'm going to live in spite of the landlord!"

No! It couldn't be like that. Love on the screen was different, it spread a film across the truth. Thank God, love was happy there, balancing itself above the dole....

She went into the chill, wet air with face prickly and dry, her head aching. Thoughts must be pushed aside, and a furrow driven straight home to bed. There would be a long enough fight for sleep.

Now it was morning. She was sitting at her desk, absently opening mail, heedless of the telephone which went on and on like the ringing in her head.

"Oh, Miss Chilton?" A round curly head was in the doorway. "May I see you before I go out?"

"But we have a conference at two o'clock."

"I know. It's terribly important, Miss Chilton."

"One moment then. Sit down while I answer this." Then crisp and cool came her business voice: "Miss Chilton speaking." In a moment a pucker gathered above the clear eyes. "Oh yes. Yes, Mr. Jones.... No, I really can't do anything further about it, Mr. Jones. What we said yesterday closed the matter as far as I'm concerned.... Well, Mr. Jones, I gave you one hour and a half of my time, if you don't think that fair. I have to think of other people too.... No, I am busy with conferences all day. I wouldn't be able to see you.... If your wife feels so badly about it why didn't she say something? I understood that she was perfectly satisfied.... Well, we won't discuss that over the telephone. I would rather see your wife alone. Yes. Yes. I will call on her tomorrow afternoon.... No.... Goodbye."

Cowardice, she was thinking. Pure cowardice to say I'd go in there again.

The girl was squirming in her seat, pretending not to listen. She probably thought things boded ill for her case. But she gathered her courage in her hands, her cheeks flushing, her candid brown eyes staring out under the shock of hair.

"Miss Chilton. It's about the Caporettis again." She was apologetic at first, as if their misfortune were her own fault. But as she went on she seemed to become unselfconscious, as if she was Mrs. Caporetti herself talking, stout and solid and determined, but perilously near the dangerline of lost control. When the worker had called yesterday Mrs. Caporetti had been like that, for the baby was sick again. Dr. Hart refused to come because he hadn't been paid for the last three times; Mr. Caporetti was off work again on account of his neuritis. He had had to keep the stove low to make the fuel last, but anyway his bedroom was simply freezing (I was in it, Miss Chilton, and I know; what can you expect when the bedroom is so far from the kitchen and no stove in the hall?) And now they were entirely out of fuel (I went out to the back porch and there was only a shovelful. It would not last the night). Here it was morning, and all Mr. Caporetti's available cash had to go for food and milk. (That's if we budget it like you said, Miss Chilton). So the girl wanted fuel ordered, and a doctor sent in from the Welfare Dispensary (because it's not a city case and we can't send a relief doctor).

Miss Chilton was fumbling with the leaves of a calendar on her desk. "But Miss Cherry, I see that coal was sent to the Caporettis only two weeks ago. It is supposed to last a month."

"I know. But it never does. Not anywhere. Three weeks at the most. And the Caporettis use their stove for cooking and everything. They have to keep it going all night so it won't be too cold in the morning for Mr. Caporetti's leg. Anyway, the have no matches in the house, Miss Chilton. They can't afford to buy matches.

"Did you put them in the budget?"

"Oh yes. But now the budget is all thrown out of kilter, with the baby sick and Mr. Caporetti not working."

"Tell me, Miss Cherry. Have you every really investigated whether the relatives could not help in this case? I mean her relatives? I know his are on relief."

The girl flushed a little, biting her lip. "But Mrs. Caporetti doesn't want me to see her relatives. She hasn't had anything to do with them since she married an Italian. They were so mean about it before."

"I realize that. But now that times are so hard all around, do you really think they would blame her, if they were approached the right way? Don't you think they might be willing to help a little, in times of stress, like this one?"

The girl would not answer her, but sat silently looking at

her lap. For all the world like Mrs. Caporetti herself. Really, Miss Cherry was too emotional. She was undoubtedly letting her clients become too dependent on her. All Mrs. Caporetti had to do was tell a hard luck story and Miss Cherry flashed back to the office like a telephone message. She had no sense of proportion. She wasn't letting her clients develop any self-reliance. It would do no harm to pull her up sharp, right now.

"Isn't it just possible, Miss Cherry, that Mrs. Caporetti has been in touch with her people all along? I mean" (As the girl shook her head stubbornly) "that if she were left to her own devices now she might quite naturally turn to her mother? I am sure they would help her out with a little fuel; or certainly they would send their family doctor. After all, if you were to tell them that their grandchild was ill, can you believe that they would be hard-hearted?"

"There are plenty of hard-hearted people in the world," the girl said.

"Well, Miss Cherry, I am not insisting that you see the relatives right now, in this emergency. But I would feel, would you not, that it might be well to carry on with the case with that step in mind?"

"Oh yes."

"Well then. Visit the family, and if the child is not better, send a doctor from the centre. But I certainly do not believe we can afford to send in fuel again. We've done it too often every two weeks. We have to think of other families."

"Yes, Miss Chilton."

"Ask them what sources they have. Find out if they couldn't borrow from neighbours until next week. Or perhaps the store would give a little charcoal on credit."

"All right, Miss Chilton. Thank you." In a whisk the girl was gone.

Miss Chilton opened the window wider, then plunged into her mail.

Automatically, she slipped the letters into files, or made notes on little cards. She would have to telephone the city relief and report that new family, before Miss

McQueen called her in for conference. Ten o'clock that was to be. But Miss McQueen had an erratic sense of time. It happened that she was just in the middle of her report when a secretary came to the door and told her: "Miss McQueen is waiting."

So be it. She arose, gathering pencil and paper and two files, and walked through the noisy stenographer's office down the hall to the big end room. "Come in." Miss McQueen, heavy and imposing, with white hair plastered neatly over one side of her forehead, was talking to Miss Dogherty, the other case supervisor. She was a big-boned woman, with a dour face and sallow complexion, her straight black hair as usual falling down over her eyes. Sometimes Dogherty seemed to be aware that she was a failure; at other times she was indifferent to that and to everything. Trouble just slid away from her as she stalked through the office with her mind somewhere far off.

Today Chilton could see she was flustered. And when Kay Dogherty was flustered the whole office could be counted on to get into a panic—especially her particular flock of workers and students.

Miss McQueen was speaking in her heavy, emphatic way. "We had a Board meeting last night, as I expect you know. I had to report that the budget in this district had exceeded the quota by almost one third. One third. And we haven't reached Christmas yet or the first of the year. Fortunately the other districts were almost as bad. But not quite. Still, those businessmen were quite stunned. Mr. Farrow said that if he ran his business that way, he would have been bankrupt years ago. Mr. Tuthill mentioned that in his opinion the only solution was to put a businessman in as head of each office. You know what that would mean: The end of our case work approach, our professional standards.... Just imagine, for instance, Mr. Tuthill or Mr. Augustus Brown sitting here in my place. Just how far would you get? No, my friends, we have to maintain our standards, even at the expense of being more severe in our distributions. Every source of saving must be checked up once again; in particular I think the emergency fund must be watched carefully; and wherever a client can be turned over to a religious organization or an institution, it should be done. We have to catch up on that budget."

"But we are not a business organization." Dogherty was speaking as if she had only heard Miss McQueen's first sentence.

"We would be nowhere without the help of business, Miss Dogherty. Please remember that. You owe your position to it. I am not concerned here with what we are, but with what we can do. We have a vital function to perform and it must be performed with the least possible sacrifice—on all sides.... Miss Chilton, have you any suggestions?"

She remembered Miss Cherry's silence. "Now that winter is here, Miss McQueen, I was thinking we would need *more* money for fuel and medicine—not less."

"Well, we can't have it. And you must convince your workers of that. These young ones must be pulled up sharply. It is they who are putting in a little extra, here and there—perhaps without your noticing it, Miss Dogherty. I think we will have to call a staff meeting on the subject. Now concretely, let us come to the point, where can we cut down? On service or relief?"

Service is relief, Chilton was thinking, nearly all the time. But she must not say that. Neither of them were expected to say anything. As long as they listened meekly to Miss McQueen, carried out her suggestions, they were safe. So she went on talking, planning, for upwards of an hour. Dogherty was getting restless, she probably had an appointment. Dear knows what she might not say....

Finally it was over. Dogherty pounded her way out. At the door Chilton was recalled. "One moment." The small glassy blue eyes were inscrutable. "I noticed that your expenditures were lower than Miss Dogherty's, Miss Chilton. I am glad to observe that you are aware of your responsibilities."

She smiled in a faded way, and hurried out. Damn! So

they were being compared like two mice. And good old Dogherty was in danger again. Dogherty whose heart was like a sieve, anyone could flow through it, even though she hadn't any scientific training.... She would have to get together with Dogherty—they could sign each other's slips, if necessary. She would do anything for Dogherty ... but not for Mrs. Caporetti? Dogherty herself would only be interested in Mrs. Caporetti. She wouldn't care about her job.

Damn. She must stop thinking. Her mind was getting fuzzy again. Crisis. Crisis. Hang onto yourself, old girl. Watch out. Now. At your desk. Turn around. Smile. Good morning Miss Svenson. Yes, I can see you now. (Even though she lies to me and swears she isn't pregnant, I can still smile.)

At noon she came down late for lunch. Miss McQueen must have gone out for lunch, if the sound of laughter and the sense of relaxation had any meaning. But when Chilton entered the girls stiffened up perceptibly: and this, although Dogherty was present. It was like a school room, this restraint which Miss McQueen had so carefully built up between supervisors and juniors. Only Dogherty ignored it.

Food was passed politely, coffee gulped in a hurry. An hour and fifteen minutes was their right, according to regulations, but Chilton couldn't remember when they had more than three-quarters of an hour. Today she wanted to sit and sit, to gossip with Black and Dogherty. Young Cherry, as they called her, had not come in. So she felt relaxed, puffing at a cigarette. Then there came an urgent telephone call, and it was all over.

Conferences. Two full hours of conference with different workers. She wouldn't be able to make a single call that day. And Mrs. Harris had to have.... Stop getting like this, she told herself. Mrs. Harris can wait. Everybody can wait. Everything can be done tomorrow. Nobody can starve in a day. "It takes weeks to starve," Black had said, or was it Dogherty? "But one night can cause pneumonia."

She felt the workers lined up outside her door, as at a

lavatory, "I've got to get in there first" someone was saying in a fierce whisper. "I'm taking the trolley out to Greenfields, and you know it takes all day." "But I have an appointment downtown at 2:30 and it's nearly that now. I'm first on the list, you know it, Dolly."

Supposing she called it off, let them scatter? But no, they had things to ask her, they might make mistakes. She opened the door, looked surprised to see them there in the hall, and asked them all in together. "Unless there is something specially important, we will just discuss finances," she explained.

It had seemed easier to cope with them all at once. Now, with four pair of eyes staring at hers, it was more difficult to sound convincing. "You must cut your budgets, cut your extras, cut your coal orders." They couldn't accept it.

"But Miss Chilton...."

"What about Dora O'Brien's arch support?"

"And the Brown baby?"

"And Mrs. Saunder's convalescent care?"

"Miss Dogherty said...."

She pounced on that one. "What did Miss Dogherty say?"

"I don't remember."

"I do. She said we couldn't really make any big changes in our plans or it wouldn't be social work we were doing, but police work."

Chilton flushed. Dogherty had reached them first, Dogherty had sowed rebellion. She was right, oh yes, but this wasn't a question of right and wrong. This was a practical question, a "business proposition." She would have to make them see it that way. She began talking, coldly and sensibly.

She could feel their chill growing, their distrust. Fortunately, Miss Cherry wasn't there (where could she be?) But there was someone to take her place, Jean Vronsky.

"That is quite understandable, Miss Chilton. But what we would like to know is this: who are *you* for? For the people we are trying to help, or for the Board?" There was a gasp and a silence after it had been said.

Chilton was angry this time. "There is no question where my sympathy lies," she said. "As a social worker of some years' standing I do not have to explain myself to you."

There! She had done it. Lost her temper—and isolated them from her, forever. She watched them filing out miserably, her face set. A fine social worker who could not stand criticism.... A fine example.

She called a stenographer and began to dictate, so fast that the girl protested. "Sorry. Just mention it and I'll slow up. Where was I? 'Mrs. Jones then said that Mr. Jones.' Yes. Paragraph."

When the afternoon was finally over, when the new case had been attended to, when Mrs. O'Hara had been given sewing materials and Miss Mickle had received her food order in advance—when everyone was getting ready for five o'clock with a sudden quickening of tempo—then she knew that she couldn't go home to the apartment for a long, long time. She would just sit here after it was quiet and smoke cigarette after cigarette. For a second now she folded her arms on the table and laid her head down.

She scarcely heard the timid knock on the door, and only raised her eyes in time to see Miss Cherry slip through the door and close it.

"I'm sorry to bother you, Miss Chilton."

"It's what I'm here for. I just happen to forget it sometimes, that's all."

Cherry should have been warned by the ironic tone. She was too full of her own story to notice.

"I could only get there this afternoon...."

"There?"

"The Caporettis, you know."

"Oh yes. There are so many Caporettis."

"Well, these ones especially. The baby was awful sick. But luckily I was able to phone next door and got him to come right away—the Welfare doctor. The baby has pneumonia, Miss Chilton.... And all they had been burning in the stove since last night was wooden boxes. There were no more left when I got there.... I just couldn't ask Mrs. Caporetti any questions, Miss Chilton...."

"So you telephoned the coal company?"

"Yes. But it's all right, Miss Chilton. It's all right. I paid for it out of my own money. Luckily I had just had my cheque cashed."

"You paid for it...!" Chilton sat back in her chair. "But you have to live too, child."

"I can live. I can easily live. It's they who can't live."

Then Chilton's head turned away, her elbows fell upon the desk. "Go away. Go away child.... Leave me, I say!"

New Frontier (July 1936)

EMANUEL BERKENFELD

CAMP IS WONDERFUL FOR GROWING BOYS

It was a hot night in June and they sat sprawled on chairs in the kitchen in their underwear. Big Lefty squirmed and shifted on the hard chair pulling the adhered, sweated underwear from under him. Little Lefty, stripped to the waist in large running pants, giggled at the sucking sound and then lowered his eyes shyly with a childish apology for his laughter.

"Gee Pop," Big Lefty said, "when are you going to be finished with that?" The newspaper was spread wide on the table before Pop, the sides where he held it smudged with the sweat from his hands. "All right, all right," Pop said.

"Look, Pop, I want you to sign this. It's for Little Lefty."

"What's for Little Lefty? It'd better be something pretty good for my boy. Eh, Lefty?" He grinned and the shy boy's face reddened beneath the perspiration.

"You said it, Pop," Big Lefty said. "It's for a summer camp for him."

"Oh, that charity thing," Freda said. She sat near the window reading a book and fanning herself with a dish cloth.

Pop threw the printed form back at him. "No charity," he said. "We need no charity."

"Wait a minute, Pop! It's no charity. What do you know, Freda, shut up! Listen Pop, it's a teacher in the school, Mr. Anderson, who's got a camp. It's a rich camp. Rich kids go there and he picks four kids and gives them each a two weeks free vacation at the camp for nothing. See? That's no charity. What do you know, Freda!"

"What's two weeks!" Freda sneered.

Pop looked at Little Lefty. "You want to go, boy?" he said. "Shake your head yes or no."

Pop always said that to Little Lefty whenever he asked him a question. It made tight knots that squeezed something inside of Pop every time Little Lefty tried to talk, stammering pathetically to get the words out of his mouth. It hurt his heart watching and listening to him stammer. It hurt because you just had to wait and you couldn't do anything to help him work and fight with his little jaws to form the words.

"Come to think of it," Pop said, "it'll be a good thing for Little Lefty. Get him away from hanging on to Freda's skirts and it'll be a vacation for Freda too, eh, Freda?"

"Yes, but I'd rather see Big Lefty go," Freda said.

"Shut up!" Big Lefty said. "Gee Pop, it'll be great. Do you know what the kids who went there last year said? It's up in the mountains on a hill higher than the Empire State Building."

"Ah," Freda sighed. She stood by the window and her thin, yellowed nightgown clung damply to her body coning her child's bird-beak breasts. "Ah, tonight on top of the Empire State Building it must be swell and cool and sweet...."

"Get away from that window!" Big Lefty yelled at her. "You're blocking out the air."

The day had been too full for Little Lefty and he lay awake in his corner bed in the cabin for a long time, too fatigued to sleep, still too full of the tumult of new strange things that had opened to him on this first day. A field of grass as they had here he had seen nowhere, not even in the parks of the city. It was so clean and level and soft that he could not at first bring himself to tread on it and it had grieved him, then, to see the other boys, less timid, trample wildly and eagerly on it with the first intoxication of freedom. Later he too romped over the green following them feeling the softness under his feet. Laughing and shouting, the boys threw themselves to the ground and he did, too, running his fingers through the blades of grass. They felt silky and soft like Freda's hair when he had run his fingers through it once when he was sick. And the trees here were things to wonder about. You couldn't tell whether they were growing up to the sky or growing down into the earth. The branches were so low the leaves brushed the ground and you had to stoop and crawl in the woods. They were sturdier and greener than other trees anywhere. You discovered that when you climbed one and sat on a stout branch high up in it amidst clusters of green slick apples. But you had to promise not to eat the apples and looking at them close enough to touch stirred the saliva in the back of your jaws until they ached.

And the food at the table was something like a king's feast in a story Freda had read to him and he had eaten so much of it that his counsellor (his name was Pottsy) had commended him. He would have eaten more had not some of the boys at the table laughed at the amount and the rapidity with which he ate. He had stopped a bit ashamed at eight cups of milk and Pottsy had patted him on the head as an example for the others.

There was more play after supper and then when it was still light they had been sent to their cabins. The low notes of the bugle had sounded a long time ago and now as he lay between the cool sheets, his head quick with sounds and sights, he seemed to hear them again, each sweet note sending a gentle comforting shiver through his body. It was dark now and still and the others in the cabin breathed softly in sleep with the same rhythmic murmur that came from the trees outside and the smell of clean, chilled air was so sharp that it hurt him to breathe. He slid deep under the blankets to lose somewhere in the dark and warmth his sweet and aching wakefulness.

It wasn't very long before they here at camp discovered his inability to form words quickly and their taunts took the same shape as the ones he heard each monotonous day in the city. The kid with the machine gun mouth, they said. You can do a tap dance to that kid's stutter. And the boys jibed him with, "C'mon Lefty spit some bullets." Somehow it was different here and didn't hurt him as much. Somehow the taunts fell on him gently as everything did here; as the leaves that fell still green from the trees, as the breeze, as the ripples that curled around his feet wading in the lake, as the dark hills rolling in the distance. It didn't matter here and he laughed with them.

But Pottsy was annoyed and he gave him word exercises and made him practice by himself. He made him practice all day and whenever Pottsy would see him doing nothing he would work with him and teach him to form sounds. *Camp is wonderful for growing boys.* That was the sentence he had to repeat to himself endlessly throughout the day and it was painful to be bothered with it despite Pottsy's encouragement.

Still, the hardest hours of the day were the ones before meals when he lay resting on his cot, his body tingling and whipped pink from splashing about in the lake and the terrible gnawing in his stomach. Those were the longest hours, the sweetly unbearable hours, waiting for mess call to be sounded, thinking of the chunks of good, brown bread on the table, the cold, creamy milk that quenched a thirst quicker than water, and almost before the last note of the call he was dressed and out in line, first, always first and waiting. Not while there was a morsel of food still left on the table would the meal end for him and often after the others had finished eager to be out he remained behind alone eating what he could. But the day came quickly and it caught him at the end of a meal when he became suddenly conscious of his stomach, conscious that it lived and ached. It was unsafe thereafter to be far from the cabin much less to play. Pottsy noticed that and also his frequent and hurried retreats to the washroom and said he'd been afraid of that and expecting it. The doctor pointed his finger at him and said no milk and to go easy with food for awhile. And so he sat at the table doing nothing and doing nothing meant sitting next to Pottsy practicing and mouthing words and reciting *Camp is wonderful for growing boys*. The distress he suffered was as nothing compared with the graver penalty of eating little amidst plenty and twisting words with his lips.

The siege soon passed however and with freedom at the table again and hard won he gobbled his food lustier than ever and the boys at the table screamed with wonder and delight. Pottsy laughed, too, saying that if he kept up that way they'd be able to roll him home.

There were times when he would fall away from his group to wander alone in the woods losing himself there and not even Pottsy's anxious shouts drawing him back. There was too much to do, too many new things to see, too many trees to climb, too many colors, too many smells to savor. He kept away from apple trees; there was no one to watch him and the temptation was great. Other trees had other excitements. Startling screaming birds to flight as he swung from the branches set his head singing, and reaching the top with dozens of caterpillars and strange insects clinging to his hair and clothes made him feel part of the tree. There was time, perched on top with the wind seeking his tired body through the leaves, to examine them and, satisfied, to flick them casually from him, and time also to soothe his scratches and pluck the twigs from his skin.

There was an apple tree behind the cabin and its low branches pushed up against the window flap in his corner. He opened the flap and forced the branch in so that the leaves hung over his bed, and looking up at them from his pillow hour after hour he came to know their shape, their coloring, their number. He would always find coming back some leaves strewn on his pillow and yet find none missing from the ones above his head. This was another of the inexplicable wonders of the tree.

The others ordinarily quick to object to anything tending to mar the appearance of the cabin tolerated him this fearing lest oppostion change him and leave him not ready as he always was to forego during boating period his chance to row, or to be content, almost anxious, as he was, to take last place in line. He preferred to sit in back of the boat with his hands free and dangling in the water, and being last in line (except for meals) made it easier from there to slip away.

In the midst of these things there could be no thoughts of home, of Pop, Freda and Big Lefty. There was no time to sit and think of them in days short and fleet, in nights that had no beginning, sleep closing the day before dark did. And so on letter writing day when Pottsy helped them to scrawl their letters he felt a pang for them at home and he thought about the things he would write to bring them closer to him. There were many things he wanted to say. He wanted to tell them about the great lake with the picture of the sky in it, of boating with the sun beating down and the breeze always slapping the heat from it, of the plunges that left the body pink and shiny. He wanted to tell them how he could feel his legs growing longer, and most of all he wanted them to know about the cold milk and the many things that crowded the table. But somehow he couldn't explain to Pottsy all of these things he wanted so much to say and the letter went merely *Am having a good time.*

He was resting on his cot waiting to hear the mess call for dinner when Pottsy turned to him. "Say Lefty," he said, "I almost forgot about you . We've got to get your things ready. You know you're leaving today."

The bed suddenly became something hard and hurting under him and a quick sickness gripped his stomach. It was a lie, it was a fairy tale, it was a dream, it was something that never happened. He watched Pottsy getting his things together and he felt his throat tying up. He didn't know whether he was going to cry or not but his throat felt like it was the beginning. He didn't want to cry, he hadn't ever cried here. Most of the boys in the cabin had at one time or another. One because he had a bicycle at home and didn't have one here. Another was homesick, another because he had been compelled to eat something he did not like.

He ran into the washroom and there he let himself go and the thing that hurt most leaning on the basin was keeping back the sobs that made noise.

Hearing Pottsy walk in he splashed water over his face.

Pottsy put his arm around him and they walked together to the mess hall.

Big Lefty, waiting for him at the station, smothered him to his chest. "Boy, look at you!" he shouted. "Just look at you!" He kept fondling and pinching Little Lefty's tanned face and in the subway all the way home he kept shaking his head from side to side in wonderment, repeating, "Little Lefty you look great. Boy oh boy but you look good! Just wait'll Pop sees you!"

Pop got up from the chair when they walked in. The sweat glistened on his face and he stood staring at Little Lefty and swallowing lumps of nothing in his throat. Freda sprang across the room and hugged him in her arms putting her moist face close to his.

"Leave him alone," Big Lefty said. "It's hot enough. Pop look at him! Just look at him! Does he look great or does he look great? We'll have to call him Fatso."

Pop looked at him. "Hello, boy." he said. "How was it?"

Little Lefty shuffled his feet. He took a deep breath and then with merely the slightest stammer said, "Camp is wonderful for growing boys."

For a moment they stared at him in amazement as people hearing suddenly speech from a mute. Then Big Lefty jumped in the air clapping his hands and howling. Pop's body shook with laughter and the sweat slid and glistened down his reddened face and Freda hugged little Lefty to her again and screamed.

"Come on give it to us." Big Lefty shouted. "Say it again."

Little Lefty said it again lowering his eyes shyly.

Again they roared with laughter. Big Lefty ran around the kitchen holding his stomach and bellowing.

"What else can you say, boy?" Pop said, still chuckling.

And then the little face took on again the old torture. The jaws wrenched broken words from the throat. The lips twisted to sew them together and the tongue flapped about pathetically.

Pop pressed him close to his side, hushing him.

They said he looked tired now and they sent him to bed. He undressed in the dark. The night sounds of the city floated heavily through the window. He opened the package he had brought home and took from it three green apples. They felt cool next to his moist face. He played with them letting them roll over his bare chest, and then he sat up in bed and polished the wetness from them with the sheet until he could see their greenness and slickness in the dark. The blare of an automobile horn pushed its way through the opened window and hung sluggishly in the air. He lay back in bed listening to it, following the sound until there was no more of it, but he continued to listen for a long time to something it had shaped in his mind. The air in the room remained dead and heavy with moisture.

New Frontier (October 1936)

SIMON MARCSON

DREAM TRAIN

Jolt. Clack-Clack. He started out of sleep, his hand moving forward as if to pull his pillow under his head. Funny, his hand touched nothing but wood. Very hard wood. With iron bolts here and there. All covered with something fine and sandy—felt like soft coal. He sat up. He felt a wall behind him. The continual rumbling noise—was wheels passing over miles of ties. Ha, he was travelling à la freight. The train was slowing down for a long curve.

What was it that kept coming before his eyes—as if he had been trying to remember something, and couldn't? Clack-clack. Streaks of moonlight across a freight car—a coal car. Travelling in the night. Out of an ocean of darkness. Ocean of darkness—he played with the phrase.... Approached the doorway. Take a breath of fresh air. That's better! Sit down—his feet dangling out. Breathe fast. Take in pure air. The thick coal dust inside had nearly stifled him. Funny him travelling. Why?

The engine lights flickered in the darkness out there. Taking a long curve. A vast sea of yellow stalks in front. Wave upon wave of wheat. Grain fields—Canadian grain fields. Like so many faces—turned towards him.... Why faces? Jolt.

He shook his head—what clouded his head so?—A face like a night of stars. Yes—a face like a night of stars.... Why the face that had flashed for a moment in the yellow light of the cafe—as he had sat at his coffee waiting for his freight train. That had done it. Hers, too—long ago—had been a face like a night of stars.... Clack-clack.

It brought visions of a new world—it seemed—much younger than this. He had been young then—at college. All life before him, and the world at his feet. Life and living had been one great passion bound up within him.....

Jolt.—Years of early youth spent in a city. Life—only a wondrous fairy castle, of knights, beautiful damsels, and dragons. Continually protecting the weak—risking one's life for their right to live.

This scene slowly merged into a new one. One of desks, and reflections of oneself—doing the same tasks, at the same time. Life, was a maze of papers, pencils, crayons, blackboards and teachers—it was school; one more mind beginning to function for itself.

Books—open up a new world—the paths to civilization's treasure-houses. Everything else takes on a different colour—for a time there is no food, drink, nor sleep.

Slowly reality forces itself upon the tender new mind. Conditions exist that should have gone by the wayside at the time of Jesus. Namely, that in a comparatively enlightened age, man lives like the animal—fighting, clawing, and gnawing one another; the strongest winning, or perhaps the cunningest or slyest thriving—the weaker or perhaps the kindlier being driven out of existence.

The young mind is amazed—here was Darwin's theory being enacted before his very eyes, and with it, all the stench and reek of the animal kingdom.

Visions become ideas. Ideas—bring in their course—moulding of character, and a course of life. College meant something entirely different—than a course in making dates—dances—and rugby. But romance is part of every visionary mind, and coupled with vigorous youth—finis love. Hers was a beauty that pervaded every part of her, and shone in lustrous warmth about her face.... Poets described it—as a face like a night of stars.

Machine makes its inroad upon man—displacing the

needy. These grow in number. Dissatisfaction—becomes front page news. 'Employees dissatisfied with employers.' 'Employers dissatisfied with employees.' Headlines scream 'The unemployed'—breadlines form—everywhere men, hands in pockets, walking the streets—'We demand bread.' More headlines—'Man starves to death—family now being taken care of,' 'Man freezes to death in own home.' These run rampant across wet pages, which until now have known of death—only as murders and wars. Things far-fetched. Now death occurs in their own backyards. Uncomfortable feeling. Shivers run up and down their backs. The new mind tempered with romance, and an insight into life—makes all this part of himself.

Strikes. Speeches. Youth and intelligence—dangerous. Sightseeing for a time in a state prison. Exiled from home. One becomes old, very old—after such a tour of sightseeing.... Work appears at times. Jobs grow fewer. One's belt grows longer....

Jolt! Oh, why didn't they put springs on these damned cars.—Oceans of wheat heads before him. Faces. At his window. The box car door his window. Those were faces below. Milling thousands. Inhabiting hundreds of cities. He was out of a job. They were out of a job. Comrades? Why, yes, comrades. Brotherhood of unemployed. Over there, oh, those were statesmen. They conducted the affairs of these thousands, these millions. That—those were wires—strings—attached to these statesmen with little groups of men at the other end—trying to get a word in. Interests. Fat men. Their own interests. Mines, battleships, oil, wheat. Wheat?—that was bread! Bread these millions ate. Oceans of loaves piled high in monstrous cement fortresses. Thousands attacking these fortresses. All had one look in their eyes. It was their battle-cry—hunger.

Window. His window. Streaks of moonlight across a coal car sailing through an ocean of flour. Each jolt a wave striking his ship.

A queer smile on his lips. 'Why couldn't they see what he saw?' The answer loomed before his eyes. The writing upon the wall....

The train had taken the curve, it was gathering speed. Jolting increased. Train passing through night. Yes, the phrase, out of an ocean of darkness. His dream train. Taking him on. Must go on. But—Ocean of darkness....

Canadian Forum (November 1933)

A Note on the Type

The text of this book was set, via computer-driven phototypesetter, in a face called Baskerville. The typeface was developed by John Baskerville (1706-1775), an English engraver, calligrapher, and printer who lived and worked in Birmingham. His interests in the development of printing technology extended from the design and founding of type, to composing and printing, as well as to improvements in paper and ink. Baskerville was part of the English declaration of typographical independence from imported continental matrices which had dominated printing until the eighteenth century. He built on the work of William Caslon whose types were the first expression of an independent English design. Baskerville's roman is a face of excellent readability and of a rather broad design. He ignored the tendency to compactness, enhancing the contrast between the main and connecting strokes. His commitment to typography as the means of achieving a fine book was displayed in some fifty productions beginning with a quarto *Virgil* in 1757. His masterpiece, the folio bible of 1763, was printed under the licence of Cambridge University and is regarded as one of the finest book productions of the eighteenth century. After he died in poverty, his widow sold his punches, matrices, and presses to Beaumarchais in 1779 for use in the Kehl edition of Voltaire. In subsequent years,

Baskerville types were sold to many French foundries and attained a wide use even as their originator was forgotten. Baskerville type design was also influential in the evolution of roman typefaces in the eighteenth and nineteenth centuries. Following the rediscovery of the original punches in 1917, Baskerville faces have enjoyed a revival in the twentieth century.

Typeset by members of Victor Hugo Assembly at the offices of New Hogtown Press in Toronto and at Dumont Press Graphix in Kitchener. Book design by Russell Hann. Assembly and cover design by Richard Wright. The assistance and advice of Steve, Bill, Shirley, Michael, Alison, Kae, Moe, Eliza, Jane, and other members of the Workers Union of Dumont Press Graphix were instrumental in the production of this book; they deserve a large measure of the credit for whatever is good enough in this production to evoke the memory of John Baskerville. Printed and bound in Canada by Webcom, Limited, Scarborough, Ontario.